Bar Down

Copyright © 2025 Stef C. R.

All rights reserved. No part of this book may be reproduced in any form except for the purpose of brief reviews or citations without the written permission of the author.

This is a work of fiction in which all events and characters in this book are completely imaginary. Any resemblance to actual people is entirely coincidental.

Cover designed by Lorissa Padilla.
Book edited by Ciara Lewis.

ALSO BY STEF C.R.

Grand Marquee Manticores
The Love Penalty (#1)

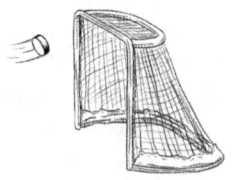

BAR DOWN
bar - down (adj.): When the puck hits the crossbar and goes down into the net. Also called 'bar south'.

Playlist

Intro – The xx
Please Notice – Christian Leave
THE LONELIEST – Maneskin
Please Don't Be – Hazlett
I Can Do It With a Broken Heart – Taylor Swift
Constellations – Jade LeMac
Down Bad – Taylor Swift
Home – Good Neighbours
Hello Love – Benson Boone
The Roads – Jonah Kagen
BIRDS OF A FEATHER – Billie Eilish
Ultraviolet – Aidan Bissett
i am not who i was – Chance Pena
It Only Cost Everything – Victor Ray
Lose Control – Teddy Swims
Belong Together – Mark Ambor
Please Don't Say You Love Me – Gabrielle Aplin
2 friends – Troy Ogletree
My Home – Myles Smith

To those who were ever made to feel like they weren't enough.

You are.

Author's note

While this book is a fun and sexy hockey romance, please be advised that there are explicit sexual scenes and other triggers such as: daddy issues, toxic family members, consumption and mentions of alcohol, as well as on page violence and mentions of blood.

Note to my family: *Maybe just skip this one altogether!*

Bar DOWN

PROLOGUE

Eight Months Ago

ASH

I FIND myself on my best friend's doorstep even though I'm not supposed to be here until tomorrow for the New Year's Eve party. A very irritated Robbie opens the door and scowls at me.

"What the hell are you doing here?" he all but growls, but I know it's just his playful side coming out. When I got traded to the Manticores a few years ago, Robbie was the one who immediately took me under his wing. Not only is he our team captain, but he's one of my best friends.

"Nice to see you too, grandpa," I quip, bringing up the nickname I know annoys him. I give him a wink as I walk inside his ranch-style home on the outskirts of Grand Marquee like I own the place. Messing with Robbie is one of my favorite pastimes. He's the fucking best, but his reactions are so predictable, making it easy to get a rise out of him. Sometimes I wonder why he lets me stick around with all the crap I give him. Any other guy would get annoyed and cut me out of his life, but not Robbie, he's the male equivalent of a mother hen. *He's a father hen.*

"Where's my favorite girl?" I say to him with a smirk and move out the way when he attempts to punch my shoulder.

"Stop hitting on my girlfriend, you dipshit," he says halfheartedly. Robbie knows I'd never actually make a move on Olivia. I'm not stupid, or blind. That girl is so gone for him. I'd tease her endlessly if we were closer, but since I don't know her on a deeper level like I do Robbie, I keep my remarks to myself.

Walking into his large, open kitchen, I say, "Never, you need some healthy competition."

"Ash, you're here?" Olivia greets me from the massive island where she's currently arranging appetizers on a charcuterie board. Robbie's entire kitchen space is currently taken up by chips, dips, drinks, meats, cheeses, veggies, and other pans filled with appetizers that still need to go in the oven. The man really knows how to throw a party.

"I can't believe he's making you work," I scoff. "You know he can afford to hire someone to do all this, right?"

Robbie swats at me with a towel before placing it on his shoulder. Wannabe Jamie Oliver over here walks up to Olivia and gives her a kiss on the cheek before saying, "I'm not *making* her do anything. Food is our shared love language, so we like cooking together." Olivia blushes and gives Robbie a look that says *you're totally getting some later*.

I fake a gag and take a seat on one of the leather bar stools at the kitchen island. I place a few slices of cheese on a platter just to stop looking at the two of them. They're cute as hell together, but their love is kind of making me sick. I didn't think I'd ever be jealous of one of my friends being in a relationship, but here I am, moping. Since when do I mope?

"Is there something on your mind, Ash? You seem a bit quiet," Olivia says, looking up from the board she just finished arranging.

"I don't have a date to the party," I say, sounding like a teenage girl not having a date to prom. Robbie laughs and we both look over at him with questioning looks on our faces.

"What?" I prod.

"Come on, man. There's gonna be plenty of people here. I'm sure you're gonna find someone to hook up with." He doesn't say it with malice, but his words hit me like a brick just the same. Is that what I've always done? Hooked up and given everyone the impression that I don't want more? Maybe I didn't before, but lately I've found that I do want it—lovey dovey bullshit and all.

"But I don't want to hook up," I whine, like the petulant child that I am.

"Then what do you want?" Robbie asks, exasperated.

"A date. Like, someone to date. For longer than a few hours." And I know exactly who I want—pale blue eyes and light blond hair, built like a viking—but I can never admit to it out loud.

"And you thought waiting until the day before to find that was a good idea?" he deadpans. Olivia sighs and elbows him, which makes me smile. This little firecracker has got my back. A small smile makes its way to my face, but it quickly drops when Olivia questions me.

"Ash, did you have someone particular in mind?" she

asks gently, and for a second I almost want to tell her everything.

I think I have a huge crush on one of my best friends and I don't know what to do about it.

Need advice, please and thank you.

But I can't tell her that, so I pout instead and rest my chin in the palm of my hand. The next moment, Olivia is by my side, giving me a hug. I turn so I can hug her back tightly and look up to see Robbie staring at us. I can't help but tease him again, so I smirk over her shoulder at him.

There's a stark contrast between Robbie and Olivia; he's more blunt with me and knows when to call me out on my bullshit, while Olivia is gentler with her advice. It's no surprise they work so well together.

She pulls back and puts her hands on my shoulders, giving me a stern look. "Ash, I think you need to tell whoever you're pining over how you feel about them. I know it's not easy to open up to someone like that, but if you just hang on to those feelings and don't vocalize them you'll just regret it later."

I sigh and bite the inside of my cheek as I look down at the floor. "But what if they don't feel the same way?"

"Then it's their loss, because you're amazing and you're going to do great things. But also, you deal with it. It won't be easy, but in time you'll move on." I take a moment to appreciate her sage advice then muster up the resemblance of a smile and bring her in for a hug again. I do my best to blink back the tears that threaten to spill, but when Robbie throws down his towel and joins in on the group hug, a traitorous one escapes anyway.

"If you need a wingman, you know I got you, man," Robbie says lightheartedly.

I scoff as I say, "As if I've ever needed a wingman."

. . .

ELI

MY HEAD IS STILL POUNDING from last night's migraine and I take a couple of painkillers, downing a whole bottle of water on my way to Robbie's front door. He's left it unlocked as he sets up for the party and I make my way down the familiar corridor. The place looks impeccable, as always.

I greet everyone with a wave and a mumbled hello and make myself busy hanging up "Happy New Year" garlands in the dining room and large kitchen. I'm sluggishly moving through the motions, willing my headache away.

Robbie is always the host of the group, taking care of us, but he rarely asks for help. I feel bad not being able to give this task my all when my friend needs me.

Olivia and Alice, Robbie's sister, took over the decorations earlier and there are black and gold ornaments and balloons all over the living room, dining room, and kitchen. The island is full of drinks, from champagne and tubs of beer on ice to bottles of liquor and mixers for cocktails. The dining table is elegantly decorated with candles and green vines surrounded by dozens of plates of party food.

Robbie assigned me to furniture duty with Jordan, one of my best friends and teammates. We moved the furniture around in the living room so there's space to mingle and also made sure to lock the doors to the bedrooms, leaving only the mudroom and the two bathrooms accessible to guests.

Once everything is ready, we take a moment to admire the newly transformed living and dining room as we gather in the kitchen. We all grab a drink, smile, and cheers to a job well done and the start of a new beginning. Robbie looks around and asks, "Where's Ash?"

My friends shrug and I zone out of the conversation as I think about the last member of our group.

Ash.

Out of all my friends, he's the one I have a soft spot for. Ever since he got traded to our team, only a few months after I joined, we've been inseparable. We have this running joke that Robbie all but adopted us into the family, but truthfully, I don't know if I would have opened up to anyone if it wasn't for Ash and his incessant line of questioning.

It probably helped a lot that we ended up living across the hall from one another in the same apartment complex. At first, I found it annoying that he constantly wanted to hang out, but now I can't imagine spending our days any other way.

Whether it's going to the gym, coming over to play video games, or simply driving to the arena together, at this point, it's our ritual. I don't think I could imagine playing hockey without him by my side.

I catch snippets of the conversation and try not to daydream as I often do. I hear them talking about the lodge and figure they must have been talking about the all-star break that's coming up.

"Olive, we'll rent a snowboard for you to try and if you hate it, we have plenty of other things we can do. The resort is huge," Robbie says.

"Sounds good. Besides having to teach me, I won't keep you away from the slope, don't worry," she says in a chuckle.

"We're not worried, we all plan to take turns and teach you," I say, joining the conversation.

Robbie called me the other day and wanted to get my

opinion on inviting Olivia to the lodge. I appreciate him asking, but it's not like any of us would say no. She's a really great referee, making all the fair calls on the ice—whether we like them or not—despite having only joined the AHL a few months ago. And even though their relationship is new, she's a great girl who makes him happy. As his best friend, that's all I need to know. Olivia is always welcome in our circle.

I was surprised how quickly Robbie fell in love. He always wears his heart on his sleeve and cares deeply about the people in his life, but I've never seen him quite as happy as he is around her. It's like this little switch was flipped and he became *more*—more attentive, more honest about what he wants. Robbie is determined to make this relationship work and he's determined to play his best, even while considering retirement.

One of the reasons I like Olivia so much is that I can relate to her. I was just as closed off and weary about joining this group of friends and this family, really, until Robbie made me realize how important it is to have a stable foundation and people to rely on. Especially when the world feels so lonely sometimes. I could see that weariness in Olivia too, but I think she's starting to come around more.

AS PEOPLE START TO ARRIVE, the whole place changes from a cozy home to a post-game after-party, which is generally not where I find myself after a game. I like peace and quiet and that's not what I'm in for tonight. There's a faint headache that still lingers, even though I slept most of the day away to recover from my migraine.

I'm not usually one for drinking, but I grab a beer anyway and take a seat on the edge of the couch while I listen in on conversations and people watch. I spot Alice shyly making her way over to Jordan where he's messing around with the computer he hooked up to a surround sound stereo, deciding he's in charge of the music for the night. She tucks a few strands of hair behind her ears with both hands as she tells him something. I'm too far away to hear it, but Jordan laughs and gives her a once over when she's not looking, and the way he's checking out Robbie's little sister is a little more than friendly.

I take a sip of cold beer and let my eyes wander around the room where I see Trip, one of our forwards, with his wife Mackenzie. The two of them are always touching when they're near each other, like they can't possibly keep their hands to themselves. I see Robbie reaching out to put his arm around Olivia as the four of them chat, but he pulls back at the last second and pretends to stretch. Since Olivia is a referee in the same league and region as our team, they're trying to keep their relationship on the down low so neither of them gets in trouble. But anyone with a brain could tell they're smitten with each other just from one glance.

I look around hoping to see a certain redhead, but he's nowhere to be found. I pull out my phone to message him and notice I have a few missed texts. I sigh and scold myself for my annoying habit of keeping my phone on silent.

I've never really been into texting. I prefer to hang out with my friends in person instead. Most days Ash just walks across the hall and lets himself into my apartment when he needs to tell me something, so there's no need to text or call one another. I notice my phone is on do-not-disturb from last night which is probably why I didn't get a notification for Ash's texts.

> this might sound kind of weird, but would you want to go with me to coach grandpa's party?
>
> i know you're already going, obviously, but i mean go together
>
> not just drive together, but like as a date
>
> i'm fucking rambling. srry. had a couple of drinks
>
> i guess i'm just tired of always being dateless at Robbie's parties. thought we could
>
> make it fun
>
> nvm.

I sigh and try to make sense of his ramblings. The guy texts like a highschooler and I always scold him about it. I think about texting back and telling him it might all just be gibberish, but my heart skips at the word I spot. *Date.* Is he —? Is Ashton Meyers actually asking me out on a date?

I read the texts again and again. *Thought we could make it fun.* What the hell does that mean? Before my brain can process what he meant or how I feel about it, someone takes the phone right out of my hand.

"Hey, I was reading that," I say, straightening up on the edge of the couch and coming face to face with Alice.

"Eli, this is a *social* event, you can't just sit in a corner and be on your phone the whole time. And also, since when do you even look at your phone, aren't you like anti-technology?" Alice says, and I swear, sometimes she talks a mile a minute.

I blink at her a few times and squint. "Since when do you care if someone is not participating in a social event?

Aren't you the one that brings your Kindle to every single gathering?"

Alice scoffs at me and looks down at her hands, admiring her manicure. "That's not the same thing," she mumbles and I laugh.

"If you must know, I was checking on Ash. He's not here yet," I say, reaching over and prying my phone from her dainty fingers.

"Oh, you know Ash. He never misses a party, I'm sure he'll show up soon," she says and looks around. Finding what—or who—she was looking for, Alice grabs my arm and pulls me up to stand. "Come on, I want to introduce you to someone."

"Al, no. I don't have the bandwidth to meet new people."

She turns around and gapes at me, "Then what the hell are you doing at a party, Eli?"

I roll my eyes and relent, following her across the room where she's being hugged by another tiny human. Why are girls so small?

"Eli, this is Hannah. I told you about her at Christmas, remember? She's my artist friend, the one who made that Lord of the Rings painting that you loved and stole from me," she says sweetly, but her eyes are narrowed on me.

My smile shows even as I shake my head at her. "I did not steal it from you, *lapsi*." She glares at me harder and I can't help but laugh out loud. Alice hates it when I call her *kid*.

"Well, regardless, this is the genius behind it," she says with another flick of her dark blond hair that's wavy today instead of her regular straight look.

I turn to face Hannah and shake her hand. She's even smaller than Alice. Jesus, she's probably only 5'2", which compared to my 6'3" frame is baffling. She has to tilt her head all the way back to look at me. When she does, I notice more details about her. She's got a nose ring and plump red lips that stand out since she's wearing all black, from her Doc Marten boots, to her leggings and dress, which is tight in all the right places. For any other guy in here, she'd be the perfect catch.

Things would be so much easier if I was attracted to girls.

Hannah gives me a dazzling smile and blushes all the way down to her collarbone. She sways a little as I let go of her hand and I steady her by gently grabbing her shoulder. I realize the effect I have on women, and if I was straight, I wouldn't have an issue leaving the party with someone on my arm. I'd be like Ash.

Ash.

Did he really want to come here with me as his date? Is he insane? What would our teammates think? Most of them are here tonight with their girlfriends or wives. Unlike Ash, who has no problem talking about the girls and guys he's hooked up with, I like to keep my personal life private. Even if he did just ask me as a joke or because I was his last resort, I still would have said no. I care about him and I don't want any of the lines to blur between us.

There's an electric charge in the room and, as always, I can feel Ash's eyes on me. I turn around to look for him and it takes me a second to realize he's at the kitchen island, which means he's already had some drinks. Our gazes lock for a moment and I lift my eyebrows in a silent question of *are you good?*

Ash breaks the contact first and walks away with Robbie who is leading him to the darts board. What the hell was that about? Is he avoiding me because I didn't respond to his messages?

Alice elbows me in the ribs and I whip my head around to look at her. Her lips are pursed and she's giving me an admonishing look. She normally looks so much like Robbie, but I don't think I've ever seen this kind of expression from him before. I frown and glance from her to Hannah who is looking at me expectantly. Shit, did she ask me a question?

"Sorry, I zoned out for a second. What was that?" I say with a fake smile on my face.

"No problem, I asked if you wanted to grab a drink with me?" she says, biting her lip and looking me up and down.

She already has a drink in her hand.

I internally groan and mentally promise to throw Alice in the snow for trying to set me up after I explicitly told her I wasn't interested.

"Um, sure," I say and shuffle on my feet for a bit. Alice gives me an over the top thumbs up but I just shake my head and walk away with Hannah.

"So, I hear you play goalie," she says as we approach the makeshift bar area. I lift a bottle of wine and point it in her direction. She holds out her red solo cup and I pour, waiting for her to tell me to stop. Except she doesn't, so I end up pouring to the brim. *O-kay.*

I shouldn't judge the poor girl, maybe she's shy and needs something to take the edge off, loosen her up a bit. "I do play goalie," I say, opening another beer and taking a sip.

"I bet you're *really* flexible. Can you do the splits?" she asks and I promptly choke on my beer and have to cough into my elbow to regain my composure. Yeah, she's not shy *at all*.

I barely get myself together before she takes a step towards me and places her free hand on my abs, bunching the shirt there. I frown down at her tiny fist, annoyed that she's going to leave wrinkles on my nice button-up.

She leans further into me and goes up on her toes to whisper in my ear, "Maybe you can show me." I lean back slowly, trying to put some much needed distance between us. What is she even talking about? Show her what?

I get distracted by Ash pulling up next to me and grabbing a whole bottle of whiskey off the table before glancing my way.

Hannah pulls back and repeats, "Will you show me how flexible you are?"

My cheeks go red and I look at Ash, but he's already walking away. "Sorry, I don't think I will." I pry her greedy hands off of me and move to follow Ash, but I'm met by a frantic Robbie.

"Hey man, I need your help," he says and pulls me aside. "Can you go hang out with Trip and Mackenzie for like five minutes? I just need a break from socializing."

"Where's Olivia?" I ask.

"My bedroom, waiting for me," he says, smirking.

Ugh. I give him a shake of the head and a fake scowl. "Seriously, you want me to entertain your guests while you *entertain* your girlfriend?"

"What can I say, I'm fucking whipped."

At least he can admit it.

"Okay, fine. You owe me, though."

Robbie smiles and hugs me. "I know. Thanks man." He starts walking away but then turns back, "Oh, can you also keep an eye on Ash? He's been a bit off since yesterday."

"Yeah, sure," I say, mentally preparing myself to go talk to people. Once that is taken care of, I need to talk to Ash and figure out exactly what his message meant.

PART 1

ONE

Present Day

ASH

IT'S funny how much a year can change a person. Last September, I was in the same exact place in Traverse City, Michigan, chugging beers and making fun of Robbie for being old and talking about retiring.

While he may have let me use his parents' cabin for the weekend, Robbie is not here to keep me in check this time. But it's not just him that's missing; Jordan is gone too. He was traded to the Texas Coyotes at the end of last season, right before the Calder Cup playoffs.

Our group has slowly been falling apart, and I can't help but feel responsible for some of it. If we had performed better as a team earlier on in the season, maybe Jordan wouldn't have been traded, maybe Robbie wouldn't have had to retire.

I stand on the back patio of the lakeside cabin and close my eyes, breathing in and out, trying to get my brain to relax. I knew being back here would bring up all the memories of the last year.

I need a drink.

No. I need another appointment with my therapist.

I reach into my pocket with shaky fingers and pull out my phone. The smoke from the neighbor's bonfire wafts over to me, and it brings on a wave of nostalgia.

I want to go back to that night.

When we were all together.

When everything was lighthearted and fun.

When we didn't have all this baggage.

When Eli was still talking to me.

When I didn't fuck everything up.

As I open the contact information for my therapist, my phone starts buzzing. I let it ring a few times, compose myself and then answer. "Hey, *grandpa*, aren't you and Olivia supposed to be on vacation?"

Robbie sighs so loudly, I can almost feel his exasperation through my phone. That makes me smile. "Are you ever going to stop calling me by that stupid nickname?"

I laugh as I pick up my bag from the patio, unlock the back door, and head inside the spacious cabin. "Never, man. You retired, how can I let that go?"

"You're such a shit," he says, but I can hear a hint of a smile in his voice.

"You love me," I tease.

"Yeah, yeah. Did you get in okay?" Robbie asks.

I swallow and drop my bag in the living room of the cabin. The place is cozy as fuck. The living room is large, with two brown leather couches and a chair that faces the fireplace. The mantel has tons of pictures of the Elliots and their kids, and above it, on the wall, is a 70" TV. The kitchen is not quite as large, but it looks spacious. There's even a small kitchen island with a butcher block countertop and pots and pans dangling above it from the wood beam ceiling. The place screams *rustic* and I'm definitely into it.

"Yeah, just got here. Planning to get some rest and be at training camp in the morning," I say, and grab a bottle of water from the stocked fridge. "Who stocks this place, by the way?"

"My parents pay someone to take care of the place, especially when they rent it out or have guests."

"Nice. Tell them thank you, by the way. For letting me crash here."

"Of course, anytime man. Are you feeling better? I know I haven't been around as much with the non-profit taking off and the trip Olive and I planned."

I don't answer right away, but Robbie doesn't press me for an answer. Robbie has been by my side through everything in the last few years. He knows I struggle not just with my depression, but also with my sobriety. I feel bad for making him worry, but when I tell him I've been doing really well lately, I'm not lying. "I'm better. I promise. It's not easy, but I'm not going to let myself down again."

"Good. I'm proud of you, I hope you know that. It took courage for you to ask for help."

I take a deep breath and nod, even though he can't see me. "Yeah, thanks man."

"Alright, I gotta go, but keep me posted on what's happening at training camp. Did you talk to *him* yet?"

"Nope," I say, quickly.

"Okay, well—I hope you know it's inevitable. You'll definitely bump into each other since you're—"

"Yeah, no. I got it. It's all good. Thanks for checking on me Robbie, I'll text you updates, okay? I promise."

He sighs, but says, "Okay, have a good time."

"You too. Say hi to Olivia for me."

As soon as he hangs up, my shoulders relax. I look around the spacious living room and pick up my bag again.

The cabin is quite large and can accommodate at least six to eight people. In the winter, we like to take a weeklong vacation during the all-star break and come up here. The cabin is only twenty minutes away from the slopes where we like to unwind and snowboard every year. There are two medium-sized bedrooms, a loft, and one of the main couches is a pullout, so this place is perfect for our big group of friends.

I walk down the narrow hallway that has even more pictures of young Robbie and his siblings, Alice, and Michael. All of them look happy and are smiling while out on the slopes or the water. They really are a wholesome family, unlike mine ever was. Growing up in one of the rich neighborhoods of Boston as an only child was kind of terrible, if I'm being honest. My parents were never the type to dote on me or show much affection. It was all about tough love in the Meyers household.

I shake away the image of my childhood and I continue down the hallway. I choose the bedroom closest to the bathroom and begin unpacking for the week—mostly shorts and T-shirts, but also some nicer clothes for going out in case I don't feel like cooking while I'm here.

When I'm done, I walk around the empty cabin and I'm hit by a pang of loneliness. This is all wrong. My friends should be here with me. Robbie, Jordan, Eli, Olivia, hell, even Alice. All of us haven't been in the same room together since April when we had a going away party for Jordan.

Actually, now that I think about it, Alice wasn't even there that day. So the last time we were all in a room together was probably the day Olivia got out of the hospital after she was injured on the ice.

That was such a messed up game. One of the players on our rival team, Mitchell, ended up checking Olivia so hard that she hit her head and broke a couple of ribs. That was also the one and only time I saw Robbie completely lose his shit. He wasn't one for violent fights before, but when he saw Olivia unconscious on the ice, he gave Mitchell the beating of his life. Mitchell was fired after being found to hit Olivia with intent to injure, and Robbie retired from the team a month before the season ended, which is a shame because that was the season we made it to the Calder Cup. He doesn't regret his decision though, as he's able to spend more time with Olivia now. And he started a non-profit hockey organization for kids called Blue Line Brigade that's starting to take off.

My phone buzzes and I see a text from Olivia. It's a picture of Robbie asleep on the couch with both cats on top of him—Beans on his lap and Caramel on his chest. I send back a heart and realize it's late and that I should probably go to sleep. Training camp starts in the morning and I need to give it my best this season.

I toss and turn more than usual and my brain keeps coming up with scenarios of what my reunion with Eli will be like.

Will he talk to me?
Will he even look at me?
Will he forgive me?

ELI

. . .

AFTER A SERIES of delayed flights and lost luggage, I finally landed back on familiar ground. Training camp starts tomorrow and my plan was to get to Traverse City early and get some rest, but the universe must be against me because my trip back to the States was a mess.

I spent the last couple months back home in Finland, training and clearing my head. My parents and little brother, Edvin, were ecstatic to have me home, if only for a short amount of time. I feel bad that I picked a career that's so far away from them, but at the same time, I need to chase my dream.

My trip home also gave me the space and clarity I needed after a wild season in Grand Marquee to figure out what I want for myself going forward. I feel like I am more confident in my goaltending capabilities now after training all summer with my father, the person I trust most when it comes to my career. But I also feel more confident in who I am as an individual and I'm ready to take more chances this year. While it was nice to see my family, I am definitely excited for a new season, even if it will be a weird one.

I don't make friends easily, and two of my closest ones are gone—Jordan is starting his first season in Texas and hasn't been answering my calls and texts recently, and Robbie is focusing all his time on the non-profit. And after everything that went down between me and Ash, things kind of soured between me and Robbie as well. As the protector of the friend group, let's just say he wasn't happy when he found out about our falling out.

I get out of the taxi and grab my small backpack, disappointed that I decided to travel light this time. I only brought my laptop and a book and I don't even have a change of underwear, let alone clothes, which means I will need to go shopping early in the morning.

I glance at my watch and notice it's past two in the morning. I have to be up at 6 a.m. if I want to shop and make it to training camp on time. I sigh and scrub my hand over my face, feeling more scruff than usual.

Damn it, I don't even have a razor.

My phone battery is at 10% and I wearily turn on the flashlight to look for the key to the front door. It's exactly where Alice said it would be, under the potted fern on the porch. Robbie's little sister has been more of a friend to me recently than Robbie himself has. She and I have been texting over the summer a lot more, and she's been helping me navigate some of my anxiety and feelings. It helps that she's a good listener and always gives me great book recommendations too.

Fumbling with the keys, I almost drop my phone, but catch it at the last second. The door finally opens and I rush inside, locking it behind me. I head straight for one of the bedrooms down the hall, hoping my phone won't die overnight. Just in case it does, I set an alarm on my watch. I don't even have time to overthink what tomorrow will bring, and what I'll say to Ash when I see him again, because sleep pulls me under instantly.

TWO

Eight Months Ago

ASH

I'VE LOST count of the drinks I've had throughout the night, but I'm not passed out yet, which means I haven't had enough. I brood miserably at the table and recount everything that happened yesterday.

After my conversation with Olivia and Robbie, I went back to my apartment and freaked out twenty different ways about how I should ask Eli to be my date to the party.

I was distracted during the game too, and I kept to myself, even when Eli tried to make conversation in the locker room. I faked a smile and pretended like nothing was up, like my feelings weren't all over the place. Because what the fuck?

I thought about the day I met Eli at training camp two years ago. He was quiet and brooding and barely said a word to me when I introduced myself. That attitude seemed to be his default mode for the first few months, and at first we thought he was just really anti-social. Looking back on it, I know he was just nervous to make new friends, especially as he had just moved here from Finland and experienced quite the Midwest culture shock. But slowly, he started opening up to Robbie, and indirectly to me, because I was trailing them around all over the place.

During the past two years, Eli and I went from teammates, to friends, to—well, *more*. We spend basically every single moment together, whether it's at practice, in the locker room, at the gym, at his apartment across the hall, on road trips, and even on our days off. Is it really that crazy to wrap my head around the fact that I started having *feelings* for him?

But here's the thing. I don't do *feelings*. I never have. I hookup, I have friends with benefits, but I don't do *this*. I don't become this mess of a person who doesn't know how to ask for what he wants.

Lately it's been really hard to be around him and pretend like I don't want him. I catch myself watching him more. The way his muscles shift when he's getting undressed in the locker room, the way his pale blue eyes sparkle when he makes a joke, the way his ass looks when he does squats at the gym.

Fuck. Fuck. Fuck.

Eli was quiet during our drive to our apartment building last night, so I didn't bring up the party. He said goodnight and headed to his apartment and I went to mine. After having a few drinks for liquid courage, I went across the hall to his apartment, but the door was locked. It was only a quarter past eleven and Eli should have been up.

Normally I would bring over a few beers and we'd sit together on the couch and chat.

I knocked hard a couple of times, but after not getting a reply, I headed back to my own apartment. After pacing around what felt like an eternity, I decided to text him. *Worst decision ever.*

I stare at my phone again and notice the messages haven't even been seen. *Gee, thanks.* After waiting around for hours last night in my drunken state and realizing I wasn't getting a reply, I went to sleep. All throughout today I've checked my messages, hoping he at least read them, but there's nothing.

I feel like a fool.

What was I thinking?

Thought we could make it fun.

Eli is not some guy that I can just hook up with. I don't even know if he's into guys, although I have my suspicions.

Although, seeing that girl draped all over him at the kitchen island is now making me question things. I caught the last question she asked him before I walked away with a bottle of liquor.

Will you show me how flexible you are?

Will he?

Trip asks me something and I shake my head, coming out of my daze. I'm about to fake a smile and reply to whatever he said when I see Eli making his way towards us at our corner of the dining room table. He takes a seat at the head of the table, where Robbie was perched before.

"Hey guys, how's it going?" he asks Trip and Mack with a genuine smile. I brood quietly next to him and watch him as I nurse my sixth or seventh drink of the night. Perfect Elias is looking a bit rumpled. The blue dress shirt he's sporting tonight has some wrinkles in it, which I'm sure he's annoyed about. I've rarely seen Eli in any sort of disarray. His apartment is always perfectly put together, his bathroom is squeaky clean and looks more like a fancy restaurant bathroom than a hockey player's bathroom. My apartment on the other hand is in a chaotic state with clothes and bottles strewn all over the place. No wonder he never comes over to my place.

Eli introduces Trip and Mack to Alice who immediately starts chatting them up about their most recent vacation. He turns to look at me and his gaze is contemplative. Pale blue eyes are bouncing all over my face and he suddenly frowns. "Can I have a word with you?" he asks low enough so only I can hear.

I lean in closer to him and some of my pettiness shows as I whisper, "Where's your puck bunny? She was dying to see how flexible you are."

Eli's jaw is set and I see a muscle twitching, which makes me smirk. "Don't tell me you didn't show her your stretches. Especially that one where you look like you're humping the—"

Eli stands and grabs me by the elbow so quickly that I nearly knock a glass off the table. I manage to catch it just in time and I shoot the whiskey before placing it down. The next thing I know, I am being dragged across the room. Is it spinning or is that just me?

"What, man? Where are we going?" I ask, annoyed that he's taken me away from the party. The last thing I want is to be confronted about my idiotic texts.

Eli opens the door to the small laundry room and all but shoves me in there. I stumble a bit and he notices, so he steadies me with a hand on my shoulder.

Then he closes the door.

. . .

ELI

I'M SO mad at Ash, I don't even know where to start. I want to scold him for the comments he was making at the table. While he thought he was whispering, the truth is everyone could clearly hear what he was saying about Hannah, and Alice was right there, looking at me with wide eyes. So I panicked and dragged him here. Not my finest moment, but here we are nonetheless.

My annoyance flares as I think about the texts from last night. What the fuck was he going on about? I doubt I will get any straight answers from him right now though, he's a drunken mess. I sigh and deflate a little when I see Ash looking at me. He looks so lost and scared. What is he afraid of?

"Are you okay?" I gently ask him.

"I'm fantastic. Don't I show it?" he smiles, but it's all wrong. It's not his charming, beautiful smile. This one is all tense and lopsided.

"Tell me what those texts were about," I hear myself say, even though I know he's gonna deflect.

"I'd rather not. I'm drunk," he says, looking past my shoulder at the door.

"Tell me. *Please.*"

Ash shakes his head and looks up at the ceiling, crossing his arms over his chest. Alright then.

"I don't know what's going on with you recently, but you know I'm always here for you, right? No matter what. You can tell me anything."

He rubs his hands over his face and starts pacing around like a cornered animal. I get the feeling I'm somehow making it worse so I say, "I'm sorry, Ash. I'll leave you be."

I open the door a crack and can hear people starting to count down the thirty seconds until midnight.

"Why was your door locked?" Ash says before I can walk out. I turn around to face him and he's slowly walking up to me. His fingers are clenching and unclenching at his sides and for a moment, I'm distracted, until I realize he's asking about last night.

"I got a migraine, so I went straight to sleep. My phone was on do-not-disturb until I got here." I see his lips part at my admission, and his eyes find mine. Did he think I was ignoring him on purpose?

"Oh. Was it a bad one?"

"I managed," I say with a half shrug. The truth is, it was a bad one. I don't get them often, but when I do, they knock me out on my ass.

Ash nods, his shoulders relaxing just an inch. "I came over to talk to you. I wanted you to be my date to the party," he says.

Shit. I stop breathing for a moment because his honesty takes me by surprise.

"Why?" I hear myself ask as I grip the door handle tighter.

Ash laughs and shakes his head. He looks at the crack in the door for a moment and we both hear the countdown.

10, 9, 8…

His hand comes up near my head and he shoves the door closed, his body pressing into me.

"Because," he says, keeping his right hand propped on the door as his left hand lifts up to grab the back of my head and all I see is red hair, freckles, dark blue eyes, and full lips. Everything is still and I hear the muffled noises through the door. "Because I like you," he whispers and I can feel his warm breath on me.

3, 2, 1...

And then—his lips are on mine, and I freeze. I didn't expect it. Never in my wildest dreams did I think there was a possibility of him liking me back. Even though my head is telling me this is a bad idea, that he's drunk and I'm not what he needs, my heart and my body are telling me something very different. Because when Ash's tongue touches my lips I open up and deepen the kiss.

He tastes like whiskey and cherries and I feel fucking intoxicated. I match the fervor of his kiss touch for touch. When he pulls, I pull harder. When he pushes, I flip him around and back him against the door. His hands move over me frantically like he can't believe this is happening, like he doesn't want to let go. *I don't want to either.*

I don't know how much time has passed, but out of nowhere, the door starts to open. Before it can hit Ash in the back, I slam my hand against it and yell out, "Just a moment." My voice comes out high pitched and panicked.

"Eli, is that you?" Robbie asks from the hallway.

"Yeah, I needed a second to myself," I say, flustered. Ash's breath is hot against my cheek as we stand here and I silently beg Robbie to go away.

After a beat, he finally says, "Take your time. I just couldn't remember leaving the light on in here." I wait until I hear his footsteps retreating to look at Ash. As soon as I do, his lips are on mine again.

"Wait," I say halfheartedly. Ash's lips move to my neck and he starts to lick and suck at my sensitive skin. But I can't do this. What am I thinking? He's drunk, and I care too much about him to turn this into a one night stand.

"Just, wait," I say and gently push him away. His face falls and I already hate myself for taking away the small joy I've seen there all night. "I don't think we should do this.

We work together, we're friends." I really don't want to stop this, but I have to. "I care about you Ash, but I don't think hooking up is a good idea."

He bites the inside of his cheek and nods, turning around and leaving me alone in the laundry room. I stay behind longer than I need to, thinking of how devastated he looked.

THREE

Eight Months Ago

ELI

ASH GOT PROGRESSIVELY MORE drunk as the night went on and he's now passed out on the couch, a bottle of whiskey dangling from his hand. Once most of the guests leave, I try to wake him up and take him home, but I don't think that's an option at this point.

"Just let him spend the night here," Robbie says, joining me in the living room.

"What if he has to throw up at some point? You want him to do that on your nice carpet?"

Robbie winces and says, "No, but if you take him home he'll probably throw up all over his bed."

"I was planning on taking him to my place," I say and catch the surprise on Robbie's face. Maybe I'm revealing too much, but I trust Robbie and maybe it's time to be more open with my best friend. "What is it?" I ask.

He hesitates, but then says, "Nothing, that's just surprising. You two didn't seem to get along that well tonight. Is everything okay?"

"Yeah," I sigh, contemplating how much to tell Robbie. "It's not that we don't get along. I just don't like it when he drinks so much. It's hard to have a serious conversation with him." I shrug but take a seat on the small patch of couch that's not covered by Ash's slumped body. I reach down and take the bottle from him, then move his dangling arm up and lay it over his stomach. He doesn't stir.

"Can I ask you something personal?" Robbie asks quietly, even though no one else is around to hear. I know what he expects, for me to shut down, but I hold my breath in anticipation and nod.

"Why do you always take care of him?"

I exhale in a rush, relieved he didn't ask the obvious question. *Do you have feelings for him?* I clasp my hands so hard they turn white and say, "He's my friend. I care about all of you."

"That's a lie. I mean you care about us, sure, but you don't treat us like this. You don't cover us with blankets when you think we're cold. You don't bring us water when we're hungover. You don't rub our backs when we throw up because we drank too much. Should I keep going?"

"No." I take a moment to gather my thoughts then say, "It's hard to explain. When I met him I thought he was an idiot and he probably still is, but he's *my* idiot, you know?"

Robbie smiles and sits down on the oversized chair next to the couch. His easygoing attitude makes me relax more so I continue. "I told myself I wouldn't make the same mistakes again. I know I never talk about my previous relationship, but I was young and stupid and fell in love with a teammate." I look up at him, waiting for any judgment or negative reaction, but all I get back is a nod.

"I was twenty-four when we started seeing each other. We were on the same team in Finland and we hit it off. Both of us wanted to keep it a secret because, let's be real, gay men in hockey are not exactly respected." There are very few openly gay players in the league, if at all. So we did our best to hide it, and we did for two years, until a couple months before my trade here. "I was ready to come out, but he didn't think I should. He basically told me I'd ruin my career if I did. So I asked him where he saw our relationship going. You know what he said?"

Robbie shakes his head and waits for me to find my words. I swallow the bitterness of that failed relationship and the disappointment that came with it and say, "Nowhere. He said it was just a fun way to pass the time for a while, but he would never even dream about being seen with me in public, let alone date me openly."

"So what's keeping you from telling all this to Ash? I mean he's not exactly closeted. Sure, he doesn't publicly announce his orientation, but we all know he's bi."

My gaze strays to Ash again and I watch his chest rise and fall a few times before answering. "I just don't think I'd be good for him. He's got so much potential, and I've got a lot of baggage that he doesn't need to deal with. I don't want to put that pressure on him."

"I still think you should tell him."

"Yeah, maybe," I sigh, my fingers itching to brush Ash's hair off his forehead.

"You know what I think?" Robbie says, and I finally pull my eyes away from Ash. "I think he gets drunk on purpose so you take care of him. Because he's too scared to tell you how he feels and so he hides behind pretenses to be near you," Robbie continues, and of course he's right on the money.

Except, Ash did tell me how he felt, or tried to at least.

He said he *liked me*.

When I don't say anything else, Robbie stands up. "You should take him to the spare bedroom and stay with him so he doesn't throw up all over *my* bed, yeah?"

"Yeah, okay," I say quietly, looking at Ash and giving in. My fingers brush the soft hair off of his forehead and he sighs in his sleep.

I carry Ash to the spare bedroom and make sure he's on his side in case he wakes up and needs to throw up. I leave a trash can next to the side of the bed, for good measure. Once I'm sure he'll be okay for a few minutes, I step out again to get some water. When I get to the kitchen, I'm startled by Olivia as she closes the fridge and faces me.

I bring a hand to my heart and say, "*Helvetti!* Olivia, you scared me."

She chuckles but quietly says, "Sorry, Eli."

"It's okay," I say and approach the island, tapping it with my fingers.

"What does that word mean?" she asks and opens the fridge back up.

"*Helvetti?*"

Olivia nods and turns toward me, handing me two water bottles.

"It means hell."

"*Helvetti*, I like it," she says.

"I can teach you more, if you'd like." Olivia raises an eyebrow, surprised. I guess I should try harder to connect with her, now that she's officially Robbie's girlfriend. "That way you can swear at players on ice without them knowing. Unless they're Finnish. Then they'll know," I say, and Olivia bursts into laughter. I can't help but join in.

"What's the word for *ass*?" she asks.

"*Perse*."

She giggles again and says, "Dustin Mitchell is a *perse*."

I shake my head, "No, Mitchell is a *vittu*."

"What's a *vittu*?" she asks and takes a sip of water.

"Cunt," I say, and when she chokes on her water, I laugh.

"I like you, Eli," she says and heads to Robbie's room.

When I return to the spare bedroom, Ash is still in the same position as I left him. I take a moment to really look at him, unabashedly. He looks like a disheveled mess, but damn, he's beautiful. I swallow and lie down next to him on the queen-sized bed. Sleep doesn't come for hours, but I lie there anyway and listen to him breathe.

ASH

I WAKE up at some point during the night, but as soon as I open my eyes and try to stand I can feel the room spinning. I know I drank way too much and that I should have faced Eli and his rejection head on rather than soften the blow with liquor, but I also just wanted to stop feeling so much.

I can't ever seem to be *good enough*. Not for my family, not for my friends, not for Eli.

The thought makes me sick to my stomach, or that could just be the alcohol in my system. I stumble through the darkness of what I assume is Robbie's guest bedroom and make my way to where I think the bathroom is. Except

I miss by a whole foot and hit the wall instead. The mattress creaks behind me but I don't have the energy to even turn around and see who it is.

I hiccup and know without a doubt that I'm about to throw up all over Robbie's carpet. Warm hands reach for me and grab my biceps, then lead me towards the bathroom. The light turns on the lowest dimmed setting and I spot Eli in the mirror as he guides me to the toilet. He brings me there just in time for me to purge the old year and all the bad decisions I made. A warm hand rubs constant circles on my back and I don't know if it's the fact that I'm such a mess or the fact that he's still so kind to me after everything, that brings me to tears.

I kneel there and heave until there's nothing else coming out of me and Eli helps me up and leads me to the sink, where he wordlessly hands me a toothbrush and toothpaste. As I sluggishly brush my teeth, he heads out to the bedroom and comes back with a bottle of water that he has me chug down. The light is so dim that it starts to flicker, and I can't help but take in Eli's rumpled look.

He looks tired.

He looks *beautiful*.

He looks like he deserves better than taking care of me at four in the morning.

All my self hatred comes rushing in and I can't keep the tears away, so I lean over the sink and put my head in my hands so he doesn't see me. As much as I like him taking care of me, I don't want him to only see me at my worst.

His hand lands on my back again, resuming the soothing movements and my shoulders start to shake with my silent crying. I bite my lip so I don't make a noise.

"Do you need to throw up again?" he gently asks and I can't do anything but shake my head.

"Why doesn't anyone want me?" I whisper so quietly, hoping that he doesn't hear it but needing to say it anyway.

Eli's comforting movements stop, but a second later he asks, "What?"

I sniffle loudly and stand up fully, slowly looking at him in the mirror. Eli's eyes are worried, taking in the tears on my face. He's only an inch or two taller than me, but his broad shoulders and thick thighs make him look larger, and with the way I'm caving in on myself, I feel like a child. Both his hands come up to my shoulders as he slowly turns me towards him. I can't help but let out a sob.

"Hey, what is going on?" Eli asks again, arms squeezing me gently.

I hang on to his arms but can't quite put into words what it is I'm feeling. *Shame, sadness, self hatred.* All the things I feel on a regular basis. I want to disappear because that will make everyone's lives easier.

So I just cry. Eli brings me into a tight hug and lets me sob into his shoulder as I repeatedly whisper, "*I'm sorry.*"

After what feels like forever in his arms, Eli leads me back to the bed. Once I assure him I won't throw up again, he helps me take off my clothes so I'm left in my boxers and white undershirt. He does the same and joins me back in bed, covering us both with the duvet.

Almost like he senses I need affection, he moves us around so that my back is flush with his front, and his left hand comes around to grip mine. Eli interlaces our fingers and I bring our hands up to my chest, where I hold tight. This is the most intimate position we've ever been in together and I can't help but feel like I forced him into it. One more thing to add to the list of things I hate about myself tonight.

Drinking myself into oblivion? *Check.*

Pressured my best friend into cuddling me after being an absolute shit all night? *Check.*

Kissed him like my life depended on it only for him to reject me? *Check.*

How the fuck am I going to fix this?

FOUR

Eight Months Ago

ELI

I WAKE up to the sound of paws scratching at the bedroom door. I try to shift around but I'm trapped by a heavy arm and a body sprawled all over me. I blink down and see Ash's head on my chest, his right arm around my torso. His legs are tangled up with mine and I try to reign in my feelings. The truth is, I've kept my desires and my feelings for Ash locked tight for a while now.

There's so much about him that I like and I've *dreamed* about moments like this many times before—lazy mornings together and his body on top of mine. I swallow hard and blink back all the emotion that wants to bubble up to the surface.

God, how I've wanted this.

Ever since that first day at training camp when he barreled into my life with his friendly attitude and charming personality, I've always had a soft spot for him. I tried to keep my distance at first, the last thing I needed was to develop a crush on yet another teammate, but wherever Robbie and I went, Ash followed. Long days traveling on the road and even longer nights talking in my apartment and playing video games made me crave more. More of this, him, us, the simplicity of just being near each other, being openly affectionate. It's something I've never had before in any relationship. And I want it so much I'm willing to take it now when I know I shouldn't. He was drunk last night, and while he said he liked me and kissed me, that might not mean anything.

What shocked me the most was his breakdown. I've never seen him cry before and seeing him so sad and broken made me feel so helpless.

Why doesn't anyone want me? Is that really what he thinks? That no one wants him?

I just wanted to help him, but I didn't know how. I wanted to tell him how often I think of him. I wanted to kiss him and show him how much I want him. But there's clearly something more there for him to unpack, and the last thing I want to be is his self-appointed therapist.

When the scratching at the door doesn't stop, I slowly get out from under Ash, brushing the dark red hair off his forehead in the process. I open the door and see one of Robbie's cats, Caramel—the orange one—looking up at me with big green eyes. I bend down and pick him up, snuggling him to my chest, knowing he's about as affectionate as me and doesn't like to be snuggled often. When I turn around with the cat in my arms, I see Ash is awake and looking at me. He's turned around so he's lying on his back now, one arm draped over his torso and I bring Caramel up to my face to hide my smile.

I approach the bed and slowly place Caramel on top of Ash's stomach before sitting down next to him. I know his eyes are glued to my face, but for once he's quiet. The cat immediately loaves up on top of Ash and starts purring, so I give him pets and steal a glance at Ash. He's still looking at me, dark blue eyes unblinking while he takes shallow breaths. I can sense he's worried about what I will say.

Eventually, he starts petting the cat too, and our fingers brush every now and again with each stroke. When I find the words I want to say, I stop his fingers with a gentle touch of my hand. Caramel senses he's no longer needed so he jumps down and leaves, while our hands fall together on Ash's stomach. I caress his thumb back and forth and say, "Are you hungry?"

"Yeah," he croaks out, still looking at me skittishly.

I nod and stand up, handing him a pile of clothes from the top of the dresser. "Robbie left these for us last night before he went to bed. Get dressed and we'll go."

ASH

AFTER A LONG STARING battle with myself in the mirror, I come out of the bathroom dressed and ready to go. I have no idea what is going on with Eli or why he's not mad at me, but he gives me a small smile and says, "Let's go get breakfast."

"Where are we going?"

"You'll see," he says, blue eyes sparkling. This is...strange.

We quietly make our way out of the guest bedroom in case Robbie and Olivia are sleeping, but as we're walking by their door we hear the shower running and a muffled thumping against the wall.

I turn to Eli so quickly that it can't possibly be good for my hangover. We both look at each other with the same wide-eyed expression and when I hear the thumping sound again, Eli has to slap his hand over my mouth to muffle my loud laugh.

"Shh," he says, face close to mine as his hand still covers my lips. There's a smile in his eyes and the next thump has him chuckling so that I end up covering his mouth too. We stand there for a second, giggling against each other's hands. Our gazes lock and I catalog every tiny brown fleck that surround his irises. The contrast is stark against his light blue gaze and I wonder how I've never noticed it before. My gaze drops to his mouth covered by my hand, and I can feel his warm breath on my fingers. Slowly, Eli releases me, and with one last look that borders on lingering, he drags me away to the hallway.

We put our jackets on and have a laughing fit as we get in his car, but once Eli starts driving, the lightheartedness seems to dissipate. An awkward silence takes its place and for the first time in a long time, I don't know what to say. Eli doesn't turn the radio on and neither do I, and my hangover headache hits me in full force.

The rest of the car ride to downtown is just as quiet and I'm starting to get antsy. Is he buttering me up with food before telling me we can't be friends anymore?

"Can you at least give me a hint as to what we're eating?" I ask, stealing a glance at him. His hands are relaxed on the wheel and he has an expression that I can't quite decipher. He doesn't look mad, but he's also not smiling anymore.

"That honey biscuit place you've been pestering me about for months," he says nonchalantly and I immediately perk up. Eli and I got brunch together every Sunday over the summer and I always suggested this place but he always refused because it's always packed with people and he doesn't enjoy crowds.

"Seriously?"

"Yes, *kultsi*," he says with a small smile. My head snaps over to the driver seat. What did he just call me? I don't often hear Eli speaking in his native language, so this takes me by surprise. I take longer than needed to respond to him since I'm stuck on the foreign word. Is it a nickname? No one's ever called me anything other than Ash or Ashton. I don't hate the idea of him calling me something else—something meant only for me.

"You must really care about me if you're taking me there. I've only been talking about it for months," I say with a scoff.

Eli's smile falls and he takes a glance at me before returning his eyes to the road. He grips the wheel a bit tighter and says, "Of course I care about you. Do you really believe otherwise?"

I fall silent for the rest of the drive and Eli doesn't say anything else either.

When we get to the restaurant, it's surprisingly not as busy as usual. Must be because it's New Year's Day and people are either sleeping off their hangovers or spending time with their families. The waitress is all smiles as she leads us to a booth in the back where it's nice and quiet. Thank god, because I'm starting to develop a massive headache after all the drinking last night.

"Can I get you anything to drink to get you started?" she asks, and I don't miss her flirty attitude or the way her eyes roam over me. Any other day, I would flirt right back, maybe even get her number and invite her over to my place. But my head has been so fucked up recently, even the thought of it makes me queasy.

"Water, please," I say without paying her any more attention.

"Two waters, two coffees, and two glasses of orange juice," Eli says and gives the girl a smile. What the hell? Since when does he smile at strangers? I feel like the roles are reversed here and I don't like it one bit.

"Coming right up!" she says, all chipper.

We quietly look over the menu and the waitress comes back with all of our drinks. I gulp down the water immediately and pour myself some more from the bottle she left on the table.

Food doesn't even sound good at the moment so I don't mind when Eli takes charge and orders us both breakfast. I'm too distracted by my headache and the decor of the restaurant to even pay attention.

The place is very sleek and modern looking, but comfortable at the same time. The walls are navy blue, the upholstery on the chairs and booths is steel gray and all the art and decorations are a nice, soft yellow. There are even fresh yellow flowers in vases on all the tables. Must be expensive this time of year.

"*Ilo*. Did you hear me?" Eli says, pulling me out of my stupor. I narrow my eyes at him. This is the second time he's called me a foreign word. They sound different, but I have no idea what they could mean. It's not *kusipää*, which is the only Finnish word I know. It means *fucker* and let's just say Eli uses that one a lot on the ice.

"What do you keep calling me?" I ask before taking another big swig of water and sip the coffee. My grimace must be quite ferocious because Eli laughs and takes my coffee away. Before I can complain about it, he rips open two packets of sugar and a packet of vanilla creamer and adds them to my cup. My brain short circuits in the face of his kindness and I'm left with nothing else to say or do, except stare at him. Eli's long fingers are lightly gripping the spoon as he stirs my coffee. He's so fucking good, and kind, and pretty. Everything about him is pale: his skin, his blond hair, his blue eyes, and yet, *he shines so fucking bright*.

I take my time and admire his movements. Eli's hands are big, but not meaty like one would think for a goaltender. His fingers are long and deft and he keeps his fingernails trimmed and proper, just like the rest of him. His hair is soft but not too long, and his eyebrows are thick and pale. I don't think I've ever seen him with scruff, let alone a beard, and his clothes are always clean and crisp. He's so put together and it bothers the shit out of me. I want to rumple him up. Make a mess of him.

Would he let me?

He says something and my gaze drops down to his mouth and his pink, kissable lips. His bottom lip is slightly plumper than his top and all I can think about is how good he tasted last night, how I wanted to run my teeth along that lip and tease it.

My gaze snaps up to his and I realize I've been caught. Eli stares right back at me with a small smile and pushes the coffee back over to my side of the table.

"Drink, it will help with the hangover."

"Thanks," I mumble.

Our food arrives quickly and we eat in companionable silence. Eli ordered me a plate of *shakshuka* and a side of the famous biscuits and this is seriously the best thing I've ever eaten.

"How do you always do this?" I ask, closing my eyes around another bite of biscuit and almost moaning in pleasure.

"Do what?" he says with a laugh.

"Know exactly what I need, when I need it?"

Eli swallows a bite of his fancy egg white omelet and looks at me but doesn't say anything. He just shrugs.

"It's like your superpower. You always read people's moods and know exactly what to do or say." Eli blushes at my words and I think it's time we stop ignoring the elephant in the room.

"I'm sorry," I blurt out, "about last night."

Eli sits back in his seat and inhales deeply. "Which part are you sorry about?"

I hold his gaze and try to figure out what he might be thinking but the man might as well be out there on the ice. He's an immovable block. Unreadable.

I bite my lip and reluctantly respond, "All of it." I think I see the smallest of shudders in his facade so I decide to take a leap. "All of it, except for the kiss."

There. It's out now. I may not recall everything I said last night, but I remember telling him I liked him, and I remember him taking care of me when I got too drunk. *Like he always does.*

Eli links his fingers together and rests his elbows on the table. His head drops down as he rests his forehead on his hands and I let him process what I just said.

After what feels like forever, I start to talk. Because I hate silence and I can't fucking help myself. "Look, if this is too weird, or too much, I get it. I'm a lot to handle and you definitely deserve better, and—"

"Stop," he says, lifting his head and looking at me with such a fierce expression that I immediately clamp my mouth shut, "Stop putting yourself down like that."

I open my mouth but nothing comes out. So I close it and do my best to swallow. I didn't expect him to say *that*.

"You are not too much to handle, and you don't know the first thing about what I *deserve*," he spits the word out with such malice it's like I personally offended him with it. Damn, maybe I have.

I lift my hands up and say, "Okay. Alright. All I'm trying to say is that I like you. I *want* you. But if you don't feel the same way, that's totally cool."

What the hell is coming out of my mouth?

Totally *not* cool.

I might fucking die if he doesn't feel the same.

"Of course I like you, Ash," he says, and I nearly leap out of my seat and into his lap, "but—"

No, no *but*.

Damn it.

Eli looks around the restaurant for a bit and then back at me. "But I'm not ready to be out. I don't know if I will be anytime soon."

I sigh and my shoulders slump. I can understand him not wanting to come out, but it's not like I'm asking for his hand in marriage. So I try my best to convince him. "Look, I'm not asking for a relationship. Hell, I'm not asking for anything, really. But maybe we can have some fun, you know? We can keep it casual. No labels."

Eli shakes his head and I feel like an ass for even suggesting all we do is hook up. "Why, then? If you feel the same way, why would you deny us both?"

"Because I've been through this before, okay?" he says, exasperated.

"You have?" I ask, confused. Eli never talks about his love life. As curious as I am, I don't know if I want him to tell me now. Not after our kiss last night. I don't think I could bear thinking about him with someone else.

Eli rubs a hand across his face before moving to his jaw. His eyes meet mine again, and this time I can see how sad he is about all of this. "When I was playing back home in Finland, I was seeing someone. A teammate. We were together for a while and we kept it a secret, but when I mentioned I wanted to come out, he freaked out. He said it wasn't a good idea, that it would ruin my career. After all that, even though I changed my mind and listened to his advice, he still dumped me."

I reach my hand out and hold his, trying to offer some comfort. I want to say: *This will be different. We'll be different.*

But I don't get the chance as he says, "I just don't think it would be a good idea to go there. I promised myself I wouldn't make the same mistakes as before. And also, you're one of my best friends." Eli squeezes my hand in his before pulling back. "I don't want to lose your friendship. You mean too much to me."

Well, shit.

I've just been friend-zoned.

FIVE

Present Day

ELI

I SLEPT LIKE A ROCK. As soon as my head hit the pillow, I immediately fell asleep. Thankfully, my watch alarm woke me up. Making a bad impression by being late is the last thing I want to kick off training camp.

For us AHL players, this is our chance to show the higher ups in the league that we can hold our own—that we have what it takes to be in the NHL—so that when the team gets plagued by injuries in the middle of the season, we are the ones called up.

Last season, I was called up once when one of the two NHL goalies had a personal problem come up. Unfortunately, I wasn't the starting goalie that night, and I spent the entire time geared up on the bench. But it was nice to practice with the "big guys" at least.

The other goaltender, Juuse, was also from Finland and it was nice to have someone to speak with in my native language. He was also very helpful during practice and gave me lots of pointers. Though he's only a few years older than me, I appreciated him taking me under his wing, even if it was short lived. We haven't really kept in touch since, but he texted me yesterday, asking if I wanted to grab a coffee one of these days since we're both in town for the camp.

I haven't responded yet, but I think I would like that. Outside of our main group of friends, I'm usually shy and reserved. It's not that I don't like people, I just find it hard to connect to anyone outside of hockey.

They always say goalies are a different *breed*, that we must be a little crazy to willingly put ourselves in front of a puck moving more than 80 mph. To that I say, *bring on the craziness*. There's nothing more exhilarating than being in front of the net and making that perfect save, especially if it's the game winning one.

I check my phone and see it still has 6% battery. I send Juuse a text, telling him we can grab coffee tomorrow, and while I'm bleary eyed and tired as hell, I decide to make my way to the shower and let the cold water wake me.

I rub the sleep away from my eyes with my knuckles and don't realize something is wrong until I reach the bathroom door, which is ajar. There is steam coming out of the bathroom and all I can do is stand there, puzzled.

Is someone else here?

Before I can turn around and head back to the bedroom to find yesterday's clothes, the bathroom door swings open the rest of the way and a very wet, very naked Ash is standing in front of me.

Fuck. Me.

I was wondering how our reunion would go, but this scenario never crossed my mind.

ASH

I BLINK a few times to make sure I'm not imagining things. While I may have pictured Eli in the shower earlier, I didn't think I had magical conjuring powers.

He's here, and somehow, he's naked too. I stare at him and blink some more before reaching out and pinching his cheek.

"Ow. What was that for?" he says, with a hint of a smile on his face.

"Making sure you're real," I say, still in a daze.

"That's not how it works. You're supposed to pinch yourself," Eli says, reaching out and pinching me back. At first, I don't even feel it, I'm too focused on the sight of him naked in front of me. But then I lift my hand and rub at my stinging cheek.

"You're really here," I say, heart pounding.

Eli's light blue eyes soften on me and I stand as still as I can, not even breathing. We just stare at one another, eyes roaming over each other's faces. After what feels like forever but was probably only a minute, Eli says, "You got a haircut."

I nod and notice that his hair has gotten longer, falling into his eyes and curling around his ears. There's stubble on his face which seems unusual for him. The shadows around his eyes make him look older.

"You didn't," I say and give him a small smirk. I'm not trying to be flirty, but seeing him with his hair longer reminds me of a conversation we had a few months ago, when I told him I needed him to grow it out so I could have something to grip on to.

His eyes widen and he looks away, but I see him blushing from his cheeks all the way to his collarbone. I guess he remembers too.

Eli clears his throat and reluctantly brings his eyes back to me. "I'm sorry, I didn't mean to accost you in the bathroom. I actually didn't know you would be here." He opens his mouth again but doesn't say anything else.

I nod, trying very hard not to look below his chest area, knowing very well what I would find. Strong, muscular thighs, long legs with fine, pale blond hair on them. Looking at his abs and chest is not any easier either, since he's built like a goddamn viking. So I focus on his face instead. He looks very tired.

"Robbie said I could stay here for the week. I'm surprised he didn't tell you." I frown, wondering if Robbie offered this place to both of us as a ploy to get us to reconnect and talk.

"I haven't spoken to Robbie since—" He pauses and looks away grimacing. "In a while, I guess."

"But he's your best friend."

Eli turns his head toward me again and brings his hand up to rub across his jaw. When he puts it down, I notice the way he flexes his fingers. "No, he's a close second," he says softly.

Our eyes lock again and I give him a genuine grin. At least he still considers me his best friend. Eli slowly grins back and ruins the moment by saying, "Jordan is my best friend, of course."

I roll my eyes and groan. *Yeah, right.* "I missed you, Eli."

Eli softly chuckles and says, "I missed you too." He bites his lip and shyly asks, "Can I hug you?"

I raise my eyebrows, knowing damn well this man is not the hugging type. *How can I deny him a hug?* Especially when I want him near me. But the one brain cell that is still intact takes over and I say, "Maybe we should put some clothes on first."

Eli blushes again and looks down. Right at my crotch. My smile threatens to take over, but I bite slightly on the inside of my cheeks. Eli whips his head back towards the ceiling so fast I think he might be seeing stars. He shakes his head a couple times then says, "Funny thing, really, I don't have any clothes."

SIX

Seven Months Ago

ELI

A FEW WEEKS AGO, Ash and I got a call from the Manticores staff telling us that we'd been selected to attend the all-star weekend event in California. I'm still pretty bummed about it, since that means we have to miss the cabin trip up north that Robbie organized. I was looking forward to spending a few days with my friends, snowboarding and having fun. Instead, I need to be on a flight to Anaheim, of all places. At least I'll have Ash with me, although recently he's been kind of distant.

After our conversation at the restaurant on New Year's Day, he hasn't been hanging out with me as much. I think I hurt his feelings by putting him in the friend-zone, but I really think it was the best decision and I hope he'll understand it someday.

But then why do I feel like shit?

I look around the gate at the airport and notice every seat is full. Everyone must be avoiding the snow that's supposed to hit this week. Not me—I prefer it. I will be miserable in Anaheim.

I look at my phone but don't see any replies from Ash.

> Where are you? Boarding starts soon
>
> Please tell me you're not skipping out

I look around once more, hoping to spot Ash's dark red hair and his freckled face, but he's not here. The attendant announces that boarding is now starting and I make my way to join the line. As I inch closer to the gate, I keep my head down, staring at my phone and willing Ash to at least have the guts to reply and tell me he ditched me.

"Why are you looking at that phone like it personally wronged you?" a deeply amused voice says from behind me and I spin around so quickly I almost drop my backpack off my shoulder.

"You made it," I say, looking Ash up and down. He looks terrible. His dark red hair is curling slightly on top, and his scruff is longer than I've ever seen. The dress shirt he's got on is buttoned up the wrong way, his collar askew. He either looks like he came from a hookup or the bar. Knowing his pattern lately, I'd bet it's the latter. Maybe even both.

I scowl at him and say, "Why do you look like you haven't showered in a week?"

"Wow, you haven't even seen me all week. How do you know I haven't showered?"

"Because you look like that!"

"Like what?" he croons, amusement written all over his

face as he leans into my space. I can smell the alcohol on him and I take a step back. This is the pattern I've been talking about. Ever since I told him nothing can happen between us, Ash has been drinking more, partying after every game, and sleeping god knows where. Most days he's not even at his apartment.

We had an extended road trip last week and all of us could tell how much his partying was affecting his game. Robbie tried to talk some sense into him, but that didn't seem to do much. I want to be honest with him and maybe give him some tough love, but I know I can't. He'll just take it the wrong way or put even more distance between us, and that's the last thing I want. I missed him these last few weeks.

"You look miserable," I say, and notice the smirk fall off his face.

"Maybe I am," he mumbles. Ash looks so dejected and sad right now that I contemplate my next move. I sigh and drop my backpack on the floor, taking a step towards him. My arms immediately go around his shoulders and I pull him into me. I don't usually enjoy hugs or physical touch, but I know Ash does. And maybe I'm playing dirty by pulling him in close when I know that nothing else can happen between us, but he needs to realize that I still need him around. I need my best friend.

So I opt for some truth and vulnerability when I say, "I missed you." Ash is quiet but I can feel his body go rigid in my arms. Maybe that was the wrong thing to say.

"You saw me last week," he says, pulling out of my arms but looking everywhere but at me.

So that's how it's going to be then, he gets to ignore me, and when I try to have an honest conversation with him, he deflects.

"You know what I mean," I say and grab my backpack.

Two can play at this game.

The line has moved up, so I head closer to the gate and I hand the attendant my ticket. A minute later, I'm seated by the window with my headphones on and remain that way for the entire flight.

ASH

MY HEAD IS POUNDING and the pressure from the plane is not helping one bit. I dig around in my backpack for some painkillers and gulp down an entire bottle of water. I may be hungover, but I need to look presentable for this stupid event. At least the weather will be nice, and I'll get to see some old friends from the Vermont Vortices. I'm trying to look at the bright side here, if there even is one.

I steal glances at Eli who is seated next to me in first class. His eyes are closed and his pale blond lashes are fanned across his cheekbones. As soon as he sat down, he started listening to music, making it very clear that he doesn't want to talk to me.

I'm an idiot. I should have told him I missed him back instead of being a smart ass. But that's just my knee jerk reaction when I feel too overwhelmed by my own feelings. And the truth is, as soon as I saw Eli standing there in line to get on the plane, all the feelings I've been trying to repress for the last month started to bubble up to the surface.

Because I *did* miss him, quite a lot, and it made me realize that I don't know who I am without my friends. Jordan is the shy one in our group and crushing hard on

Robbie's sister, but besides the fact that he's oblivious to the fact that she likes him back, he's one of the most observant and smartest people I know. I'm pretty sure he was going to be a doctor if he didn't have a career in hockey. Robbie is our leader and captain, and he loves us all unconditionally. Especially me, and especially when I don't deserve it. Recently he's been completely whipped by his girlfriend, but I honestly don't even care. Olivia is awesome and she fits right in with our group.

As for Eli, he's my fucking rock, but after he rejected me last month, I decided it was best to distance myself. It can't possibly be healthy to hang out 24/7 with your best friend who is also your teammate and who you ~~possibly~~, ~~maybe~~, *definitely* have feelings for.

Except I really hate this part—the one where I've been an ass to him all month, ignoring him, not coming over to watch movies or play video games with him.

I hate that he keeps reaching out a hand when all I want is to sink and drown. Why am I so self-destructive? I can't even blame him for choosing to ignore me this time. I deserve it. I knew it was coming at some point. There's only so much a nice guy like him can take, and I *knew* I was too much for him to handle.

I begrudgingly drag my eyes away from Eli's gorgeous face, squeeze them shut, and try to get some sleep for the next few hours. I need my beauty rest, because California is going to suck major ass.

SEVEN

Seven Months Ago

ASH

BY THE TIME we get to the hotel, Eli still hasn't said another word to me. I even tried to make small talk in the ride share but he just nodded along to what I was saying and continued to look at his phone, all but dismissing me.

I know I love to be the center of attention and fill the silence by talking all the time, but the fact that he's trying so hard to avoid me is starting to piss me off.

"Are you gonna avoid me all weekend?" I ask as I catch up to him by the front desk.

"I'm not avoiding you, I just have nothing else to say," Eli tells me without even looking in my direction, and honestly, that really fucking stings.

"I can check in the next person in line," the concierge says, and Eli moves up to the counter, leaving me behind.

I blow out a frustrated breath and rub my temples with one hand. My headache never really went away and I definitely need a nap soon. Maybe I can skip some of the afternoon activities in favor of a nice comfy bed.

"Sir, I can help you over here," says another concierge. I move up to the right of Eli and give her my ID and let her know I'm here for the all-star weekend.

After she types in my name, she gets a really confused look on her face and she starts asking her colleague questions about the reservation system.

Eli is still waiting for his room keys when one of the ladies says, "I think there's been some kind of misunderstanding with the reservation."

"Which one?" Eli asks.

"Well, both, really. It seems there was only supposed to be one person checking in, and then a change was made to the reservation to add a second person."

"Okay, that's not a big deal. We've shared rooms before on the road, we'll be fine," I say, smiling to myself. I get to annoy Eli all weekend when he's trying to avoid me? This is the best case scenario. Maybe I can get under his skin.

"Well, since the initial reservation was made for one person, that means we assigned you to a room that only has one bed. Normally we'd be able to swap rooms, but we are extremely busy this weekend with the event and won't be able to accommodate that change."

My smile falls and when I look back at Eli, I can see he's frustrated with the news.

Well, fuck me sideways, this is not what I expected. Not when I know exactly what Eli's body feels like next to mine and how much I crave us being together like that again.

. . .

ELI

OF COURSE there's only one bed. Could this day get any worse? My phone dings and I look down to see a reminder that we're supposed to be at the arena in an hour. Ash and I ride the elevator in silence and I use my key to unlock the door to *our* hotel room. The place is nice, fancier than I expected.

The room is clean and modern with muted beiges and grays, but it's also smaller than I expected, and the bed is not a king size as the concierge said, but definitely a queen.

I'll be fine.

Totally fine.

I think.

I drop my duffle and backpack on one side of the bed and pick out a business casual outfit I brought to change into. "I'm taking a shower before heading to the event," I say, carrying my small bundle of toiletries to the bathroom. As I walk by him, Ash's hand reaches out and catches my bicep. I stare down at it for a second before making eye contact for the first time in a few hours. I feel bad for ignoring him, but I'm just so fed up with his attitude. If he doesn't want me to help or be his friend, then I can't force him.

"Are you okay with this arrangement?" he asks, nodding towards the bed.

"I'll be fine."

He gives me a soft look and says, "I know you like your space, Eli. So if you need me to spend a few nights somewhere else, I'll figure it out."

"I appreciate the offer, but I'd rather have you here," I

whisper and then to not make the moment too raw I add, "Besides, someone needs to keep you out of trouble."

One corner of Ash's mouth lifts and he says, "Oh, I can get in *plenty* of trouble in this room."

What a little shit. I roll my eyes and tell him, "Stop flirting and get ready. We leave in twenty minutes."

WHEN WE GET to the arena for the first event, Ash is immediately jumped by two of his friends. Dylan and Max introduce themselves to me, but I remember them from last season. They both play for the Vermont Vortices, one of our biggest rivals.

Just bringing them up makes me think of Dustin Mitchell, Vermont's biggest dickhead. Remembering how he picked a fight with Ash a couple months ago at a bar makes my blood boil. I couldn't get the image of Ash's bruised face out of my head for a while after that. How young and vulnerable he looked, and how much I wanted to protect him.

As a goalie, fighting is not something I generally condone. I don't understand the point of it, since all it does is bring both teams penalties during a game. When the fighting happens off the ice though, that's even worse, and it shows that players are unprofessional.

"Are we hitting up some clubs after this, or what?" Dylan asks. I take a deep breath and try hard not to roll my eyes. Of course, this is what they care about.

"Hell yeah, we need to catch up. Isn't that right, Ash?" Max follows up with a smirk and a light shove to Ash's chest.

Maybe I can condone *some* fighting if it means this guy stops flirting with Ash.

Before Ash can reply I say, "Who could possibly catch up at a club? You won't even hear yourself, let alone someone talking to you."

Dylan snorts. "What, are you too old to have some fun? We're on break, let loose a little and enjoy California."

"Give him a break, he's a goalie. You know how weird they are—he probably doesn't even know the definition of fun," Max says, poking at me.

Like I give a shit what they think. I raise an eyebrow at Ash but he's not looking at me. Fine. Whatever. It's not like I thought he would side with me, but it would be nice if he put his focus into something other than drinking every now and then. I roll my eyes at their childish behavior and simply walk away.

After a few interviews and photo shoots, Ash and I are ready to participate in the afternoon's event. There are a variety of mini games for us to participate in, where we need to work together as a team to win.

The first is to play a version of mini golf, except instead of using a putter, we need to use a hockey stick to hit the golf ball. I grimace and look around for the cameras, hoping to angle myself in a way that won't show how bad I am at this.

"What's that face for? Already regret spending time with me?" Ash asks.

I scowl and say, "I'm terrible at golf, there's a reason I never go when Robbie suggests it."

He laughs and it's bright and happy. I can't remember the last time I heard him laugh like this. "I think you'd really like it, if you stopped being stubborn and actually let us teach you sometime."

"How did you learn how to play golf?" I ask, trying to keep my voice low so no one else hears.

"My father taught me. It's kind of a requirement for being born rich. If you're born into old money, you *must* know how to golf," Ash says, some of the laughter and happiness already dimming away.

He doesn't talk much about his family, but I thought that's just because they're high profile and private. Ash's dad is Nelson Meyers, one of the best defensemen in hockey history. He won five Stanley Cup championships during his time with Boston and is now the current general manager for the team. Ash never talks about him though. All I know is that Nelson Meyers has never been to a Manticores game.

"What about your mom?" I prod.

"What about her?" he glares at me.

"You never talk about her."

"There's nothing to say. I don't get along with my parents, and that's that."

"Okay, I'm sorry I brought it up," I say, and continue to fumble with the hockey stick, trying to hit the ball.

"Try holding the stick lower and position yourself above it," Ash says, dropping his and helping me position mine. His hands are warm and I'm sure I'm blushing just from his proximity. "Make sure when you look down, your eyes are level with the ball. At least that's what you want to do with an actual putter and golf ball."

I clear my throat. "Cool, thanks." Ash looks at my pink cheeks as he straightens to his full height and smirks. Great, now he knows I'm flustered by his touch.

AFTER WINNING the putt-putt mini game, we went up against the other winning team, which happened to be Max and Dylan. This time, we had to get a hole in one to win the game.

Max went first and he hit the ball so hard it hit one of the photographers in the groin. After some apologies and making sure the guy was alright, Ash took his turn. He hit it perfectly, except as soon as the ball approached the hole, it rode along the edge and continued rolling down the other side. Dylan was smug about it and said, "You guys have no chance of winning this. My short game is impeccable." As soon as he lined up the shot though, he hit it too softly and it only traveled halfway to the hole. The smile fell off his face quickly and I inwardly cheered.

I couldn't believe the game was up to me. My hands were sweating and I kept brushing them on my shorts. Ash came up to me, put a hand on my shoulder and whispered, "You got this, pretty boy." I'm pretty sure my brain short circuited, but oddly, that was exactly what I needed.

Instead of overthinking the shot, my brain was stuck on what Ash said.

Pretty boy.

I smiled to myself and took the shot.

Hole in one.

As much as I dreaded this trip, I have to admit I'm actually having fun.

And if Ash happens to hug me when we win, I won't complain about it.

EIGHT

Seven Months Ago

ASH

THE SECOND MINI game we are forced to play is even more ridiculous than the first. After drawing the short stick, I'm blindfolded and led to a mini obstacle course. The coordinator of the game explains what I need to do and I try not to fidget too much. Truth is, I don't love the blindfold. It makes me feel powerless and I don't know how to let someone else guide me around when I feel so vulnerable.

"So, the goal is to be the first person to complete the obstacle course, grab the stick and shoot the puck into the net. If you win, you'll move on to the next round and swap places with your partner," the coordinator says.

"I got you, don't worry," Eli leans in and says over my shoulder. Completing the obstacle course requires me dodging, rolling, crouching, all while blindfolded and with only Eli to guide me along.

"I trust you," I say as the coordinator gives us 30 seconds to set up. Eli's hands grab both my shoulders from behind and I involuntarily lean into him.

"You need to walk straight ahead for about twenty steps and then crouch to go under a beam. It looks rubbery, but at least you have a helmet on, just in case it's not."

I can hear the smile in his voice and it makes me smile too. "Anything else?"

"That's it for now, I'll walk along the rest of the course and tell you more directions," he says, repositioning me so I'm facing the right way.

"Go, go, go!" yells the coordinator.

I follow along with Eli's directions and duck, reaching a hand up and brushing it over the rubbery beam as my head narrowly avoids it. As soon as I straighten up from my crouch, I start slowly moving, arms out ahead of me. "Eli, now would be a great time for some more directions." I chuckle nervously.

I hear him from somewhere to my right when he says, "You got this, *kultsi*. Keep going straight for another five steps—there you go, now you need to step over an obstacle, so make sure you swing your leg wide."

"Oh, the jokes I could be making right now if we weren't technically working," I say under my breath. Eli laughs softly as he moves along the course with me. I don't know if it's because of our bond or something else, but we clearly work well together. He navigates me through all the obstacles and I'm the first person to reach the hockey stick.

"Yes! That's it, *kultsi*! You need to set up a little bit more to your left—just like that, now make sure you add some flex to it and lift the puck. Give it some flare." I do as

I'm told and I hear cheers erupting around me. I drop the stick and take off my blindfold just in time to see Eli rushing at me with a huge smile on his face. I grin back at him and he hugs me tight before realizing where we are and that everyone is looking at us. He lets go sooner that I would have wanted, but I don't care.

I have to admit I'm having a lot more fun than I thought I would, and that's all thanks to being around my best friend again.

ELI

BY THE TIME we wrap up the mini games, I can feel my social battery draining. There's only so much an introvert like me can take, and after a few hours of socializing and putting on my game face, I am exhausted. I can't wait to get back to the hotel, shower, and unwind. If I weren't sharing a room with Ash, I might be taking care of other needs as well. Although, with his behavior recently, he might spend the night elsewhere.

"Eli! Wait up!" Ash says, jogging up to me. I notice Max and Dylan walking behind him, also approaching. My eyes start to roll before I catch myself and put on a smile.

"What's up?"

"We're headed out to a club nearby," Ash says, tucking his hands into his khaki shorts. The movement makes his biceps flex and his tight blue polo stretches over his broad chest. I bite down hard so I don't do something stupid, like tell him how good he looks. Ash looks at me sheepishly before looking back at his pals. "Do you want to join us?"

"I—what?" I ask, dumbfounded.

"C'mon, *champ*, you need to blow some steam after all those games," Dylan says.

I frown at the nickname he gives me and look over at Ash. He seems nervous, but I can't figure out why. Does he not want to go out with his friends? Is he inviting me as a buffer?

"We ordered a car, let's go," Max says, putting his arm around Ash and giving me a smirk. "Unless you're too good to hang out with us?"

My eyes narrow on Ash's shoulder where Max is rubbing his thumb back and forth and, while I think it's a terrible idea, what I say is, "Lead the way."

I guess I'm going to a club.

The car ride is loud as Max, Dylan, and Ash relive the excitement of the first day of all-star, but I keep to myself again. I'm thinking of ways I can get out of this hangout.

Can I fake a migraine so I can leave early?

Maybe I can get one drink and leave?

Maybe they'll be so busy they won't even notice.

Not even ten minutes later, we're inside a fancy club, loud music blasting from the speakers, dim lights making it look dark and sultry. A reservation must have been made because we are led up the stairs to a more private part of the club.

We take up a booth with low seats that's right across from the dance floor. When the waitress comes around, I point at a drink on the menu, not even caring what it is. Everything is so loud and I feel a headache coming already. Maybe I won't need to fake anything to get out of this.

I sit quietly and listen to the guys' conversations as much as I can over the noise while I sip on what turns out to be a mai tai. Max is sitting close to Ash in a way that makes me think they might have hooked up at some point in the past. And that maybe Max is trying to make a move again.

My thoughts are interrupted when a couple of girls come over to our booth. "Do you mind if we join you guys?" one of them yells out over the loud music. Dylan nods enthusiastically and she all but plops down in his lap. The other girl moves between them, focusing all her attention on Max and Ash.

I continue to sit there, by myself, on one side of the booth and watch their interactions. Ash shoots me glances every now and then like he has something to say but doesn't quite know how to. Soon enough the two girls drag Max and Dylan out to the dance floor and Ash and I are left alone together.

I order a second drink even though my head is pounding. What am I doing here?

Did I only come here because I was jealous of Max? I don't have a right to be jealous, Ash can do whatever he wants. I was the one that told him we should just be friends and nothing more.

"Are you okay?" he asks, sliding closer to me on the cushion.

"Fine, just have a headache," I mumble.

Before Ash can say anything else, Max runs over and says, "Let's dance, ginger boy." Really, Max? *Ginger boy?* Now I do roll my eyes at him. Ash shakes his head no, but Max is insistent, reaching over and grabbing him by the arms. I swing my legs to the side and give Ash the space to exit the booth, which he does.

There's a sour feeling in my stomach as I watch them make their way to the dance floor. Dylan is dancing with both the girls that came over to our table, and Max and Ash are dancing together. The more I watch them, the more my jealousy flares. And after a few minutes, when Max pulls Ash closer and his hands move down his back, lower, and lower, I can't take it anymore. I slam the empty glass on the table, leave some cash next to it and stand up.

I should just walk away and not look back, but I only make it a few feet, my head pounding, when curiosity takes the best of me. My head swivels around to look at Ash and I expect to see them dancing close together, but Max is all over him, kissing his neck.

When Ash opens his eyes, he looks right at me. For a moment, he looks confused, like he didn't expect me to watch him dance with another guy. His eyes widen the slightest when he takes me in, ready to leave. I'm not sure what my face portrays, and frankly, I don't care.

So I walk away.

I order a car to take me back to the hotel as I make my way out of the club, all the while trying to ignore the sinking feeling in my gut that I may have lost any chance I might have had with Ash.

You did this to yourself, Eli. I had my shot and I blew it. Ash told me he liked me, he told me he wanted me. And I wanted him too, more than anything. But I got so lost in the thought of what others would think of me, of us, that I didn't take the chance. And now he's in there, finding someone else to spend his time with, and I remind myself that I don't have the right to be jealous.

I pace on the sidewalk and pinch the bridge of my nose, willing this headache to go away. My ride share arrives quickly and I get in the backseat of the Mini Cooper, but before I can shut the door, a hand comes down on the inside handle and stops me.

"Wait."

NINE

Seven Months Ago

ASH

"WAIT."

I don't know what the hell I was thinking, running after Eli like this. Has my last brain cell completely abandoned me? I didn't even have that much to drink tonight.

"Mind if I get a ride with you?" I hear myself ask in a daze.

"Hey kid, this ain't a taxi. Beat it," the ride-share driver yells at me, but I don't budge. My eyes stay fixed on Eli and his frozen state, like he can't believe I chased after him either. But how could I not? Especially after seeing that wounded look on his face when he saw Max kissing me.

Fucking Max. Why did I let him get so handsy with me?

I don't know what this hot-and-cold back and forth with Eli is doing to me, but I need some kind of explanation.

Or closure.

Or *something*.

He can't just keep rejecting me, reaching out, only to ignore me later and then get mad when someone else is making a move.

"It's fine, we're going to the same place," Eli says to the driver, eyes still glued to mine. I hop in the backseat, only now realizing how freaking tiny this car is. Both of us are big and take up the majority of the backseat, and when I spread my legs to get more comfortable, my knee bumps into Eli's.

I pull it back like I've been burned, knowing he doesn't care for physical touch, especially not in public. His body goes still and my knee starts bouncing. After about a minute of awkward silence, I feel Eli's hand stilling my knee. His touch is soft and warm, and *fuck*, I want nothing more than for him to grip harder, and higher. But he doesn't.

I fully expect him to yank his hand away as soon as he stops my bouncing leg, but his hand lingers. His long, gentle fingers run circles over my bare knee and I want to melt right here in the backseat of the world's tiniest car. My eyelids flutter and I turn my head to face him.

Eli is already looking at me, so much hurt and longing showing in his pale blue gaze. His fingers stop circling on top of my knee, and he just lets his hand rest there, with a light grip. Not breaking eye contact, I move my own hand to slowly cover his. His gaze drops down to our hands and moves back to my face, and more specifically, my lips. My tongue peeks out to lick them and I see him track the movement.

He still wants me.

. . .

ELI

ASH KEEPS his hand on top of mine the whole ride back to the hotel. I can't stop stealing glances at him. I don't know if I want to stop. Seeing Max all over him made me so irrationally angry.

I didn't think I was the type to get jealous, but just thinking about the way Max's hands were roaming all over Ash's body is making me grind my teeth. *That should have been me.*

I still don't know what exactly it is that we're doing, and I'm in no way ready for a relationship. But maybe we need to get this out of our systems. Maybe all this tension can just go away and we can go back to how things were.

The car drops us off and our hands no longer hold as we walk inside the hotel. We're both quiet on the elevator ride up. Quiet is not usually Ash's strong suit, but I don't say anything for fear of ruining this. Whatever this is.

As soon as we get to our door, my mind is made up.

One night.

This needs to happen. We need to get this out of our systems so we can move on.

I unlock the door and gesture for Ash to walk in first, which he does. As soon as I get inside as well, I kick the door shut, reach for the collar of his polo with both hands and push him up against the wall.

For a second we're both stunned, just looking at one another, but then our bodies move of their own accord—heads tilting, lips parting.

As soon as his lips are on mine, I let my desire take over.

He tastes like the fruity cocktail he was drinking at the club and I chase that, touching my tongue to his seam, begging to be let in, and it feels all consuming. I'm starving and the only thing I want is *him*.

Ash's hands grip the back of my shirt so hard I think he might rip it off me, but as soon as my hand grabs a fistful of his hair and I tug, his grip loosens. He gasps and that's all I need to deepen the kiss, angling him right where I want him.

And fuck, do I *want* him.

I'm hard already and I let him know it as I bring our hips flush together and I grind once, twice. I do it again until we reluctantly break for air, panting hard. Ash's dark blue eyes are blown wide with desire and his lips—they're pink and swollen. *Fuckable.*

"Is this really happening?" Ash asks, one hand moving to my chest and trailing down, down, down. It lingers at the waistband of my pants and he looks up through his lashes for permission.

My cock twitches at the touch and it takes everything in my power to remain in control. I swallow hard and say, "Just once. I need to know what you taste like."

"We've kissed before," he says with a small smirk on his face.

I grin back at him, pulling him into me. As I leave a trail of kisses from his lips to his jaw to his ear, I hear myself say, "That's not the kind of taste I'm talking about, *rakas*."

Ash sways on the spot and I can see a glimpse of his eyes rolling back in pleasure. I bite down on his earlobe, getting an immediate reaction from him. But right as he's about to shove his hand down my pants, I step back and muster all the confidence I can to say, "Take off your clothes."

. . .

ASH

I DON'T THINK I've ever heard Eli use such a commanding voice before, but it's hot as fuck. I swallow and very enthusiastically pull off my blue polo shirt, my hands moving so fast I almost get tangled up in it. It ends up somewhere on the floor. My hand hovers over the zipper of my shorts when Eli suddenly grabs it.

"Slower." His raspy voice does things to me and I can't help but oblige. He lets go of my wrist and I can tell by the tightness of his muscles and the way he clenches his fists that he's fighting hard to stay in control. *Good.*

I reach down to take my shoes off instead of my pants. I perch on the edge of the bed and slide off my boat shoes and no-show socks, my gaze staying fixed on Eli the whole time. Then I sit up straight and do a slow shimmy dance. If he wants a show, he'll get a fucking show.

I try to keep my smirk off of my face so he doesn't think I'm laughing at this interaction. It's fucking hot, and I need him to keep going. He's right, this needs to happen between us, even if it's just once. I reach down and palm myself through the pants, knowing I'm already fully hard.

With painful slowness, I pull the zipper down and lean back on the bed, lifting my hips just enough so my pants and underwear can come off. Once they drop to my ankles, I kick them off, getting fully situated on the bed as I lean back on my elbows.

As if he's in a trance, Eli takes a few steps toward me, eyes not once leaving my body. He categorizes every muscle, every scar, every tattoo. He's seen most of me—in locker rooms and joint hotels, and in my apartment—but he's never seen me like this. Thoroughly and completely naked for him. My cock twitches just from his proximity.

"Is that one new?" he asks, voice deep and dripping with desire. I look down at where he's pointing—the honeysuckle tattoo that's inked right above my heart. I falter for a second, thinking about why I got this tattoo in the first place. Like all my other tattoos, this one has a special meaning.

"Yeah," I rasp out and keep my gaze averted. *Please don't ask. Please.*

I feel the mattress dip on my left side and lift my head to see Eli hovering above. I feel his knee sliding between my legs and pushing against my thigh. One of his hands rests on the bed above my shoulder, his other reaching up and leaving feather light touches over my tattoo.

"Beautiful," he says, laying his palm down flat over my heart. The traitorous bitch is beating a mile a minute and totally giving away how nervous I am. Eli's lips hover over mine and my breath catches, because holy shit, is this really happening? I've been imagining this moment for so long.

This time, when he kisses me, Eli doesn't hold back.

ELI

ASH IS INTOXICATING. I might be addicted to kissing him because I can't seem to stop. I press my full weight into him, pinning him to the mattress under me and take my time exploring his mouth and gliding my hands all over his body. He's perfectly sculpted, all smooth skin and hard muscles—muscles that clench when I run my hand over them.

"Are you going to take off your clothes?" he asks with a heavy sigh. My mouth moves down his neck, nipping and licking at his collarbones. Ash's breath stutters and I feel his hips pushing up, searching for friction.

"Not yet," I say, giving him an intense look before moving my mouth lower, kissing his tattoos. His body is a piece of art, and every single tattoo is a part of him. A part of his story.

I start with his newest one, right above his heart. I'm curious to know what it represents and why he got it, but I don't want to push right now. He seems nervous about telling me about it, so I decide to ask him later. *After*.

I kiss the tree that is tattooed under his ribs on the left side. The one he got in September during training camp, because it meant he could keep himself grounded. The tree is blooming on top, but underneath, its mirror image is distorted and looks a lot more like roots. I've always loved tattoos and learning about their meanings, but I don't have one myself.

There is a flock of birds taking flight on the right side of his torso, starting near his pelvis and going up, up, all the way to his shoulder blade. I remember when I first saw it, two years ago, when we all went out swimming. When I asked him about it, he said he got it when he was sixteen to piss off his dad and that it represented his desire to be free and happy. I've been slowly categorizing little bits and pieces of Ash, taking them with me everywhere I go.

His left thigh tattoo is of a beautiful butterfly, with its wings spread. This one means transformation and personal growth, something I know he struggles with sometimes. I kiss every inch of every tattoo, moving to his right arm, where he has a vine creeping up his forearm, this one also signifying growth.

By the time I'm done putting my mouth all over him, Ash is panting and writhing underneath me. When I touch him where he most needs me, he's impossibly hard and slick with precum. He lets out the most beautiful moan as I twist and stroke him. His head is thrown back in pleasure and I think I might have made a huge mistake. Because how am I supposed to walk away after tonight?

Swallowing the tight knot in my throat, I move lower until I can put my mouth on him. I lick him once, twice, before taking him in my mouth and as soon as I do, Ash's hands fly to my hair, fingers threading through it roughly.

"Fuck, that feels too good," he says, trying to make me slow down. But I'm done taking this slow. I *need* him like I've never needed anyone else before. This isn't just some hookup. I knew it was going to be like this from the first moment he suggested it.

It feels like coming home after a long day of work.

It feels like rain after a summer drought.

It feels like falling, and Ash and I—*we're inevitable*.

I pull back for a second, taking his hands out of my hair and pinning them underneath his body, before saying, "Keep them there." Ash blinks at me through heavy lids but nods along, opening his mouth to say something. Whatever it is, it dies on his lips the moment I take him back in my mouth. I swirl my tongue around his head before taking him as deep as I can.

"Fuck, *fuck*." Ash's movements stutter and he tentatively thrusts once, twice. I swallow around him, digging my fingers into his hips. It only takes a few more thrusts and me reaching down to cup his balls for Ash to let go. I swallow it all down, licking him clean before letting go with an audible *pop*. When I look up, his chest is heaving, his eyes are screwed shut and his hands are out from under his body, fisting the sheets.

I grin at how out of sorts he looks and make my way back up his body. His eyes fly open and he grins back, all but tackling me sideways. He kisses me hard, his hand fisting my shirt, undoing my buttons.

"My turn," he says, nipping at my jaw and moving down, trailing kisses on my chest. His movements are rushed as he pulls me up to take my shirt off, then immediately pushes me back down and palms me through my shorts. I groan and drop my head back, letting him take over and do with me as he pleases.

"No, I think you mean it's my turn," I say, closing my eyes in contentment. My fingers twitch when he pulls down my layers and I expect him to go for it, but nothing happens for a long moment. I lift my head to look down at him and he's just frozen. Staring.

"What?" I ask, concerned.

"Why the fuck are you so big?" Ash blurts out. I choke on a laugh and he looks at me wearily, some amusement in his blue eyes. "Seriously, that's not gonna fit *anywhere*."

"You're such an idiot," I chide and he smirks. I take it a step further and say, "You can take it, *rakas*."

"Death by giant cock. Make sure you put that on my headstone after this." I don't have time to laugh or call him an idiot again because the next second his lips are on me, one of his hands covering the rest, moving up and down in time with his mouth.

"*Perkele!*"

"Talk Finnish to me, baby," Ash says, licking up my shaft and biting the inside of my thigh.

"Fuck, no more talking," I say, and guide my cock back in his mouth before taking a firm grip of his head and showing him exactly how I like it. It doesn't take long before my body starts shuddering in pleasure. Ash's mouth pulls away and he replaces it with his hand, twisting with just the right amount of pressure as he climbs back up my body. I come all over my stomach and his hand as he kisses me fervently and bites my lower lip.

I grip the back of his head with one hand and squeeze his ass with the other as we lay there, our kisses soon turning languid and soft.

Fuck.

I wanted this so much. I thought that getting it out of our systems would help, that it would be like scratching an itch, there and gone. But this was so much *more*. How are we supposed to go back to being just friends after this?

TEN

Present Day

ELI

AFTER LAUGHING at me for a solid five minutes, Ash finally takes pity and gives me some of his clothes. "It's not my fault my luggage got lost," I mutter.

Ash chuckles and I try not to stare at his naked ass as he walks by me and heads to his room, but I fail miserably.

He always looked good, but there's something about him now that seems a little different. There are no circles under his eyes, and he seems to have put on some muscle since the last time I saw him a couple months ago. It suits him well.

Ash comes back wearing a pair of boxers with bright pink donuts on them which I'm immediately disappointed with. The frown must be showing on my face as I stare down at them because he says, "Got a problem with my underwear, Kalias?"

I do. I have several problems actually. The first being that he's wearing any underwear at all while I'm still naked in the hallway. The second problem is that in all the years I've known him, I've never seen him wear anything other than plain boxers.

It feels like there's a new side to him that I don't recognize and that feels like a punch to the gut. I used to know everything about him, all his little quirks, all his likes and dislikes. *We used to be inseparable.*

Ash clears his throat and I finally stop staring at his crotch. I muster a smile and reach out to take the clothes from his hands. "Nope, no problem."

"Here, this pair is brand new, you can have them," he says, running back into the room and coming back with a similar pair, these ones covered in little tacos.

I sigh at his ridiculous choice of underwear and mumble a thank you on my way to the shower. I can still hear Ash's chuckle long after I close the door.

WHEN I GET out of the shower, I hear Ash making coffee in the kitchen but decide to take another moment to myself and head to my own bedroom. Not only am I jet lagged, but this reunion has taken me by surprise and completely thrown me off kilter.

Realistically, I knew that I would have to face Ash at some point this week while we start training camp, but I thought I would have more time to prepare myself. After everything that happened this past summer, we are long overdue for a conversation. We both said and did things we didn't mean and I don't know how to act around him anymore.

I look in the full-length mirror in my bedroom and immediately feel embarrassed. Ash's black athletic shorts are a size too small and show off all of my muscles, but they are especially tight on my ass. And his red T-shirt with our team logo on it is so tight I can almost see my heart thumping through the material.

I look ridiculous. I can't possibly walk into training camp like this and not be made fun of. I sigh and close my eyes, resigned to stay here just a minute longer and stew in my embarrassment, but Ash knocks hard on my door.

"Are you ready to go? I have a rental car here so I can drive us to camp."

"I'm contemplating skipping today," I say miserably.

The door opens and Ash leans on the frame, his arms crossed over his chest. The bright grin he gives me makes my heart skip a beat. "Well, aren't you a sight for sore eyes?"

I immediately feel myself blush and my accent slips out a little as I tell him to fuck off. All that does is make him laugh.

I shake my head and make my way to the door, but Ash doesn't move aside, so I slow down in front of him. His grin turns more into a soft smile and he licks his bottom lip before catching it between his teeth.

"How about that hug?" he asks softly, his freckles standing out in the soft light of the morning.

I nod dumbly and Ash drops his hands from his chest. Quicker than I expected, he wraps me up in a tight hug. His arms go around my torso and clasp at my back. Ash presses his forehead to the side of my head and I can feel the relief in his shoulders. My arms go around his back and we just stand there in this beautiful embrace for longer than necessary, neither one of us saying anything.

I missed him so much.

ASH

THINGS ARE GOING BETTER than expected, considering that Eli and I haven't spoken in months. I really fucked up this summer and I honestly didn't think he'd even give me the time of day when we saw each other again. Yet here we are, tentative with our bantering but making light of what would otherwise be a really awkward situation.

I thought seeing each other naked this morning would have sent Eli running, yet he seemed oddly fine with it. What I would give to know what's going on in his head right now.

"Ready to go?" I ask, grabbing my small backpack with a change of clothes. When I look back at Eli, I see him shuffling uncomfortably in my clothes that are definitely too tight on him.

I open the door, step aside and say, "After you." Eli grumbles something but I don't catch it because I'm too busy staring at his ass as he walks down the porch steps.

The car ride to the arena is quiet and some of the awkwardness I expected earlier does creep in. I want to start a conversation and ask him about his family back in Finland, or ask him about his flight. Anything. But every time I open my mouth, I don't know what to say.

I want to apologize again, but I don't want him to be angry at me. I want things to go back to normal, but I don't know what normal is for us anymore.

So instead I drive, sneaking subtle glances at Eli and wondering how the hell I'm going to make it through this week.

THE FIRST DAY of training camp is kind of like the first day of school. Most of it is spent catching up with friends and pretending to learn new things, all while avoiding the attention of the coaches. I don't see much of Eli the rest of the day since everybody wants a piece of him.

He's the best goalie we have at the AHL level and, clearly, it hasn't gone unnoticed. While I'm more the popular kid in high school, Eli is the prince that wanted to experience a semester abroad and he happened to land in bumfuck nowhere, Michigan.

I catch glimpses of him hanging out with the other goalies in the gym, and it breaks my heart that he's over there laughing and having a good time with others while I'm left pining after him. But I can't blame him, our falling out was my fault after all. I could blame it on the alcohol, or my mental state at the time, but I don't. If therapy has taught me anything, it's that I need to own up to my mistakes, ask for forgiveness, and move on.

The asking for forgiveness part is tougher than I expected, and I don't know how to bring up the subject. Should I be blunt about it? Should I butter him up with food and conversation first?

"Hey man, are we going out for drinks after this?" Jackson, another forward on the Manticores, asks me, pulling me out of my headspace.

"I'll come out, but I don't drink anymore," I say, putting on my gear and getting ready to hit the ice for some drills. With how many players there are between the ECHL,

AHL, and NHL, we don't all take the ice at the same time. We've got scheduled slots for when to train and which of the two rinks to be on.

I'm stuck in my head thinking about drills, so I don't hear Jackson's reply until he steps closer to me and repeats himself. "Since when don't you drink? You're like the designated party boy."

"Well, tough shit, find someone else," I say in a laugh, trying to hide my annoyance.

Jackson's eyebrows shoot up. Guess he didn't expect me to be anything but the comedic relief and *party boy* of the team.

"Did you get a girlfriend or something? We can convince her you can come out with us. You seem like the type of guy to get pussy whipped." Jackson laughs at his own stupidity and I'm immediately angry. First off, fuck him, going out and drinking is not what I do anymore, regardless of if I were in a relationship or not. I wish I could just snap at him and tell him to fuck off, but I'm trying to be a better person and not the hothead of the team. So I ignore him.

"What, cat got your tongue?" he taunts me, getting all in my personal space, and I want to punch his stupid face. Out of the corner of my eye, I see Eli entering the locker room, headed for his gear. I guess we have the same training shift.

I take a deep breath and face Jackson again, swiping my helmet off the bench in the process. "Look man, I'm just not interested in drinking anymore. Drop it."

Jackson looks back at Eli, then at me with a sneer. "Found yourself a boyfriend, did you? Which one of you is the *bitch* in the relationship?" Before I realize what I'm doing, I drop the helmet and grip Jackson by his jersey, shoving him against the locker so hard it rattles.

The room comes to a complete silence and I need to be careful with what I say next, considering all eyes are on me. I bite down on what I really want to tell him and how much of a *bitch* he is. Instead, I lower my voice and say, "If you *ever* say something like that to me again, I will make sure your hockey career is over." I get closer to his ear and make sure the next words are for him alone. "You know who my dad is, so you know I'm not fucking bluffing."

I shove him once more for good measure, grab my helmet, and stalk out of the locker room without a second glance. I hate that I brought up my dad, and it's not like he'd even do anything since we're not on speaking terms, but I can't have this asshole spreading rumors among the team. He can talk shit about me all he wants, but if he brings Eli into it again, we're gonna have a problem.

ELEVEN

Five Months Ago

ASH

ELI WAS RIGHT. Hooking up, even if it was just once, helped a little. It centered me somehow and gave me a glimpse into what I could have one day. My attraction towards him didn't go away though. I still want him, like all the fucking time, but at least I know now, without a doubt, that he's meant to be in my life. Even if I'm destined to love him from a distance, I can't imagine a world where he's not in my life—a world where we're not friends.

I haven't hooked up with anyone since two months ago in Anaheim and my sexual frustration is at an all time high. Even though Eli and I didn't go all the way, I feel like nothing and no one will compare to him. His soft dominance, the way he had me panting, almost begging for him was enough to have me obsessed. Enough to have me replaying that moment again and again—in the shower, in my bed, all the while touching myself and finding my hand lacking compared to Eli's.

I'm obsessed with Eli.
Is it healthy?
Absolutely not.
Do I care?
Not in the slightest.

While nothing else sexual or romantic happened between us, our friendship did go back to some kind of normal. We've been driving to games together and going to the gym at the same time, which has helped me a lot in terms of staying active and getting a good sleep schedule in place. We've spent most of our free time hanging out with our group of friends and playing video games at Eli's apartment where I set up my PS5.

I get antsy if I'm left to my own devices for too long, and while Eli likes his peace and quiet, he tolerates me enough to keep me around. I worry that I'm too much and that he'll get tired of me crashing his place all the time, but so far he seems to enjoy my messy company.

OUR LAST GAME of the regular season is tonight and the energy is at an all time low in the locker room. After Robbie retired a month ago, Trip stepped up to take on the role of captain. While he's a good guy on and off the ice, it's just not the same and I get the feeling he doesn't like me very much. I never get invited to any of his gatherings, even though lots of my teammates do. It's not like I *need* to be liked by everyone on the team—because I already know I'm not—but I don't understand what his deal is.

Robbie isn't the only reason I'm bummed out. This

morning we got the news that Jordan is being traded to the Texas Coyotes, which is fucking bullshit. He might not be the best defenseman out there, but he was *our* best defenseman. The team is making room for new recruits that will get called up from the ECHL team, but Jordan leaving is going to crush us—especially since we made it to the Calder Cup playoffs. Our first playoff game is in about a month and we need to get our shit together unless we want to embarrass ourselves.

The last time the Manticores made it to the playoffs was six years ago. I wasn't on the team back then, but I've heard stories about how great they used to be when Alex Dionis was the captain. Not that Robbie didn't do a great job, but there's only so much one person can do. Back then, Alex had an incredible group of guys on the roster, some of which are still playing at the NHL level today and making history.

I was hoping *we* would be the same one day. Me, Robbie, Jordan, and Eli—a hockey powerhouse, meant to leave behind an amazing legacy.

Instead, we're drifting apart.

ELI

THE ATMOSPHERE of the arena tonight is more somber than usual. The team is on the ice and we're showing a highlight reel of Jordan's career on the jumbo screen. He's standing at the edge of the tunnel, in full view of everyone as we give him a standing ovation. He waves at the crowd before walking down the tunnel and likely out of the arena. I wouldn't blame him if he didn't stick around for the game.

The fact that he couldn't even play tonight due to the

timing of the trade sucked. We've had such a great season, clinching a spot in the Calder Cup, and he can't even enjoy that with us and celebrate.

We take our spots and the game begins, but it's clear none of us are at our best tonight. The passes are sloppy and the guys can't manage to score even once. Our defense is also laughable and I get screened so much, I let in four goals, which is totally going to fuck up my save percentage.

By the time we're out of the arena, I am angry and disappointed. But there's nothing I can do about it except suck it up and go to Jordan's farewell party. I don't understand why he's choosing to leave so quickly after being traded. Since his new team didn't make it to the playoffs, he doesn't need to report for any kind of training until September.

And yet, we're having a combined end of season and farewell party for Jordan tonight. He plans to head to Texas right away and look for housing and check out the area before coming back to move all of his stuff from his apartment.

I'm in my head about it all when I hear someone calling out my name.

"Eli, wait up!" I spin around and see Ash coming out of the building, looking dashing in a white button-up, dark green slacks, and his hair all damp from the shower.

"I thought you were going to stop at the apartment before meeting up at the party," I say, waiting for him to catch up. I greedily take in his forearm tattoo as he rolls up his sleeves, the black vines peeking out.

"Changed my mind. Can I ride with you?" he says, stopping right in front of me, closer than we usually get when we're in public. And yet, I don't have the strength to move away. Ever since Anaheim, I've wanted him near me a lot more. I don't know what that means, but I'm starting to regret ever saying no to his friends with benefits suggestion.

"Of course, *rakas*." He looks up at me, eyes sparkling, left eyebrow slightly raised.

"You know," he says, leaning into me, "the last time you called me a foreign name, we ended up in some very compromising positions."

I bite the inside of my cheek to keep from smiling. Compromising indeed. After sucking each other off in the hotel room, we had a repeat of it in the shower.

It counts as being "one time" if we do it the same night, right?

"I remember," I say, making a show of checking him out, head to toe. He pulls back in surprise and grabs my upper arm, dragging me to my car.

Once we get inside, he says, "Are you flirting with me?"

"Maybe I am," I say, letting out a frustrated sigh.

"What's going on?"

"I've just been—I don't know." I say, gently smacking the steering wheel.

"Frustrated?" he asks.

"Yeah..."

"Sexually?" he prods, and I peek at his face to see he's biting back a smile.

"If you laugh at me right now, I will throw you out of my car and you can walk to the party."

He makes a show of zipping up his mouth and schooling his features in a neutral expression. I narrow my eyes at him and say, "Yes, sexually."

Ash nods along, searching my face for...something. For a moment I think I've rendered him speechless but then he says, "How can I help?"

I close my eyes and sigh again. "I can't ask you to hook

up again when I was the one to push you away the first time around. It was also my idea that it should only happen once. I'm not in the business of being a hypocrite."

He laughs, bright and beautiful. "Eli, I don't give a shit about you being a hypocrite. Things change, we can still consider a friends with benefits arrangement. Besides, you're not the only frustrated one."

"Tired of all the one night stands?" I say, and it comes out with more bite than I intended. While I might be jealous, I don't want him to know it.

Ash's hand grabs my forearm and squeezes lightly before he softly says, "I haven't been with anyone since California." This takes me by surprise, because he's not the type to stay celibate for long.

"Really?" I ask.

"Yeah," he mumbles, and the car gets a little too silent. Before I can come up with a reply, Ash says, "I just couldn't get over your giant cock. I told you it would ruin me."

I burst out laughing and he joins in. Maybe this friends with benefits thing could work, if we can joke about it and still be friends.

"Are you sure you're fine with just sex? No other labels or feelings involved?" I ask when our laughter dies down, making sure he knows what he's getting into. As much as I like him, I can't focus on a relationship right now.

He swallows and gives me a shy smile. "Yeah, pretty boy, I'm sure."

TWELVE

Five Months Ago

ASH

EVERYONE IS at the farewell party for Jordan that Robbie is hosting. The whole team showed up, and it's a bittersweet feeling to say goodbye to a player while also celebrating the end of a great season. Robbie's whole family is here—his parents, his older brother Michael and his wife Tangela, who is also Jordan's sister. But there is one person missing—Alice.

I walk up to Olivia who is currently alone at the dining table, scrolling through her phone.

"Hey, girl. Where's Alice?"

She looks up at me, a smile forming. Olivia is gorgeous, with long brown hair and green eyes, but the best part about her is how smart and witty she is. I remember when she used to only frown at me whenever I tried to ask her out.

Oh, how far we've come.

"I don't know. I'm trying to get a hold of her but she's not answering. She's not even on her social media, which is a bit concerning," she says, frowning down at her phone.

I take a seat next to her and poke her cheeks so she smiles again. "How are you feeling?"

She winces a little before flipping her phone over on the table and giving me her full attention. "Better, but I'm still not one hundred percent healed. The doctor said it will take another couple of weeks before I can start doing some more physical activity."

"I bet you miss skating," I say, not being able to imagine being on bed rest for six weeks. Olivia's injury came from a nasty collision a month ago when Dustin Mitchell ran into her, on purpose, after blackmailing her and threatening to get her fired over dating Robbie.

"You have no idea. I miss any kind of exercise at this point," she says with a pout. I reach my arm out to circle her shoulders in a sideways hug as she rests her head against mine.

"I'm sorry he did that to you. I'm glad he was fired, but at the same time, I almost wish he'd be back next season so I could kick his ass."

"I think Robbie did a good enough job of that," she says, shaking her head.

"You're right. He'd do anything for you, but so would we, just so you know."

She gives me another grateful smile and a tight hug and that's when Robbie saunters over to us. "I thought I told you to stop hitting on my girlfriend, Ashton."

I give him a cocky smile in return and kiss Olivia on the cheek. She laughs and pushes me lightly away as Robbie drags my chair away from her and leans in to kiss her. He's so fun to mess with. I'm jealous of how effortless their dynamic is. I want that more than anything. Someone to be silly with, someone to kiss in a room full of people, someone to love and love me in return.

I stand up to give them some privacy as I glimpse around the room. More people are trickling in, teammates and their significant others. Robbie's house is packed. Jordan is talking with his sister, but he doesn't seem to be very social despite this being his party.

On the other side of the kitchen, I see Eli leaning against a wall, looking at me with an unreadable expression. I tilt my head for him to join me but he shakes his head no. He then nods towards the hallway and takes off. I take that as my cue to follow, so I make my way through the crowded kitchen and down the hallway. I don't see him anywhere so I just stand around for a moment, spinning in circles.

All of a sudden, a hand is grabbing the back of my shirt and pulling me inside a room. When the door closes and I turn around, I notice where we are. Eli pulled me into the laundry room. Last time we were here was at the New Year's party when I first kissed him. Eli's gaze is intense as he slowly backs me into the door. It reminds me of that night and how amazing that kiss was. Even with how drunk I was, I still remember every movement, every touch.

Eli's lips meet mine and this kiss is gentle, but bruising. It's like he doesn't believe I'm actually here, so he needs to ground me. My lips happily part for him and my hands fly to his hair, which is long enough for me to run my fingers through, but not long enough for me to grip.

"You need to grow out your hair so I have something to pull on," I groan out when he finally gives my mouth a break.

"Hm, I'll think on it," he replies before diving in again,

his hips finding mine and grinding. Eli's hands are eager and enthusiastic as he reaches down and undoes my belt, reaching next for the zipper of my slacks.

"Aren't you afraid of getting caught?" I say, wondering if this really is such a great idea.

"I locked the door this time. Just try and be quiet."

I don't get a chance to reply, because Eli drops down to his knees, pulling my layers down until my hard cock springs free and he immediately takes me in his mouth.

"Fuck!" I pant, looking down at him. His fingers dig into my ass and start kneading and I'm so fucking gone for this man and his touch. I start thrusting, slow at first, until Eli guides me faster with his hands. My hands are on his head, threaded in his hair, and I need to lean back on the door as he takes me even deeper. When his finger moves lower and finds my entrance, I tense up.

"Is this okay?" he asks, letting me go with a loud *pop*.

"Fuck yeah. Just took me by surprise."

Eli smiles up at me before licking me again. His finger stays at my entrance, gently massaging me, while his mouth moves lower to suck on my balls. His other hand starts pumping me and I can't think straight anymore. It doesn't take long for me to come all over his hand, while his finger continues to move in teasing circles. When he stands up, I kiss him hard, not wanting to let go of this bliss.

ELI

ASH KISSES me long and hard and I lose myself in it. There's something about his sexy confidence and demeanor that is incredibly alluring. Not only is he funny and charming, but he's smart too. Smarter than he gives himself credit for. I feel like I could talk to him and spend every day doing nothing and everything together. And that scares the shit out of me.

I pull back, breaking the kiss. Ash's pants are still down and while I'm painfully hard, I need to put some distance between us. "Let's get back to the party," I say.

"What? Why?" He laughs with a confused look on his face. "What about you?"

"I'm okay, *rakas*."

"You're...okay?" Ash frowns at me like he can't comprehend. It makes me chuckle.

"Obviously, I'm not *okay*. I just mean, I can wait until we get back to the apartment. Maybe you can come over?" I hear myself asking. What am I doing? I just said I need to put some distance between us and now I'm inviting him to spend the night?

"Okay, I'll come over. On one condition." Ash zips up his pants and brushes another kiss, this time on my cheek. "You have a couple drinks and let loose tonight, and let me drive us home."

"I don't need to let loose," I say with a scoff.

He laughs, hands looping effortlessly around my waist. "No, but I really liked how you bossed me around last time you had a few drinks and put aside your inhibitions."

I take a deep breath and bring a hand up to cup his head, my thumb pushing on the side of his jaw. I lean in and nip at his bottom lip before moving to his earlobe and biting down. "You like it when I tell you what to do and how to do it?" I whisper in his ear.

"Fuck. Yes." Ash's hands tighten at the small of my back.

"*Hani*, I don't need to drink to boss you around. I can

do that any time." Ash's skin is flushed, his freckles standing out when I lean in to suck on his neck and gently bite him.

"*Fuck. Me.*"

"I can certainly do that too once we get to my apartment."

"Okay, can we go now?" he asks excitedly. I laugh and give him another kiss because I can't seem to stay away. This time when I pull back, I press my forehead to his.

"We need to be here for our friend. Later though."

"Fine, but will you at least tell me what all the names you call me mean?" he pouts.

"One day," I say, smiling.

STANDING NEXT to Ash and not being able to openly touch him is pure torture. I've never wanted anyone as much as I *want* him. I don't know if this friends with benefits arrangement is good for either of us, but at this point, I'll take what I can get.

I can't afford for this to turn into something more though, because I'm not ready to come out to my family and my teammates. I know it's shitty of me, and that Ash deserves better, but for once I'm being selfish.

It's past midnight when we get back to the apartment complex and Ash is buzzed. He's had a few drinks, but not nearly what he usually consumes at parties. He's in a good mood and keeps smirking over at me from the elevator all the way up to the third floor.

We come to a stop in the hallway and I take a few steps into his personal space, forcing him to back up a bit—except he doesn't. He stands his ground and loops his arms around my waist.

I press a short kiss right below his ear before saying, "Do you have condoms?"

"Obviously," he laughs.

"Your place then," I say, turning him around so he can unlock his door. He taps his phone to it and we both step inside. The place is a mess, like usual, and normally that would bother the hell out of me and I'd start picking things up and putting them away, but I'm too wired up for that. The door swings shut and I push Ash against it, immediately finding his lips with mine. He opens up eagerly and loops his hands around my neck, fingers combing through my hair.

"Why don't you have any condoms?" he asks when we come up for air, and I'm surprised by the question. My jealousy flares and I want to say *because I don't sleep around like you do*, but that's not something I need to judge him for, especially when he told me he hasn't been with anyone else since we hooked up in California.

"Because I haven't had sex in two years, and up until tonight, I didn't think I needed them."

"Wait, two years?!" He pulls back and I feel my cheeks getting red. It really has been that long. Is he worried I don't know what I'm doing? Ash's eyes are wide as they search my face. I break the contact and look away, embarrassed.

His hands frame my face and pull me back to him in a slow, sweet kiss. "I'm honored, *pretty boy*." I smile into the kiss and bite his lower lip, dragging it down before soothing it with a lick. Ash moans and presses his erection into me, and I take that as my cue to start moving us to the bedroom.

Compared to the frantic encounters we had before, this time we take our time undressing each other. There's nothing but the sound of our shuffling and rough breathing between kisses as we make our way to the bed. The only light in the room is the moonlight coming through Ash's open blinds, and it casts him in a perfect shadow. His blue eyes are darker than usual and his tattoos are stark against his freckled skin. *He's beautiful.*

I interlock our fingers and bring our joined hands to the pillow above his head while I press into him. We're chest to chest and I take my time, slowly kissing his lips, his cheeks, his jaw, before letting go of his hands and moving lower, trailing feather touches over his arms and chest. I lick his cock before taking him in my mouth, working him up, getting him hard and panting for me.

He reaches into his nightstand and pulls out a bottle of lube and a strip of condoms, placing them next to me. I take the lube, rubbing it over my hands, making sure it's warm enough, before bringing two fingers to his entrance and slowly coaxing moans from him. My lips return to his cock and once again I take my time. Ash's hands rake through my hair and grip the back of my head every time I hit a spot he likes.

"Fuck, I want you inside me," he says, dragging my mouth away from him, and opening up a condom. He rolls it on me, adding a good amount of lube. I remember what he told me at the party, how he liked it last time I *bossed* him around.

"Turn around," I say, one hand on his hip, guiding him to get down on all fours. The smile he gives me over his shoulder is pure giddiness and anticipation.

"Fuck yes, bossy Eli is coming out." I laugh and reach around to grip him in my hand, pumping a few times, until he's leaning back into me, asking for more. I let my free hand come down and slap his firm ass cheek. The sound of it reverberates in the quiet room and the moan Ash lets out makes me impossibly harder.

I kiss a spot between his shoulder blades and straighten back up so I can line myself at his entrance. He's more than ready for me and I slowly push in, holding my breath, my fingers digging into his hips. My eyes close tight and *holy shit*, he feels too good. I need a moment to compose myself.

"You okay?" he asks, looking over his shoulder with a glimmer in his eyes. "You can move, you know. I know I said your giant cock would ruin me, but I promise I can take it."

This startles me into a laugh and I relax a bit, leaning in to give him a kiss, which only pushes me inside more and we both groan.

ASH

I'VE ALWAYS BEEN a fan of sex, but sex with Eli is on a whole other level. *Holy shit*. How have we gone this long without giving in to whatever this is between us? Just like he is with anything else, Eli is slow and methodical. He guides me in different positions, touching me *everywhere*, kissing me. There's an intensity to him now I've never seen before. Like I'm the only thing in the world that matters at this moment.

When he moves us around so he's on top, angling me so that he's as deep as he can be, he kisses me fervently and strokes me until I come with a gasp and a throaty *"Fuck fuck fuck."* He presses his forehead to mine and thrusts harder a few times before raggedly saying, "I'm going to come."

I push on his abs enough for him to pull out, before I take off the condom and put my hand on him. His arms shake above me as he comes, chest heaving and breath ragged. When he's halfway to collapsing on top of me, I pull him down and hold him tight.

"That was—" he rasps, trying to catch his breath.

I chuckle, "Good, I take it?"

His head lifts and he gives me a gorgeous smile, a dimple popping in his right cheek. "More than good, *rakas*."

"Hmm, that's good," I say, kissing along his shoulder and neck as we lay tangled up in my bed. Not long after, we shower and return to bed.

When Eli holds me through the night, it reminds me of New Year's and how he took care of me. He's always there for me, a constant ray of fucking sunshine.

I really hope I don't fuck this up.

THIRTEEN

Present Day

ELI

ASH IS RILED up during our warm ups. We ended up being on the ice at the same time, running drills and working on improving certain areas. I've been working on my RVH since it's something I rarely use. As a big player, reverse vertical horizontal lets me use my body efficiently when the play is behind the net, but it's not something I defer to unless necessary.

Ash has been working on his passes, puck control, and balance. Generally when I'm in the zone, I don't get easily distracted, but every time I take a break, my eyes stray towards him. And every time, he's caught me looking. When he gives me a wink, my stupid heart flutters in response. While he's being nice and flirty with me, I could sense some tension with him and some of the other players, especially Jackson.

I caught the tail end of their interaction in the locker room when Ash slammed Jackson in the locker, but I have no idea why. I don't know where we stand after everything. It feels like there's an ocean of space between us and I want so badly to know how he is. But I'm not even sure Ash would tell me if I asked.

After a couple of hours of training, we're done for the day. Juuse and I catch up in the locker room. He's putting his gear on as I take mine off and put on the too small shirt and shorts I got from Ash. He's looking at me in a way I can't, and truthfully, don't want to decipher right now. It's not Juuse's gaze I want on me, after all. Before I can get embarrassed or explain why I don't have normal clothes, he asks, "Do you still want to grab that coffee tomorrow?"

"Yeah, of course. Let me know where."

"There's a place called Water Bearer, they have breakfast food and good coffee."

"Sure, I'll be there at eight?"

"Perfect!" he smiles and squeezes my shoulder before heading out onto the ice.

As he leaves, I catch Ash looking between us with a furrow in his brows. When he notices me staring at him, he gives me a small smile, but I can tell it's forced. Things are feeling a bit awkward, and I don't know what to do about it, except get him to talk to me. With our track record, it's unlikely either of us will actually speak what's on our mind.

I stand up and walk over to him. "Hey."

"Hey," he says, his smile growing more genuine.

"Any chance you could drive me to a clothing store?" I laugh.

Ash sighs and, low enough for just me to hear, he says,

"Bummer, I really like you in those shorts. You should lose your luggage more often."

I sigh and shake my head, but we walk together to his car and he drives me to our favorite store, Meijer.

ASH

I TRY to swap out the pants Eli added to the shopping cart with a size down, but he catches me and gives me the *murder glare*. His face is so expressive and I can't help but smile at him. His eyes are narrowed and his jaw is set, hands on his hips. I sigh dramatically and swap the pants back. I guess now I have to live with the fact that I'll never see his perfect ass in those too tight shorts again.

It's tragic.

On the bright side, no one else will see it either. I'm not sure what I picked up on in the locker room, but the way Juuse was looking at Eli made me want to punch the other goaltender in his stupid pretty face.

And to be fair, I wanted to punch lots of people in the face today, but did he *have* to check Eli out that blatantly? And what was all of that about the two of them going to breakfast together?

Is Eli open to dating now? Or is he too oblivious to realize Juuse is into him?

Knowing him, it's probably the latter.

My thoughts spiral as we walk around the store, grabbing some groceries, along with a bag of charcoal and some other supplies to grill.

"Since when do you cook?" Eli asks all of a sudden, sounding kind of surprised. I guess he has a right to be, considering he's only ever seen me eat takeout and steal Robbie's food every time I go over.

"I started recently. Olive has been sending me some recipes that she and Robbie have tried out."

His eyebrows shoot up. "*Olive?*"

"Yeah, what about her?"

"Since when do you call her that?"

"What is this, an interrogation?" I huff, going to the self-checkout and scanning the asparagus and chicken first.

"I'm not trying to interrogate you, I just want to make sure you're not *actually* hitting on Olivia, who is in a relationship with our best friend."

I look over my shoulder, unceremoniously dropping the lettuce I just scanned into the grocery bag. "I thought Jordan was your best friend."

He's got the frustrated murderous look on his face again, but he says, "Jordan hasn't answered any of my calls or texts in a couple months."

I stop, looking at him. Eli's arms are folded across his chest and he looks sad. "What do you mean he hasn't answered? Is he okay?"

"He's fine, I guess. To his credit, he does answer sometimes, but it's all just small talk. He doesn't respond to any actual questions about hockey, or how he's doing, or if he's coming to visit. I think the trade really fucked with him."

"Shit. I should really reach out to him more. I've kinda been distracted by my own shit. Therapy really sucks the life out of you sometimes." I laugh, tapping my card to the reader to pay for the groceries.

Eli doesn't say anything as he scans and pays for his clothes, and it's not until we get back to the car, everything put away in the trunk, that he says, "You're in therapy?"

I take a deep breath. "I started going when I got back

from Finland," I say, swallowing hard and slanting a glance his way. Eli is looking at me intently, but his face doesn't show any sign of being upset or annoyed that I brought up Finland. He maintains eye contact for a moment, before nodding along in understanding.

Does he really understand though?

How fucked up I was a few months ago, and how bad I feel for everything I did and said?

We're both quiet as we drive the twenty minutes to the cabin, 90s hits playing softly on the radio. Once I park the rental car in the driveway, I take a deep breath and squeeze the wheel to steady my nerves before saying, "I'm sorry, by the way. I had no right to blow up your life and drag you through the mud."

When he doesn't say anything, I look over and see his confused expression. "Drag me through mud?" he repeats.

Right, sometimes I need to explain all the weird sayings we have that he doesn't get.

I chuckle and say, "Generally, it means I ruined your reputation, but in this case I meant that I brought you down to my level and fucked everything up."

"Would you fucking stop it?" he snaps, and I rear back, my smile dropping. The only other time I've seen him this upset, this out of sorts, was *that night* in Helsinki. I'm frozen now too, not knowing if I should exit the car and flee, or stay and let him yell at me, punch me, whatever he needs to do to just *forgive* me.

Eli's fists are tight, resting on his thighs, and his jaw is so clenched I'd be surprised if he doesn't need dental work after this. *Fuck, he's really mad.*

"I'm so sorry," I whisper, biting the inside of my cheek to keep my face from crumpling.

"Stop talking about yourself like you're beneath me; you

always fucking do that, Ash, and it's infuriating. You didn't bring me *down* anywhere. But you know what?" he says, finally facing me and pinning me with a look of such hurt, I want to curl up and die. "You did fuck up, but so did I, and I need you to stop acting like I'm goddamn perfect, because I'm not."

He gets out of the car, and opens up the trunk. I slowly get out too but don't know what to say. Eli's reason for being mad is not what I expected. He grabs his bag of clothes and walks towards the cabin, and I'm left staring at the groceries in the trunk, my eyes stuck on the lettuce poking out of the bag.

"One more thing," he says, looking over his shoulder at me, one leg on the front step. "I'm sorry too. I let you down when you needed me most."

"No, you didn't," I say quietly, but he's already walking away.

FOURTEEN

Three Months Ago

ASH

AFTER A SEASON of ups and downs, trades and injuries, we finally did it. We made it to the Calder Cup Finals.

The coach's speech is a jumble of words as I bounce my leg up and down, nerves getting the best of me. We're going into the third period tied 3-3 and my skin is buzzing with anticipation. Even though I have a goal and an assist, I still feel like there's so much more I could be doing.

Eli's hand stills my leg and even through the knee pads, his firm hold calms my nerves. I give him an appreciative smile and then we're all throwing our gear back on, ready to bring this cup home.

Sweat drips down my face as I push myself to the limit. Looking up from the bench, I see there's only a minute left in regulation and we're still tied.

"Fuck," I yell, kicking the board. "Come one, boys, let's bring this home!"

Trip gets slammed into the boards and he hobbles over to the bench, pain showing on his face. I wince just from looking at him and jump over the ledge for the shift change.

Thirty seconds remaining.

Okay, you can do this.

I stay alert during the face-off and get a hold of the puck. The rest happens in a blur as I manage to dodge the defensemen standing in my way and make it to the offensive zone. We play it safe, passing the puck a few times, but when one of my teammates fakes the shot, the goalie is caught off guard. I catch the puck and slapshot it into the net. The next thing I know, I'm being tackled by my teammates.

The final buzzer goes off and the arena erupts into cheers. The game is sold out since it's a playoff final at home, and all 11,000 seats are occupied. Well, not anymore, since everyone is standing, cheering, and hugging each other. Because we did it. We actually won the fucking cup.

I look up at the private box where the Elliots are celebrating and for a moment I feel so sad that Robbie didn't get to experience this with us. He's the reason we made it here in the first place after an amazing regular season. I lift up my stick and point it at him, nodding my thanks.

We did it for you, man.

Robbie points back at me before sweeping Olivia up in a hug and spinning her around in celebration. He then high fives Alex, his business partner, and Malia, Alex's wife.

Jordan should be here too. With how busy I've been recently, I haven't reached out to him as much as I should have. For a second, I think I see him in the stands, but that's just my mind playing tricks because he's now in Texas.

The rest of Robbie's family is there too, his parents, his brother with his wife and kids, and Alice. She's taking videos and pictures and waves at me. I wave back and drop my stick, gloves and helmet on the ice. I don't bother even trying to look for my own family, because they aren't here. Instead, I turn around and skate up to the one person that's been there by my side for the past two years. But especially these last few months.

Once my teammates let go of me, I sprint up to Eli and jump in his arms, nearly tackling him. He catches me easily, even with all the pads between us. His mask is still on and even though all I want is to fucking kiss him, I know he wouldn't want that. So instead, I kiss his mask before taking it off of him.

He sets me down and we hug each other tight. "You were fucking amazing out there, Eli."

"You scored the winning goal"—he shakes his head against me—"that was amazing."

We smile like idiots and our hug becomes a group one when all our teammates surround us to celebrate.

THE REST of the night passes in a blur of happiness. We take pictures on the ice, we get congratulated by our friends and strangers on the street. We party with the team and crew, and everyone who made this season possible, then we go *home* and Eli and I celebrate in our own way.

The last two months have been stressful and exhausting, but having him by my side has made everything better. We both understood the pressure and knew how to build each other up, whether it was a pep talk, a trip to the gym, or just silently being there for one another.

The constant sex has helped too.

And I knew I would be falling more and more for him each time I would crawl into his bed, but I still did it. He tried to push me away a few times, but I managed to convince him that our friends with benefits arrangement could still work.

The problem is, I can't tell if he was trying to push me away because he was falling too, or because he genuinely doesn't think this could work. We haven't exactly discussed the offseason, but I figured we could train together or take a vacation or something.

I look over at Eli next to me in bed and trail my hand down his naked chest, my fingers stopping on a bruise. It looks a light shade of purple and I frown. When did he get hurt? And why didn't he say anything? I scoot down lower on the mattress and kiss it gently, then move my mouth up his torso to his collarbone and neck.

Eli lets out a content hum and I continue on, leaving featherlight kisses on his jaw and cheeks, his nose and forehead. My hand trails the band of his boxers and when I palm him, he's already growing hard for me. I smile against the corner of his lips and whisper, "Are you dreaming about hockey or just happy to wake up next to me?"

Pale lashes flutter open and he stretches out, the motion bringing his bulge further in my hand. I wrap my fingers around him and squeeze lightly. "I was dreaming about that goal you scored, and how you jumped into my arms afterwards. Except in my dream, we were naked, and I bent you over the net and took you right then and there," he says sleepily.

I laugh and his eyes widen a bit, like he can't believe he just told me his ridiculous dream. "Okay, I have so many follow up questions," I say. "First off, you *took me* right then and there? What is this, the regency era?"

Eli covers his face with both his hands and mumbles something in Finnish. I laugh again and pull his hands away, dropping more kisses on his reddened cheeks.

"Second off, was the arena packed full of people or was it empty?"

"Shut up," he says, trying to swat me away, but I'm not letting up. I get on top of him, pinning him down with my hips. Eli grunts when he feels my hardness, but his hands snake up around my waist as he pulls me closer.

"I'm serious, I need to know more about this dream. What were the logistics of bending me over the net?"

He sighs. "If I tell you, will you stop bothering me about it?"

I smile wide and say, "Never."

Eli is quiet for a moment before saying, "The arena was empty, obviously, I'm not a perv. And you weren't fully bent over, more like you were facing the net, gripping the top bar, and I was, you know...taking you from behind."

"Hm, well we don't have a net here, but you could *take me* from behind by that dresser." I laugh and wiggle my eyebrows.

Eli's pupils expand and I think he really likes the sound of that, but then he says, "The dresser is too low, but we can try the kitchen counter."

"Who are you?" I stutter a laugh. I never would have thought he'd suggest something like this, since he's usually very careful about his space, always keeping it nice and tidy.

"Duke Elias, about to *take you* from behind," he jokes and I fucking love this silly version of him.

"You need to stop talking to Alice so much, she's a bad influence with those damn romance books."

"Don't complain, you're the one reaping the rewards."

. . .

ELI

ASH'S PHONE rings while we're at breakfast and I peek *Dad* on the screen before he silences it. It lights up again and again while we drink our coffee and eat the pancakes I made us.

"Are you going to answer that?" I say, taking him in. He's wearing nothing but a pair of light blue boxers and a silver necklace. I linger on his collarbones and his freckles, but my eyes always come back to that flower tattoo, right above his heart. The one he still hasn't told me about, and I haven't pressed. He notices my stare and rubs at it gently, shaking his head no.

I try not to push on the topic of his father, since I know they have a tumultuous relationship. So instead I ask, "What's the meaning of the tattoo?"

Ash stops rubbing at it and looks at me with a serious expression on his face. It cracks when he gives me a smirk and says, "When are you going to tell me what all the Finnish words you call me are?"

I smirk right back and say, "Hm, good point."

We continue eating our pancakes in comfortable silence, but his phone won't stop ringing. With a sigh, Ash picks it up and stands up, facing the bedroom. "I'll go take this, be right back."

The clock on the stove tells me it's 11 a.m., which means this is the perfect time to call my family. With the seven hour time difference, I'll be catching them right around dinner time. I grab my laptop from the coffee table and log into Zoom. From the bedroom, I can hear Ash's voice rising, talking to his dad. I don't know what his family dynamics are and he wouldn't tell me even if I asked, but from the sound of it and the fact that they didn't even show up to the final game, I don't think things are going well between them.

After about three seconds, my mom's face lights up the laptop screen. She beams at me and starts asking me a billion questions in Finnish. I laugh and respond to each one, cherishing each chat with her. She's amazing and has always supported me and my dream, and so has my dad, who pokes his head in front of the camera.

"Eli, congratulations! The game was incredible. *You* were incredible. Mark my words, they're going to call you up to the NHL in no time."

I smile and thank him, but I think he's getting ahead of himself. Sure, this season was great, and we won, but Detroit already has two amazing goalies and there's no way they would bring me up so soon.

"Wish we could have been there," my mom says.

"Yeah me too, sorry I couldn't get you tickets this time."

"Oh *hani,* don't apologize. We just didn't have the money for this trip, but we'll start saving up for the next one."

I looked up tickets for all three of them to come visit this past week and the price was insane. Even with my savings, I couldn't afford the tickets, and it killed me that they couldn't see me in person.

"How is Edvin's training going?" I ask. My brother is ten years younger than me and he's a goalie too. Just like he trained me when I was in a Finnish league, my dad is training Edvin as well.

"He's doing fantastic, shows lots of potential, just like you did. Maybe you can give him some pointers this summer."

My smile slowly fades at the mention of this summer. I haven't decided if I should go home for the offseason or stay in Grand Marquee. I really miss my family and want to spend some time with them, help with my brother's training, but at the same time, I'm finally feeling like I can be myself here, with Ash. I know this is not a relationship, but whatever it is, it makes me happy, and kind of free. Even if we are stuck in our own little bubble, in either his apartment or mine, I'm *happy*. I don't know if I want to go back to Finland and feel like I need to hide who I am again.

"I'll let you know soon, *isi*."

He sighs, "Okay, we miss you, Eli."

"I miss you all too," I say, a knot forming in my throat.

As soon as the call ends, Ash pulls open the bedroom door. He's wearing one of my T-shirts and his own sweatpants and he stomps over to the front door, phone and keys in hand.

"Everything okay?" I ask before he can reach the door. He doesn't fully face me, but stops, jaw clenched, hands clenched into fists at his sides.

"Nothing to worry about, I just need to blow off some steam," he huffs out.

"And you can't do that here? Why are you leaving? Where are you going?" I ask, surprised that he's all of a sudden taking off.

"None of your goddamn business, Eli," he snaps before leaving the apartment, slamming the door behind him. I sit there, confused, and maybe a little hurt as well.

Here I was thinking this summer would be focused on *us*, spending time together, training together, but the truth is I don't know what Ash's plan is, if he even has one.

Maybe he feels trapped by this arrangement and needs

to take back some control. Maybe he wants to go back to partying and hooking up with new people. I can't blame him, he's young and fun after all.

As I sit at the dining table, pondering everything, I think that maybe I need to think about myself more than I do of others. So I pull up flights to Finland and book myself a round-trip ticket for the summer.

FIFTEEN

Three Months Ago

ASH

MY FATHER'S words come back to me, again and again as I pour myself another glass of whiskey. It's not even the afternoon, and I'm already trying to drink myself into oblivion.

What a disappointment.

You were sloppy and waited until the last second to score the winning goal.

If you were really serious about your career you'd be putting in more effort into your training.

The audacity of that asshole to call me the day after my championship and tell me how shitty of a player I am. How I could never live up to his legacy. Maybe if he pulled his head out of his ass for once, he'd realize I gave up on following in his footsteps when I got traded to Grand Marquee.

I haven't been home or seen my family in two years since I moved here from Vermont and I don't plan to see them anytime soon. I realized a long time ago that I could never measure up to my dad. No matter how many awards or medals I got, he'd never be happy with my accomplishments. And my mom, well, she never took my side in anything. She'd try to make peace between us but eventually she'd get yelled at by my dad and then she'd drop it.

So I always found a way to piss him off, whether it was underage drinking, accepting a position on a team in Vermont instead of Massachusetts, or dating not just girls, but guys too. The truth is, my father would never approve of me, no matter what I did. And yet, I can't shake off the feeling that I'm not good enough.

Never good enough.

Because if my own family doesn't love me, then who ever will?

I down the rest of my whiskey, but before I can pour myself another, there's a knock at my door. I close my eyes and silently beg them to go away.

They don't. The knock comes again.

"Ash, can we talk?" Eli's muffled voice comes through the door and I groan. No, actually, the last thing I want to do is talk. But I stand up and make my way to the door anyway, flipping the lock and opening it wide.

Eli takes one look at me and purses his pretty lips. "You've been drinking."

I scoff, "And?"

He sighs but doesn't say anything else. The hand that's tucked in his front pocket comes out and holds something out to me, a key. I stare at it, confused. Is he giving me a key to his apartment? I didn't think he'd want any kind of commitment between us.

When I don't take it, he fidgets with it, turning it every which way. After a moment of silence he says, "Can you look after it for the summer? You don't have to clean it or anything, I already did that, and I'm almost done packing. I just need someone to water the plants and take the mail in."

Wait. What?

My mind snags on one word, drowning out the rest. Packing?

I frown and say, "Where are you going?"

"Home. For the summer."

"This is home," I say moronically.

"I mean back home. To Finland. I need to spend some time with my family, I haven't seen them in two and a half years," he says, carefully watching me for a reaction. My chest constricts because *of course* he wants to see his loving family who misses the hell out of him. I thought the best part of this summer would be that I got to spend it with him, but clearly I was mistaken.

"Right," I say, swallowing the lump in my throat. I reach out and take the key from his hand, but before I can pull it back, he grabs my fingers and intertwines our hands over the key.

"I'm sorry. For leaving on such short notice. I didn't think I wanted to go until I called them earlier and—"

"You don't owe me an explanation, Eli. It's fine," I say, looking over his shoulder at his apartment door. The place I think of as home because *he's* there.

"Just listen," he says, squeezing my hand and running his thumb over the back of it. "I really like you, Ash. I want us to be okay, because you mean so much to me. And me leaving has nothing to do with you. I very much want to spend the summer with you, but I'm homesick. I need this trip."

My eyes finally search his face and I can see the truth there. He does care, even though he probably shouldn't.

"I understand," I say, my voice wavering. "I'll just miss you, that's all, and it's gonna be really lonely around here without you."

He swallows and leans in, kissing me softly. It feels like a goodbye kiss and I want to cry, I want to punch a wall.

What if he forgets about me?

What if he moves on while he's away?

What if he doesn't want me when he comes back?

"Wish I could come with you," I say before realizing. The last thing I want is to be clingy and annoying. "Sorry, I shouldn't have said that."

Eli tilts my chin up so he can look me in the eye and says, "What if—" He stops and looks away in thought. "What if you do come with me?"

My eyebrows shoot up. "Really?" I ask, unable to keep the hope and longing out of my voice.

Eli nods, convincing himself. "Yeah, yeah—it would be good. My parents always ask me about my friends, they'd love to meet you. You can stay with us, we have a spare bedroom—"

I smile and cut him off with another kiss, my free hand tangling in his hair, which has been getting longer. "If you're sure, I'll come with you, *pretty boy*."

"I'm sure," he breathes against my mouth before diving in for another kiss, this one more intense and pressing. "There's just one thing."

He puts some distance between us and leads me to the couch. Eli holds my hand in his lap as he says, "I don't want you to think I'm trying to end things between us, because

I'm not. But, we need to be careful around my family. They can't know about me yet, and I'm not ready to drop that bomb on them, honestly."

"I know, I won't say anything to them, I promise."

Eli watches me for a moment, contemplating. Then he nods, "Okay, *hani*. Let's get you a plane ticket."

SIXTEEN

Three Months Ago

ELI

TWO DAYS LATER, Ash and I are about to board a plane to Helsinki. After leaving our apartment keys with our friends, Alice, Robbie, and Olivia drive us to the airport. If they think it's weird that Ash is coming with me, they don't comment on it.

At check-in, we request that our seats be assigned next to one another and the lady is nice enough to grant our request. Once we drop off all our luggage, we say goodbye to our friends. When I'm done hugging everybody, Ash pulls both Robbie and Olivia into a group hug, saying, "I'm gonna miss you guys. Please don't have too much fun without me."

"We wouldn't dream of it," Olivia says with a small smile and Robbie rolls his eyes at Ash's antics.

Alice pulls me aside near the security area and pulls out

a book from her tote. "I got you something, it's a hockey romance." I take it and curiously flip it around. She's been lending me some of her favorite books and giving me recommendations. She knows I like to read when I travel.

The paperback has a dust jacket on it that's a solid red cover and no title. I pull the jacket off and look at the blue cover underneath with the bright red title *Time to Shine* by Rachel Reid. My cheeks flush when I realize it's a romance between two guys—two hockey players, to be exact. I cover it back up and shove it in my backpack.

When I look back at Alice, she's got a knowing smile on her face and gives me a wink. "Don't worry, your secret is safe with me," she whispers and gives me a quick hug and peck on my cheek before walking over to Robbie and Olivia. I'm left a little dumbfounded.

How does she know I'm into guys?

Does she know about me and Ash?

I can feel a glimmer of panic starting to set in, but then I realize that if anyone is going to accept me for who I am, it's Robbie's family. They've been nothing but kind and supportive of me. But still, I don't think I'm ready for people to know.

With another wave back to our friends, Ash and I head to security.

"Are you sure you wanna be away from them for two months?" I ask, worrying that maybe Ash's decision to come with me was a little rash. He seems to be running away from something and that might not be the healthiest choice. Can I really be what he needs when I don't even know how to handle my own shit?

"I can survive without Robbie keeping me in check, if that's what you're worried about," he says, eyebrows knotting.

"No, I didn't mean that. Just—you don't exactly get along with your family and Robbie is the closest thing you seem to have to one here. I want to make sure I didn't push too far by asking you to come with me."

"First off, I more or less invited myself, so don't pretend like I didn't jump at the opportunity to see your hometown. And second off," he trails off as he takes off his baseball hat and runs his right hand through his hair. The vine tattoo is on full display on his forearm and like usual, my eyes are glued to it. "Second off, *you're* my family too. Not just Robbie."

It's the way he says it that has me all twisted up in knots. He says it soft and quiet, shrugging like it's the most natural thing in the world.

You're my family too.

I swallow hard and watch him go through the metal detectors, putting his shoes back on. I stare after him for so long that the TSA officer has to wave at me to get my attention and have me move along.

Once I catch up to him, I want to say something back, I want to assure him that I feel the same way. Because I do. In the past few months, he's been a constant in my life, and I can't even imagine what it would be like to not have him around.

There's a strange feeling taking root in my chest, making my heart beat faster the closer I get to Ash. And I want to give into it, I want to wrap my arms around him and never leave.

Instead, I squeeze his shoulder and say, "There's so much I want to show you when we get to Helsinki. We still have to train, of course, and I bet my brother is going to be super excited to share the ice with us."

"I can't wait to meet him."

"My family is going to love you."

"I hope so," he says, putting his hat on backwards and giving me a wink.

"Is there anything you're looking forward to?"

"Are there museums?" he asks as we take a seat at our gate.

"Plenty. Although I'm surprised that's the first thing you're asking about."

"What, you think all I want to do is party?" he jokes, but I detect an edge of vulnerability in his tone.

"No, *hani*. I thought you'd ask about the tram or the ferris wheel. That's what all the tourists want to do, anyway."

"There's a tram??"

"There is. And there are lots of artists coming to Helsinki over the summer. We can also go to a concert if you want."

"Hell yeah, that would be sweet!" he says, nodding and bouncing his leg in excitement. He's kind of like a dog sometimes. Cute and enthusiastic.

I smile at him and want so badly to reach out and touch him, to kiss him. But I made the damn rules, and I need to stick to them. So I settle for looking at him, basking in his brightness and making plans for the summer.

After a short flight to New York and an even shorter layover, we board the second flight. Ash passes out for the entirety of it, and I read the book Alice gave me, crying over how much I relate to the main character, Landon, and his story. I know my life is nothing like a book, but maybe I need to get over this fear I have and just tell my family that I'm into guys.

Would they react badly? Or would they accept me?

SEVENTEEN

Three Months Ago

ASH

AFTER FOURTEEN TOTAL hours of travel, we *finally* land in Helsinki. I was able to sleep the entire flight, which is not an easy feat for me, so by the time we go through customs and pick up our luggage, I am awake and ready for the day.

Eli, on the other hand, looks more tired than I've ever seen him and his pale blue eyes are bloodshot and a little puffy. "Hey, are you okay?" I ask, gently stopping him by hooking my hand around his elbow.

Eli looks down and smiles tiredly. "I'm good, I just don't really enjoy long flights. Couldn't sleep."

I nod and let go of him. We each grab a cart and pile our hockey equipment bags, suitcases, and backpacks on them before making our way out of baggage claim.

Maybe I should have been more worried about what Eli's parents would be like when I first met them, but I can tell right away that I'm going to love them. I could spot them from a mile away. His dad looks how I imagine Eli would in 30 years. He's just as tall and imposing, with dark blond hair and the same color eyes as his son, except he has the slightest glimmer in them when he reaches out to hug Eli.

His mom is shorter than I expected, her head barely reaching Eli's chin, but the fierce hug she gives him shows how strong she is. I stand by, watching their reunion, not knowing what to expect, but it doesn't take long for them to notice me.

Eli's father smiles as he shakes my hand and says, "Ashton, welcome to Finland. Is this your first time here?"

"Yes, sir," I say, trying to sound more confident than I really am in front of this man that Eli looks up to so much. *I am meeting Eli's family.* This is a huge step for me and some panic finally starts to set in. What am I doing here, intruding on Eli's time with his family? Does he truly want me here?

His mom wraps me up in a swift hug as Eli looks at us with a soft smile. Our gazes catch and I take a deep breath. This is fine. He *does* want me here, he wouldn't have suggested this otherwise.

An hour later, we get to Eli's childhood home, which is not far outside of the city. The mint green house looks more like a duplex, with two separate entrances, except it's connected together through the living room. The ceiling is high and the kitchen is on the right side of the house, with a small dining room tucked in a corner by the door to the back patio. The left side of the main floor of the house has a large master bedroom and bathroom. This is where his parents sleep.

Upstairs there are two more bathrooms, and three bedrooms. One is Eli's old room, one is his brother's, and the last is the spare bedroom. Except, when we get to the spare bedroom, it looks more like a craft room than anything else. There's definitely no bed in here.

"Mom, what happened to the spare bedroom?" Eli asks, frantically looking around.

"I turned it into my office. I paint and sell things on Etsy now," his mom says proudly, showing off her work area.

"Since when?" Eli asks. Is it just me or does he seem panicked?

"Since last year, *hani*." Eli's mom says something else but my mind is stuck on that word, *hani*.

Eli calls me that all the time, and I still don't know what it means.

"What does that word mean? *Hani?*" I interrupt quickly, before the conversation can move to another topic.

She smiles at me and says, "It means *honey*. It's—what do you call it—a term of endearment?"

I feel a flutter in my chest and I can't stop smiling. When I look over at Eli, I see his face is beet red and he's looking everywhere but at me.

"Why do you ask?" Mrs. Kalias says.

"Oh, I'm just curious to learn more of the language," I say with a smirk. "I have more words to ask you about. What does *ilo—*"

Eli jumps in at this point and distracts his mom. "Do we have a spare mattress then, can we set it up? I won't have Ash sleeping on a couch for the whole summer."

His mom looks almost offended. "*Hani*, of course not. He'll be staying with you in your room. We switched your twin bed out for the queen size. I'm sure you can share."

Eli's face looks so red, I'm afraid he's not even breathing at this point.

Well, well, well. We get to share a bed after all, it seems.

"Of course we can. Thank you so much for having me, by the way. I really appreciate it! I'm excited to see more of the city," I say, trying to get into her good graces. She seems like a lovely mom. I know she likes me immediately because she won't stop beaming at me.

"There is so much to see, and I can show you later, there's a hiking path right behind the house, you can go on walks or run. It's beautiful."

"Sounds incredible," I say, genuinely excited to be here.

Eli still has not said anything since finding out we'll be sharing a bed, so I pat him on the shoulder and ask, "Where's our bedroom?"

He throws me a glare and I can't help it, I laugh. He's so cute when he's flustered.

"Eli, are you okay? You look a little red," his mom says, reaching up to feel his forehead.

"Fine. I'm fine," he says, swatting his mother's hand away playfully.

I join in on the concern, having my own agenda. "Maybe you need to lie down for a minute, it's been a long trip."

"Yes, good idea, Ashton. You two go lie down, and I'll have some dinner ready when you wake up from a nap."

Two minutes later we're in Eli's bedroom, the door closed and locked behind us. He pins me with another glare and I smile and shake my head.

"It's not funny, what if they figure it out?"

I put on a sympathetic expression and slowly approach him, looping my arms around his waist. "*Hani*, I can read the room. She doesn't suspect anything, she thinks we're two best friends who can share a room together because, let's face it, we've done that before."

"I guess," he says, rubbing his hands down on his face. I gently pry them away and give him a tentative kiss, nipping at his bottom lip.

"We'll be careful," I say, "I promise."

Eli nods, unlocks the door in case anyone tries to wake us later, and we both fall into the bed, on separate sides, exhaustion pulling us under.

ELI

I AM HOME for the first time in two years and I feel like something in my chest has loosened. Like I can breathe a little easier and I don't have to feel guilty for leaving my family behind to chase my dream, thousands of miles away.

And yet, I'm still hit with a wave of anxiety. How do I tell my parents that I may be in love with my best friend?

I've been in love once before, even if that love was unrequited, so I can spot the signs. How I feel lighter when Ash is near me, more like myself, how I want to spend every waking moment with him because he's funny, and lively, and beautiful, and all I want is to be around him, hearing his jokes, and listen to him babble about anything and everything.

I might have fallen a little more in love with him when I saw him giving my mom a big hug and thanking her for the hospitality, or when he shook my dad's hand in gratitude. When my dad praised him for his winning goal in the Calder Cup, I could see a shine in Ash's eyes.

This is surprising since he's usually not one to shy away

from pride. His jersey is #1, after all. Cockiness might as well be his middle name. And yet, I wonder if he knows how incredible and amazing he was on the ice this season. Did we not tell him that enough?

My brother, Edvin, is away with some friends for the weekend so we won't get to see him yet, but it's nice to catch up with my family. The house is unchanged, with the exception of the spare bedroom being turned into a craft studio now. When the hell did that happen?

While my apartment in Grand Marquee is nice, it doesn't always feel like home; it doesn't feel cozy and lived in. I have so many memories in this house, of family meals, of mom and dad helping me with homework, me helping my little brother in return. The truth is, I missed them like crazy.

When we wake up from our nap, we venture downstairs, following the smell of *karjalan paisti,* a traditional stew with pork, beef, lamb, and vegetables, served with mashed potatoes. I give my mom another hug and say, "You didn't have to go through all this trouble for dinner. We would be fine with anything, really."

"As if I would feed my son anything but the best when he comes home." She shakes her head at me but gives me a soft smile.

"I missed you, Mom," I say with a sigh and kiss her cheek.

"I missed you too, *hani.*" She pulls out of my hug and grabs the stew pot, placing it on the table. I grab the mashed potatoes and bread and help her.

"Ashton, take a seat. Make yourself at home," my dad says, coming in from the living room where he was watching a game of *jalkapallo,* or as the Americans would call it, soccer. When I look over at Ash, he's standing demurely in a corner, wringing his hands.

I frown at him and tilt my head in a motion to join me. He tentatively approaches and takes a seat next to me. While my parents are busy grabbing drinks for us all, I squeeze his leg and give him a wink. He seems to relax a little, but his smile seems tight. "Are you okay?" I ask.

"Yeah, just jet lagged, I guess," he replies, fidgeting with a napkin. I slowly take my hand back but keep my eyes on his face. He does look tired and a little sad even.

"Do you want to go on a walk after dinner? Get some fresh air?"

"Sure."

My mom peppers me with questions as we eat and Ash keeps quiet, but he does nod along to all my stories of work and life in Grand Marquee. He has two helpings of stew and my mom fawns all over him. It's cute, I think. He fits here, with them. With me.

My dad gives us a run down of the training facility where we'll be working at, which happens to also be where my brother trains. As a goalie developmental coach, my dad has helped train me and my brother growing up. He talks us through some of the drills he wants to set up for us, and I can see the excitement in Ash's eyes dimming.

I make a mental note to ask him later what exactly about this arrangement is bothering him.

AFTER DINNER, we help clean up—I wash the dishes while Ash dries them, and my dad puts them away. My mom heads upstairs to work on her crafting—since she's got some orders to fulfill— and the three of us sit and watch the remainder of the soccer game.

My dad takes the reclining chair while Ash and I share the couch together, and our legs touch from knee to thigh, but neither of us moves. I crave to be near him and I keep thinking that sneaking around here is going to be unbearable.

As soon as the game ends, my dad hands me a key to the house. "A copy for you, for the summer. Make sure you lock up after your walk."

"I will. Thanks. Are you headed to bed?"

"Yeah, it's been a long day. Get some rest tonight. Good night, boys."

Ash and I say in unison, "Good night."

Once my dad rounds the corner and I hear the door shut, I turn to Ash on the couch and slowly lean in. He watches me, amusement written all over his face. "What are you doing?" he says, nervously chuckling.

"Honestly, I didn't pay attention to most of that game. All I was thinking about was kissing you," I whisper. My eyes drop to his lush mouth and, even tired, he looks so damn good. His dark red hair is getting longer on top, and even his side fade is growing out a bit. And the stubble he has right now makes me want to touch him—every inch of him.

There's a furrow between Ash's eyebrows and he looks at me, searching for something. "I thought you wanted to be careful. No offense, Eli, but you're kinda giving me mixed signals here."

I pull back and realize that—he's right—I was the one who came up with all the rules and asked him to keep us a secret so my family wouldn't find out. Can I really not keep it in my pants after just one day?

"I'm sorry, you're right. That's really shitty of me." I

drag my hands over my face and internally scream at myself.

Ash sighs and places his hand on my thigh. "Let's take that walk."

WE DON'T GO TOO FAR since it's dark outside, but we do take the illuminated path to one of the lookouts with a fishing pond. Our shoulders brush the entire time and every now and then I run my fingers over the back of his hand. As always, Ash notices and looks at me sideways, a small smile playing on his face. When we get to the pond, we take a seat on the bench, and for a moment I just take it all in.

It's a little chilly, to the point that I grabbed a sweatshirt, but Ash refused when I offered him one. He's in his signature white T-shirt, a color that brings out his freckles and tattoos in the moonlight.

I try to stop, but fuck it, I can't.

I can't stop looking at him.
I can't stop thinking about him.
I can't stop loving him.

I take a deep breath and it catches when Ash turns to look at me. "What's up?" he asks.

I slowly let out a sigh and say, "I don't know, maybe I'm just feeling jet lagged."

"And horny?" Ash waggles his eyebrows at me seductively.

"Shut up." My hand reaches out to lightly push him away but he catches my wrist in his hand and brings it up to his face. Not once breaking eye contact with me, Ash kisses my wrist and my palm before turning my hand over and kissing the back of it too.

"The jetlag is an excuse and we both know it," he says,

too observant for his own good. My shoulders slump and I drop my head in the crook of his neck. Ash lets go of my hand and hugs me, even though it's at an awkward angle and we're sitting on a bench. One of his hands rubs up and down my back and the other tangles in my hair.

"I'm just—" I start, but I need to take a moment to compose myself. What am I trying to say?

I'm confused, and scared, because I really like you.

"Whatever this is between us, it's not just sex anymore. I'm not sure how to tell my family, but I do *want* to tell them."

Ash doesn't say anything but continues to rub his hands up and down my back. Eventually he pushes me back to look at me and I can see his blue eyes are shining. "This isn't just sex for me anymore either." His face is soft and full of emotion and I don't think I can handle him saying the words. "Eli, I—"

My lips crush his in a kiss that I hope conveys everything.

Yes, yes, yes.

You love me, and I love you. But this thing between us is too complicated, and we just got here, and I don't want to fuck it up. *So please don't say it yet.*

Ash opens up to me, his hands gripping my hair at the nape of my neck, my hands fisting the collar of his white T-shirt until I think I might have stretched it out permanently.

God, I want him. So much.

When we come up for air, we're both smiling, and a little shiver goes through Ash. "Cold?" I ask.

"Just a little. No, Eli, you don't have to—" I grip the back of my sweatshirt and take it off in one swift movement. Ash swallows and it gives away that, yes, he was turned on by that little move. I pull the sweatshirt over his head and bring my face closer as I tug it into place.

"I like seeing you in my clothes," I murmur, kissing the corner of his mouth.

Ash kisses me back, letting out a small moan. "*Fuck*," he says, "it's gonna be really hard keeping my hands off you for the summer."

"I never said you should keep your hands off me. Just that we need some ground rules. Nothing around my parents or brother, but maybe when we go visit the city or if we take a train somewhere, we can spend the night away. Just us?"

"That sounds perfect."

We stay on that bench for another hour, talking about summer plans and making out until we're breathless. We walk back to the house hand in hand, holding on until we're ready for bed. Even then, my hand finds his under the covers and I don't let go until the morning.

EIGHTEEN

Present Day

ASH

EVEN IN HIS ANGER, Eli is quiet. The door to his bedroom closes with a soft thud and I'm left staring at the kitchen counter. I try to put the conversation out of my mind and instead focus on mixing together a quick marinade for the chicken.

I get my headphones and listen to a playlist I found that helps me focus. The glass mixing bowls are in a bottom cabinet next to the stove and I pull them out, measuring the ingredients—lemon juice, olive oil, Italian seasoning, paprika, salt, and pepper—before mixing them together. I carefully butterfly the chicken and throw it in the marinade too. I move my head around in time with the lo-fi beats as I prepare a side salad and slice up a few strawberries.

I text Robbie and Olivia a few pictures and thank them

for the recipe. The response is immediate as Olivia's face lights up my screen with a video call. I swipe to answer and take the call outside so I don't bother Eli.

"Hey," I say with a smile.

"Hey Ash, how was the first day of camp?" Olivia asks with a big smile on her face.

"Well, *mom,* camp was fine, although I did shove a kid into a locker. Does that make me a bully?" I joke.

Olivia's smile fades and she gets a concerned look on her face. "Ash, what happened? Are you okay?"

"I'm fine. Some asshole was talking shit about me not going out to drink anymore and wouldn't let it go. I had to make some empty threats to let him drop it."

"Please be careful, Ash," she says.

"I know," I sigh. "I won't do anything stupid, you and Robbie need to stop worrying."

"We're not worried about you doing something stupid, man, we just want what's best for you," Robbie says, popping into the frame and pulling Olivia into his chest.

"I know, I love you guys."

Robbie rolls his eyes, but smiles and Olivia says, "We love you too." She hesitates for a moment, but then asks, "How is Eli doing?"

My eyes dart to the side, towards the window of his bedroom. What is he doing right now? Is he still angry?

I swallow and say, "He's fine. The airline lost his luggage in Chicago so he had to buy some stuff from Meijer. We drove to practice together, then went to the store before coming back. Now I'm getting started on dinner."

"Is he joining you for dinner? Have you talked at all?" she prods.

I sigh. "I don't know if he'll join. He was kind of mad at me earlier," I say, thinking about how angry he looked. Did I mess this up beyond repair? "We haven't talked about Finland yet, but I tried bringing it up."

"But you will, right?" Robbie asks in a hard tone.

"I'll try," I relent and he nods in understanding.

"Well, if you need us, we're a phone call away," Olivia says, giving me a soft smile.

"Tell him I say hello," Robbie says and I nod, eager to change the subject.

"How's it going with the Blue Line Brigade?" I ask.

"Really good, we've had a few events already and met some of the kids that signed up. They won't get to start training until October, so we're finalizing things now, getting them fitted for gear and stuff." Robbie could talk for days about his non-profit and it makes me happy that he found something to love just as much as playing hockey.

"That sounds awesome. Let me know if I can help in any way."

"I will, thanks. Olive and I need to get ready for a fundraiser, so we'll catch you later?"

"Yeah, have a good time. Miss you guys."

"Miss you too. See you soon," Olivia says with a wave goodbye before ending the call.

I don't know what I would do without the support of my best friends. I sit outside for another moment, pondering everything good that I have in my life—a job I love, friends that I adore—and, Eli. I hope he still wants to be in my life.

When I'm done contemplating, I grab the food from inside the cabin and get the grill started.

ELI

. . .

THE CONVERSATION from the car is still on my mind. Maybe I shouldn't have lost my shit on Ash, but it pisses me off when he puts himself down like that. I genuinely wanted to talk about what happened in Finland, but after the way I reacted, I feel like I shut down any conversation between us.

I get an email from the airline that my luggage was found in Chicago and is being shipped to me in Traverse City. Sounds like I'll be without it for a couple more days, but at least I got some essentials from the store. A few pairs of shorts, some athletic, some more decent for going out, some T-shirts, and toiletries.

I've stubbornly closed myself in my bedroom, a combination of modern and rustic style, with a queen size bed taking up most of the room. All my belongings are tucked away in the small dresser. I grab the book I bought while at the store and sit in the rocking chair by the window, hoping to relax and let go of the lingering anger before going out there and facing Ash again.

Even sitting down, the window gives me a perfect view of the back of the house—the fire pit where Robbie would have bonfires for us every year at training camp, where he and Jordan would give Ash advice and talk excitedly about the new season and how we were going to crush it.

I miss that the most. Our tight knit group of friends. All of which are scattered now.

Maybe it's time to open up to new things, new friendships, and move on. I've never been a fan of change, and taking this step seems impossible. But I promised myself I would work on my issues and face my fears head on this season.

My pocket buzzes and I take it out way too fast, hoping

for a text from one of my friends. Instead, it's a message from Juuse.

> Great job today at training. I watched some of your drills from the gym, you're improving a lot!

Thanks, I'm ready to give it my all this season.

> I'm sure you will ;)

If you have any advice for me, it's greatly appreciated.

> Of course. We'll chat more at breakfast.

There's at least one friend I can make while I'm at training camp.

When I look up from my phone, I see Ash outside, fussing with the grill. He's added charcoal to it and got it started, and has moved to the pop-up prep table to work on the vegetables. It looks like he has some marinated chicken already in a bowl, and I'm still shocked that he's taken up cooking, of all things.

With his back to me, I take the opportunity to savor the sight of him. *He looks good.*

Better than good. He looks fit. His shoulders are broad and the white cotton T-shirt he has on stretches across them, accentuating his muscles. His tattoos peek out and I swallow hard. I move my eyes down and notice a new one on the back of his calf. Unlike his last tattoo that was in color, this one is all black and about the size of a puck.

When I realize what the tattoo is, I stop breathing and my eyes burn with the threat of tears.

Ash's tattoo is of a sailboat.

NINETEEN

Three Months Ago

ELI

WHEN EDVIN WALKS in the door after his weekend away, I'm pretty much shocked into stillness. He's so... grown up. When the hell did that happen?

The last time I saw him, he was just a skinny sixteen year old struggling with his reaction time in the net. Now he's tall and big—almost as big as me. And what is that on his face? Is he growing a beard?

"Eli!" he drops his bag, abandoning the task of taking his shoes off, and runs up to me, tackling me into a hug.

I squeeze him tight and say, "Hey, *lapsi*. I missed you."

He pulls back with a huff. "Not a kid anymore. I'm taller than you," he says, trying to straighten up and going on his tiptoes.

I laugh and bring him into another hug. "Sure you are."

"Both my boys are home, I'm so happy," mom says, joining in on the group hug. Dad comes in too and pinches our cheeks, trying to be annoying. Joke's on him, I've missed this like crazy. When I look up, I see Ash hovering by the stairs, watching us with a small smile.

"Ed, I wanna introduce you to my friend—"

"Ashton Meyers, hell yeah!" Ed walks up to Ash and reaches out a hand. "You scored that amazing goal that won the Manticores the Cup."

Ash smiles, albeit a little tightly but says, "It was a team effort. Nice to meet the famous Edvin, I've heard a lot about you this past weekend."

"Ugh, did Mom pull out the baby pictures and embarrassing stories? If so, in my defense I was a little kid, it's not my fault I was always naked."

"Yes it is, you kept taking all your clothes off. And no baby pictures were shown," I say, clapping Ed on the back.

"Are you telling me all this time I could have been looking at baby pictures?" Ash asks with a sparkle in his eyes. "Mrs. Kalias, you've been holding out on me."

My mom laughs, charmed, and says, "I'll bring them out."

"Mom, no!" I groan while Ed starts laughing. At least he's the naked one in the pictures.

"Ed, how are you?" I ask, taking in my brother. He's really changed so much in just two years. It makes me wonder what else I missed.

"I'm good. Enjoying life as a high school graduate, excited for college," Ed says with an easy smile. Mine comes with a wince as I say, "Sorry I couldn't make it to your graduation."

"Are you kidding? You were playing in the Calder Cup, who cares about a silly graduation?" he says, dropping onto the couch and resting his legs up on the coffee table.

I take the spot next to him and Ash walks over to us, but before he can sit down with us, my mom comes bounding down the steps with a stack of photo albums. His eyes light up when he sees them and all but bounces on his feet in excitement.

My mom places them on the coffee table and sits on the floor. Ash joins her and the two of them flip through page after page as she tells him every embarrassing story of my childhood, like the time I played in a mud puddle in the backyard and refused to come inside the whole day. The picture shows me covered in mud from head to toe, wearing my biggest smile. Or the time I broke my arm jumping off the stairs because I thought I could fly just by wearing a cape, like Mario.

Ash laughs at my mother's animated recounting of the story and I can't help but feel relieved and happy that he's here. He belongs so easily by my side and I want so badly to tell him that.

At some point, my dad steers the conversation to hockey and comes up with a plan for practice. Ash is quiet while my dad talks about it and I'm surprised. The sport has always made him excited and happy, but lately that doesn't seem to be the case anymore. His smile is always tight when someone brings up the Calder Cup.

Ed groans and says, "Dad, I just got home, can we maybe not talk about hockey yet?"

"You know how important training during the offseason is," my dad says, putting on his serious face and I nod along. Ed shrinks into himself a bit and I feel bad. Maybe we should talk about something else.

"Okay, enough hockey talk," my mom says, collecting the albums and putting them away.

"What do you want to do for your birthday, *hani*?" she asks when she comes back a moment later.

My gaze snaps to Ash and I see him grinning at the term of endearment. I knew something would go wrong bringing him here. I figured that my family would find out we're into each other before I got the chance to tell them, but I never considered that he would slowly learn the meaning of all the secret nicknames I've come up with in the last few months.

"I was thinking we could go to Helsinki. Maybe rent a hotel so we can sightsee a few places. Ash wants to ride the tram."

"Woah, woah, don't make this about me," Ash says, standing up and stretching. I catch a glimpse of skin as his shirt rises up and do my best not to stare at it, but I fail miserably. He notices and gives me a subtle wink. "It's your birthday in a few days, what do you want to do?"

"That is what I want to do," I say, frowning. I've never cared that much about birthday celebrations. It's just another day to me, so why make a big deal about it?

"Okay, so the three of you go, get a hotel for a night or two, it will be fun," dad says.

"Do you two not want to come?" I ask my parents, hoping they will say no so I can get more time alone with Ash.

"We can celebrate you here when you come back. I'll make your favorite cake," mom says and I straighten up in my seat.

"German chocolate cake?" I ask

"Of course," she responds, patting my shoulder as she walks by to the kitchen.

"Ugh, what is it with you and coconut? It's not even that good," Ed says and I smack him in the chest with a decorative pillow.

"Alright, let's get the hotel and train tickets. Are you excited?" I ask Ash as I stand up from the couch.

"Hell yeah!" Ash says, turning around and running for the stairs.

"Pack light, we're only downtown for one night," I yell after him.

"Yeah yeah," he says, bounding up the stairs to our room. His excitement is infectious and my brother runs up after him to pack his own bag.

ASH

EVEN THOUGH THE man I love is turning twenty nine today, he doesn't want to make a big fuss about it, so we keep our excursion lowkey. We walk over to Fleet Park where we see all kinds of boats, but the sailboats are by far the most interesting ones.

Sailboats are fucking cool.

Growing up in Charlestown—one of the rich neighborhoods of Boston—means I've seen and been on my fair share of boats. I remember begging my dad for months to get a sailboat when I was fifteen. I was so excited when he finally said he'd purchase one, it was probably one of the few times I actually liked hanging out with him, touring different boats together. But when the time came, he bought the biggest, most expensive yacht he could afford instead.

My father has never been a man of his word. I don't know why I expected him to actually follow through when he never seemed to care about me or my interests before. I should have known better.

I'm lost in my own thoughts when Eli steps up next to me, leaning on the fence that overlooks the bay. Ed joins on my other side and for a moment we take it all in. The sun is out and a small breeze picks up and it's enough to ruffle Eli's hair, which has been getting longer.

"We should go on a sailboat," I say wishfully.

"My friend Mikko has one, I'm sure we could at some point."

I gasp and turn to Edvin. "Are you holding out on me, Ed-man?"

"We'll get in touch," Eli says, walking closer to me. He's been doing that more since we got here. Finding ways to be near me. I expected him to put a mountain of distance between us, but he's been more casual than usual with his affection. I look over my shoulder at him. He's so close I could kiss him.

Instead, I just look at him. I keep telling myself that I need to stop staring at him all the time, but it's not easy to peel my eyes away, not when he looks so good in a pair of navy blue shorts and a white button up short sleeve shirt. When he winks and puts on his RayBan sunglasses with a smile, I go a little weak in the knees.

The three of us have been walking around for the last half hour, after getting coffee and pastries at a nearby cafe. From the pier, I can see the ferris wheel, which is smaller than I expected, but still impressive. When Ed tells me one of the gondolas has a sauna, I am blown away. A sauna on a ferris wheel? How cool is that?

I'm reluctant to leave the sailboats, but Eli says, "This isn't the last you'll see of them, I promise."

So we keep walking until we get to one of the tram

stations. I don't know why I'm so excited about public transportation of all things, it's not like we didn't have trains in Boston growing up, but my dad always had a driver take me to school and practice, so I never really got to experience it. And while we have buses in Grand Marquee, it's such a small city that I don't really need to ride the bus.

The tram is more modern looking than I expected, each seat attached to a swivel and posted in front of a small table. There are even a few TVs located above the large windows but I pay them no mind, looking at the buildings as we pass them by. Helsinki has an interesting architecture and history from what I've seen so far. Older buildings made of colorful red bricks—like cathedrals—look like they're straight out of a history textbook, while the newer buildings have a more modern, minimalistic look to them. It's such a stark contrast, but somehow it works.

Eli and Ed do their best to give me a rundown of what everything is, but there's so much to see and learn about, that we start looking up architecture tours for tomorrow before we head back to their house. While Ed is spending the night with a friend tonight, Eli and I got a hotel room. I'm hoping we can also celebrate his birthday today in a fun way, with a bed that's not directly above his parents' room.

We end up seeing two museums—one of art and one of history—and by the time we are done it's already evening. Eli takes me and Ed to one of his favorite restaurants with outdoor seating by the water. This gives me a great view of the sailboats, so I'm extra happy.

When Ed goes to the restroom, I place my hand on Eli's thigh under the table and lean in just a little. "Thank you, for today. I've had a lot of fun."

"Are you sure? I didn't bore you with all the history and museums?"

"Are you kidding? This is your home. I want to know all about it! Plus it's your birthday, so we had to celebrate you in your own way."

Eli's smile is big and I spot some pink in his cheeks. I want to kiss him so badly, but instead I squeeze his thigh again.

"I know you didn't want to have a big birthday celebration, so I didn't get you a present, but there's plenty of things we can do later to make it up to you," I say, wiggling my eyebrows suggestively.

"I have you here with me, I don't need anything else." Eli's serious gaze is piercing and I can't fucking wait to get to the hotel. My hand twitches, wanting to move higher up, but I let go when I see Ed walking back to the table.

"Just got a text from my friend, he said there's a new club nearby and I think I'd want to go. What do you guys think?"

"No, thank you," Eli says before I can reply, and I look at him from the corner of my eye. His grip is tight on his fork and he's digging into his appetizer like it personally offended him. Ed gives me a questioning look but I just shrug. This isn't my business, even though I have an inkling as to why Eli doesn't want me around clubs.

The conversation moves to hockey and I zone out, like I do every time the topic comes up recently. I'm too much in my head about it and I can't shake off the disappointment my dad expressed after the Calder Cup. I keep my eyes on the sailboats while Eli gives Ed advice and tips on training.

When I return to the conversation, Ed is looking a little bored and chastised. The poor kid just wants to have a little fun with his brother and instead is getting a lecture.

When the waitress brings our meal, I order a bottle of

champagne for the table and change the topic to something more lively.

"So Ed, what fun plans do you have for the summer?"

Ed perks up and says, "I have tickets to a music festival at the end of August. It's a huge line up of DJs but also some popular pop artists. Wait, do you guys wanna come? I could totally find some tickets."

"We're returning to the States before then," Eli says, and I can't figure out his tone. Is he disappointed that we're not staying longer? Or is something else bothering him?

"Oh, right. Well, maybe I can save some money and come visit you next summer?" Ed asks shyly.

Eli looks startled for a moment. "That would be nice," he responds with a smile.

WE SPEND hours at the restaurant, ordering more wine and dessert, and for the first time in a long time I think I'm really happy. We part ways with Ed, who is meeting up with his friend, and Eli and I head over to the hotel. I'm feeling buzzed and happy but some of that happiness dims when I get a text from my dad.

> Have you started training? You better not be wasting time partying god knows where.

My initial reaction is to throw my phone away and go party, just like he expects me to. But I try to put him out of my mind. Why should I still give a shit about what he thinks of me and my career?

> yep

I lie and put my phone away right as we get to the hotel.

"Everything okay?" Eli asks.

"Fine." What's one more lie?

As soon as the elevator doors close, Eli takes hold of my hand and threads his fingers through mine. He doesn't let go, not even while he opens the door to our room, not while he backs me up against the wall, not as he unbuttons my shirt and my pants, and not as he reaches into my boxers and makes me see stars.

After, we make love on the bed and shower together, taking our time to kiss and appreciate every part of each other's body, knowing we won't have this kind of privacy or time together for the rest of the trip. Eli falls asleep on his stomach, one arm slung over me, his head on my shoulder and his legs entwined with mine.

My phone buzzes again on the nightstand and I want to ignore it, but ultimately I give in and look. I expect my dad to yell at me and tell me again what a disappointment I am, but instead I see a text from Ed.

> My friend and I want to go to that club. We're on the way, but we don't really wanna go alone since we've never been before. I know Eli doesn't want to, but is there any chance you'd wanna join us?

I close my eyes and blow out a breath. I shouldn't, I know I shouldn't. But he wants someone there to more or less chaperone. Eli is exhausted and won't wake up until the morning, I'm certain of it. I slowly pull myself away from his arms and text Ed back.

> Send me the address.

TWENTY

Two Months Ago

ASH

THREE WEEKS LATER, my phone pings with another text from my dad and I grit my teeth, begging for him to just drop it. My gut tells me to just block him, that I'll be better off if I'm not in contact anymore. And yet, I still read all of his messages, again and again. It might be a kind of self torture at this point.

> Fourth of July is coming up. You need to be here. We have some important people coming and we need to be a united front.

I scoff at his ridiculous request from a couple weeks ago and read on.

> not happening. in Finland for the summer

> Of course, instead of taking your career seriously, you're out gallivanting in Europe. You're such a disappointment.

> nothing else is new, dad

> Clearly. What a waste of space.

Eli stirs next to me in bed and I decide to take a gamble. I put my phone away and walk quietly to the bedroom door, flipping the lock. I know his parents are awake since I can hear them downstairs, making food and chatting in the kitchen.

When I return to bed, I cuddle up behind Eli, pressing myself into him, my erection painfully hard. I skim my hand down his body and grip him, rubbing his cock through his boxers. As he wakes up, he grinds back into me and turns to kiss me but hesitates.

"We shouldn't. Not here."

I groan, needing to touch him again. We haven't had a moment of privacy since that night weeks ago at the hotel. "I locked the door, and we can be quiet," I say and slip my hand inside his boxers, tugging. Eli's response is to buck into my hand and kiss me.

"We don't have any condoms here," he says.

"Just a quickie then. Hands or mouths?" I ask and he lets out a low growl, pushing me back and repositioning himself so that both our mouths are lined up with our cocks. We've never sixty-nined before and I get a thrill just from the anticipation. Then Eli's lips are on me and I moan before I catch myself.

"Shh, take my cock like a good boy and don't make a sound," he commands in a whisper and I shiver from his tone alone.

"Yes, sir."

With how sexually pent up we both are, and the fact that we haven't had the chance to do much together over the last few weeks, it doesn't take long before we both come, panting and gripping each other hard.

ELI

ONCE THE ICE clears out at practice, my dad skates out to where Ash and I are taking a break, over by the bench. We both noticed that Ash was struggling today but my dad probably felt like it wasn't his place to give out unsolicited advice.

"Everything alright, guys?" he says now, stopping in front of us.

Ash's helmet is off and he takes a frustrated swig of water, not looking in our direction. He's been standoffish all week, but especially today. Even after we got each other off this morning.

"Hey Dad, we still have the rink for another thirty minutes, right?"

"Yes, I figured you didn't want to overdo it though."

"How about Ash and I run some drills? Just us two."

My dad looks over at Ash before turning back to me and nodding in understanding.

"Okay. You can leave the equipment in the locker, like you always do. Do you want to take a rideshare back home?"

"No, we can walk, grab a pizza on the way back. We'll need the fresh air."

"Okay then, we'll see you at home."

"Thanks, Dad."

I catch Ash as he tries to head to the bench. "How about you take some shots on me?" He turns around, looking confused and angry.

"I don't need your pity party, Eli, let's just go," he says, eyebrows low and his mouth twisted in annoyance.

I skate up and block the tunnel entry. With all my goalie equipment on, Ash definitely can't get around me. "You think I pity you?" I ask, gaze narrowed.

"Yeah, I do. And it's fucking condescending as hell. I may be struggling but I don't need you to baby me," he says hotly.

I let out a low laugh. "No, *ilo,* I don't pity you. I do think you're being an idiot right now though. You want some tough love? Here it is: whatever is on your mind is affecting your game and you're playing like a kid in little league. Your shots are sloppy and you're not focused enough. So either drop your issues at the door of the arena or get your shit together. Don't waste these people's time." I say this louder than and angrier than I mean to, but this conversation is necessary.

Ash's chest is rising and falling, and I know he's angry and wants to lash out, but he doesn't say anything. He clenches his jaw and tries to get past me again but I push him lightly. His breaths are quick and I can tell I've riled him up, but *enough is enough*.

Ash pushes me back and when I retaliate, it's enough to knock him on his ass. I step onto the ice as well and put my helmet back on, grabbing his from the half wall and tossing it down to him.

"Put it on," I say darkly, "I don't want you to hurt your pretty little face."

Ash does as he's told, but as soon as he stands up, he checks me into the boards with a roar. We throw punches and push each other around until I take him down, making sure not to hurt him as I land on top. "Why won't you talk to me?" I ask, each word punctuated with my heavy breathing as I keep him pinned to the ice.

Ash flails around for another minute before he deflates with a sigh and all the fight goes out of him. We're both catching our breath and I give him the space to sit up.

After what feels like an eternity, he says, "My dad thinks I'm a disappointment."

His voice comes out so quiet I almost don't hear him. After a long moment of silence, he elaborates, "He wasn't even at the playoff final but he saw enough of it online. Told me I got lucky with my goal, and it shouldn't even have been a close game. He thinks I'm wasting my time here and that I should be taking my training more seriously, back home. Said I was a waste of space."

He takes his helmet back off and pulls up a knee, resting an arm on it and sighing deeply. I take my mask off too, stunned. His dad said that? What the actual fuck?

"You do know that's all bullshit, right?" I yell out, louder than I intended, and Ash flinches, closing his eyes tight.

Gentler, I say, "Please tell me you don't actually believe any of the crap, *hani*."

"I don't know what to believe anymore." His small voice comes out so sad it's breaking my heart. I shuffle closer to him and press our foreheads together, holding on to his shoulder pads.

"Listen to me. You are *incredible*, no matter what your idiot father tells you. Not only did you struggle with a lot of things this past season, but you managed to bring our team into the playoffs, something that hasn't happened in five years.

"It was *your* overtime goals and *your* shootouts that

clinched us the playoffs. So I don't give a shit that your dad is Nelson fucking Meyers; when it comes to you, he doesn't know what you're capable of. *I do*. The team does. We all believe in you."

Ash sniffs and I drop my glove to wipe away the tear that falls on his cheek. "Is there anything else that's bothering you?"

He shrugs and says, "I just feel like shit. Like I'm not good enough. Seeing your amazing relationship with your dad and your brother is just emphasizing the fact that I'll never have that."

"You do realize my family loves you, right?"

Another shrug and he looks away. "For now. But they don't fully know me. Sometimes I wonder why you even put up with my shit."

"Stop!" Ash looks back at me, startled. "Stop painting yourself in a lesser light."

We sit there for another minute before Ash says in a tentative tone, "Were you serious about me shooting some pucks on you?"

"Think you can handle it?" I ask with a smirk.

This coaxes a smile out of Ash. "Yeah, *pretty boy*. I think I can."

Fifteen minutes later, after getting twenty pucks by me, Ash and I clear the ice and head to the locker room for a quick shower. I throw my head back and groan as I think about the beautiful bar down shot he took which caught me completely off guard. The puck hit the bottom of the crossbar with such precision before falling perfectly into the net. I'm still thinking about it as I take off my equipment.

Once we're both in our underlayers, I order the pizza on my phone and strip naked, looking behind me at Ash and tilting my head for him to join me in the shower. There's no one else in the building right now, except for the guy that runs the zamboni, but he's not going to come into the locker rooms.

Ash tosses his under-layer in the backpack, grabs something from a pocket and bounds into the shower behind me.

"What's that?" I ask, nodding to his closed fist.

He smiles and kisses me hard, knocking us both under the lukewarm water. His free hand reaches down and pumps me, gripping just right and I groan into his mouth. "Fuck, *ilo*."

"What does that word mean?"

I grab his wrist and try to see what he's hiding in his hand but he snatches it away and lifts it above our heads. "Come on now, what are you hiding?" I say, taking a step into him, pulling our groins flush with one another.

He grunts but doesn't relent. "Tell me what that word means and I'll show you."

I bend down to kiss the flesh between his collarbone and neck. "It means—" I swallow, my hands running up his torso, his bird tattoo, and I think that maybe I can give him this one word, what he means to me. "—it means *happiness*."

Ash lowers his hand and cups my face before sucking on my lower lip. "Thank you, for telling me."

"Hmm." I don't get to say much else because Ash tears his teeth into the packet he was holding and rolls the condom on me so fast, I don't even have time to react.

He kisses me again, this time slow and meticulous, all the while applying lube to the condom. "Where did you even get that?" I ask, looking down at the pocket size lube bottle.

All I get is a wicked smile as he turns around and starts grinding on my cock. My hand snakes around his chest, pulling him into me as I line myself up with his entrance.

Once I'm inside him, my hand moves to the column of his throat where I lightly grip him. The moan that comes out of Ash might as well bring me to my knees.

I thrust into him, slowly at first, until he starts to move on his own, chasing more of my cock. "*Fuck*. Go. Faster," he says, grabbing my hand that's around his throat and squeezing it.

"What's that now? You think you can make demands?" I say, slowing my thrusts down and pulling almost all the way out.

"No, fuck, sorry," he says, desperately begging for more. "*Please*, I want more."

"Since you asked so nicely..." I say right before slamming back into him and picking up the pace. I let go of his throat to bend him over, Ash's hands finding a grip on the shower wall.

"*Yes*, fucking hell, Eli, you feel so good."

I pull out all the way and Ash groans in disapproval, but I quickly turn off the shower and lead him to the lockers. He doesn't expect it when I pick him up and guide him against one of them. "Hold on to the top."

Ash does as I say and he holds himself up with both hands while my cock finds his entrance again. The only sounds left in the room are the ones of slapping skin as I fuck him against the locker, my fingers digging into his hips as his heels press into my ass.

I know how hard it is for him to open up to me and tell me about his family relationships, and there's still plenty for us to unpack. But for now, right here in this locker room, all we care about is each other.

And that's enough.

TWENTY-ONE

Two Months Ago

ELI

ASH and I are in our bedroom, folding laundry and stealing glances at one another. I catch myself leaning in to kiss him more than once and I have to pull back. The door is open, my parents and brother are around. And yet, when I think about them finding out, I find that I'm not filled with as much dread as before.

I mean, how bad could it actually be?

Worst case scenario, they never speak to me again. Could I really handle that?

Then again, I guess it could be worse—they could become like Ash's dad and take it upon themselves to constantly belittle me and tell me how wrong I am, how much disappointment I bring the family.

But I know them, they wouldn't do that. *Would they?*

Maybe it's time I told someone. If I'm closer with any of them, it's probably my mom and she wouldn't cut me out of her life. *At least, I don't think she would.*

My spiraling train of thought gets interrupted when my brother walks into the room.

"Ed, what's up my man?" Ash says, fist bumping my brother and performing a series of handshakes that are too complicated for me to even follow.

"Ash-man, we need to party again. That's actually why I came in here, to tell you—there's a party I know about, a friend of mine is hosting. And the best part, it's on a sailboat," my brother says, waving his hands around and fist pumping.

I pause halfway through folding a sweatshirt. I realize it's the sweatshirt Ash has been wearing around when he gets cold and a smile tugs at my lips. I love peeling this off of him, and I love the ease with which we go about our days, the simple domesticity of it all.

But then what Edvin said clicks. "What do you mean party *again*?" I ask.

Edvin looks away quickly, embarrassed. Like he didn't mean to say that around me.

They partied together? *When? Where?* We were together every time we went out.

"We went to a club a couple weeks ago. You don't have to worry," my sweet little brother says, not knowing how much I do worry. For both of them.

"When exactly?"

"The night of your birthday?" Ed says, biting his lip in a grimace.

My anger flares, because what the fuck? They didn't

think to tell me? Or invite me? I turn on Ash and my voice comes out clipped when I say, "You took my little brother to a club?"

Ash frowns at me, holding eye contact, but doesn't say anything.

"Oh, now you have nothing to say?" I know this is probably going to end in a fight, but I can't believe he'd do something like this behind my back.

"Eli, chill, I was—" Edvin starts to say, but Ash stops him.

"Ed, don't." A muscle in Ash's jaw twitches but he doesn't look away from me. "Finish that thought. What's wrong with us going to a club together? I didn't realize I was confined to your house and the ice rink while I'm here."

"There's nothing wrong with it, and you can do whatever the hell you want, but don't drag my little brother into it. He's too young for that kind of stuff."

"I'm eighteen—" Edvin starts to say, but we both give him a look telling him to stay out of the conversation. "Maybe I'll just go," he says, backing out of the room and closing the door.

Ash rounds back on me, face twisted in anger. "What kind of stuff? What do you think happened at the club, Eli? What do you think I did, *debauched* him?"

I sigh in frustration and look around the room. "This is so typical of you. Maybe I don't want my brother around alcohol and drugs, and god knows what else. You shouldn't have taken him there. Especially not behind my back. Or on my fucking birthday," I yell, throwing my arms out to the side, still holding the damn sweatshirt.

"There it is! *You* don't want him to have any fun," he says, pointing a finger at my chest. "Just because going to a club, having a couple drinks, and dancing doesn't sound like your kind of fun, it doesn't make it *wrong*, Eli!" Ash yells.

"Edvin isn't stupid and he's not a baby. Maybe you should give him the benefit of the doubt." His face is red and angry, and I kind of get the feeling we're not actually talking about Edvin in this situation.

"If it's not wrong, why did you hide it from me?"

"Are you that fucking oblivious? When we spent the night in the city and went to dinner he kept asking us to go out with him. And what did you do? You ignored him, kept steering the conversation back to hockey, and school, and his career. The kid just wanted to have some fun and let loose with us and—god, Eli—you sounded just like my dad."

I'm about to fight back, but Ash's comment hits me like a punch to the stomach. All the air goes out of me at once and it's hard to catch my breath. I just stare at him, shocked that he'd compare me to his awful dad. He's shocked too, like he can't believe he said that, but he recovers quicker than me. "Shit, I didn't mean—I'm sorry—"

"It's fine," I say numbly. I drop the sweatshirt I'm still holding and walk out of the bedroom.

Edvin is waiting in the hallway when I walk out. "Eli, don't be mad at him, this is all my fault—" he tries to say, but I walk around him to the stairs. I take them two at a time, put on my running shoes, and head out the back door to the trail. Dusk is fast approaching, but I don't care.

I run for miles, trying to clear my head. The more I think about it, the more I realize that Ash was right. I did ignore Ed's pleas to go out to a bar or club, or do something fun while we were in the city. He's eighteen and probably bored of all the museums and tram rides. Maybe the issue was bringing him along in the first place, but I just wanted to spend time with them both.

How did they sneak around? Did they meet up at the club?

It's not that I don't want them to have fun, I'm just hurt they didn't tell me. Especially on my birthday. Even if I didn't go, I would have liked to know about it. What if something had happened and I didn't know where they were? How could they not tell me?

I get back to the house with the full intention of sharing my thoughts with them and also apologizing, but they're not there.

"Mom, where are Ash and Ed?" I ask after looking around the house for them.

"They went out," she says from her spot on the couch where she's knitting something.

"What?" I ask, dread pooling in my stomach.

They left without telling me?

Of course they did, I acted like an overprotective lunatic.

I take a seat on the edge of the couch, running a shaky hand through my hair. Fuck, I messed this up, and now I don't even know where they are.

"Eli, *hani*, what's wrong?"

"They didn't tell me they were going. I don't know where they are, Mom, I'm sorry. I was trying to look out for Ed but—"

"Eli, calm down. They went to Mikko's sailboat party. Ed said you didn't want to go and that you went out for a run instead." She frowns.

"How do you know where they are?"

She laughs. "Because just like you, Edvin tells me everything. Did you think he snuck out and kept secrets?"

"He's just a kid," I say weakly.

"He's eighteen and just graduated high school. You know, he's moving out in the fall."

"What??" I ask, appalled.

"Eli, seriously, what's up with you? Your brother is grown up."

"Since when? Did I really miss it all?" I ask, tears I didn't expect falling down my face.

Mom pulls me down fully on the couch and hugs me tight. "Eli, baby, I'm so sorry you feel like that. But you have your own life and career to worry about, of course you're bound to miss some things. The age gap between you two is pretty big, I'm sure it feels like you're two completely different people, but you're not. He's so much like you: strong, smart, determined, talented."

"I—" my sobs stop me from speaking and I relent, just crying in my mom's arms as she soothes me. Fuck, I missed so much back here.

"Your brother is fine, you don't have to worry about him. You know, he told me you didn't want to go out with him to the club. He's worried all you do is work."

"What? You know about the club too?" I ask dumbly.

"Of course. Ed said he really wanted to go, but not alone, so he took Ash with him. Why didn't you want to go?"

"I don't like the crowds or the noise. I didn't think either of them needed to be around drinking and who knows what else. Ash doesn't exactly have a great track record with alcohol. He gets—I don't know—depressed, I guess, when he drinks a lot."

She eyes me curiously. "You worry about him?"

"I worry about *both* of them," I say, swallowing hard.

"But you worry about Ash more," she says softly. It's not a question, but a statement, and as I look at her, I think that I *need* to tell her. She would understand.

I'll tell her. Soon.

First, I need to apologize to Ash.

ASH

I'M PARTYING on a fucking sailboat and I can't even enjoy it. I'm lost in a sea of strangers and I want nothing else than to be here with Eli. But he's made it very clear how he feels about me and my partying.

Fuck, I knew not telling him was a bad call, but it's not like I corrupted his brother and got wasted on a Thursday night in an unknown city.

I'm sure he thinks the worst of me, because why wouldn't he? I have a history with substance abuse and a tendency to fall off the wagon.

Always a *disappointment*.

But that night didn't go as Eli envisions it. Ed and I went out, met with his friend, had two drinks each at most, then they danced around with a couple girls while I watched dutifully from the sidelines. If anything, I was a glorified chaperone. I didn't even dance, for fuck's sake. Around 3 a.m., I walked them back to his friend's place, making sure they were safe, then I ordered myself a ride back to the hotel.

Edvin offered to hang out with me tonight once we got to the party, but I told him to go be with his friends instead. He doesn't need to see me at my worst too.

I keep drinking, but I'm in no mood to dance, or talk, or laugh. So I walk around, admiring the sailboat, sipping on my drink.

When a pretty blond comes up to chat with me, I politely turn her down, telling her I'm seeing someone.

Is that what I am doing? *Seeing* Eli?

Is he even going to put up with me much longer, or will he realize he can find someone better? *Someone who won't fuck up all the time.*

I lose count of how many drinks I've had and I'm lost in thought, looking at the harbor when someone taps me on my shoulder. I spin around and I'm met with pale blue eyes and light blond hair and I smile. He smiles back but it's different. One of his canines is a little crooked and there's no dimple popping.

Edvin keeps smiling at me as he says, "Having a good time, Ash-man?"

I nod, my smile dropping a bit once I realize I'm face to face with the wrong Kalias. "Yeah, doing great."

"That girl keeps looking over at you," he says, nodding towards the long-legged blond that was flirting with me earlier. "Are you gonna make a move?"

I laugh, but it comes out hollow and I take another sip of my drink. "Not really my type at the moment."

His eyebrows raise and he looks at me like he's seeing me for the first time. "As in you're not into blonds, or not into girls?"

I look at him and decide to test the waters. Eli doesn't want his family to know that he's gay, that's fine, but maybe I can see how they react when I tell them I'm bi.

"I've hooked up with women, and men. And I'm *definitely* into blonds," I say with a wink and his face immediately goes pink, his eyes wide. Shit, I didn't mean for that to be flirty. I straighten up and quickly say, "I definitely didn't mean you, please don't think I'm coming on to you."

"Yeah—no—of course not," he says, flustered, waving me off. After a moment of silence, he says, "But—did you mean Eli?"

I can't bring myself to look him in the face or respond, because *shit, shit, shit*, how did this backfire so badly? Me and my stupid mouth. Why can't I ever shut the hell up?

"Can we maybe have this conversation when I'm sober?" I laugh and pray to whatever god is out there that he drops it and doesn't tell Eli.

"Sure, but, does Eli know?"

"Know what?"

"That you're in love with him?"

The way he says it so casually startles me and I drop my drink, the glass breaking on the floor of the sailboat. There's no judgment on his face as he places a hand on my shoulder and gives me a nod and a small smile. "Maybe I should ask my brother directly, but something tells me he'll try and avoid that conversation. For what it's worth, I think you two are really great together. You make a good team, in and out of hockey."

"Thanks," I say quietly, and crouch down to pick up the broken glass.

"I'll go find a broom," Ed says and walks away.

I'm struggling to find the last piece in this dark part of the deck when a voice startles me over the music. My hand slides across the floor and my body involuntarily jerks. As I go down on one knee, my hand slams down to catch myself, and what do you know? I find the last piece of glass, embedded right in my palm.

I hiss out at the sharp sting but before I can stand up and take a better look at it, I feel two strong hands on me, one gripping my wrist and the other gently prying my fingers open to look at the damage.

Eli winces as he looks at my palm, his long fingers inspecting. "I'm so sorry, I didn't mean to scare you, *rakas*."

Surprise must be written all over my face as I simply

stare at his pretty face, which looks a little puffy, like maybe he's been crying. When our eyes meet, his pale blue ones are bloodshot and tired.

"What does that word mean?" I whisper.

Eli purses his lips and I know he won't tell me, so I try to pull my hand away but he's holding fast. "It means *dear*, or *darling*, I suppose."

My smile is quick to show and I mumble, "Cute."

"Come on, let's go find a first-aid kit below deck."

"We're not allowed to go below deck," I shake my head, getting a little dizzy just looking at the blood. The glass is not deep, but it sure is bleeding a lot.

"Mikko won't mind. I know him, we grew up together." Eli guides me to the opposite end of the boat and down the tiny staircase below deck. The underside is narrow, but long. There's a small bathroom and kitchenette at one end, a corridor with a couch, a TV, and mini fridge, and a double bed in the room at the other end.

Eli guides me to sit on the couch as he looks around the cabinets under the kitchenette and the bathroom sink. He finds a first-aid kit and makes his way over to me, focusing on the task at hand. He's quiet and methodical, pulling the glass out, wiping the cut down with alcohol, whispering apologies when I hiss out in pain again. He applies some kind of ointment to the cut before bandaging it, and when he's done, he gently holds my hand in his lap.

"I'm sorry for earlier. I shouldn't have yelled at you like that. I definitely shouldn't have assumed the things I did."

"I'm sorry I didn't tell you about the club," I sigh, rubbing my forehead with my free hand. "I wasn't trying to deceive you, I was just trying to appease Ed and maybe blow off some steam myself."

"I know. It wasn't my place to tell you what you should

or shouldn't do. I hope you can forgive me. I've just been mad at myself for missing so much of my brother's life, his formative years, really. And I've been trying to compensate in all the wrong ways."

"Ed looks up to you and loves you, Eli. He just wants to spend time together and wants you to show an interest in his life, not just hockey."

"I know, I'll do better. But I need to do better by you too," he says, squeezing my wrist and caressing it with his thumb.

"There's nothing to forgive. If anything, you should be mad at me for leaving you on your birthday and comparing you to my dad. That was shitty, and I didn't mean it," I say, willing him to believe me.

"It's okay. It hurt in the moment, but you weren't exactly wrong."

"Of course I was wrong. You're *nothing* like him. You're the kindest, most selfless person that I've ever met." My eyes roam all over his face and he has the most beautiful smile on his face, the soft one reserved just for me.

"Eli—" I say, but stop. I've wanted to tell him since the first night we got to Finland, but he wasn't ready to hear me then. I make sure to look at him, really look at him and when he doesn't stop me, I continue, "*Mina rakastan sinua.*"

I love you.

I've learned the words from the Kalias family. From Eli's dad when he whispers them to his wife as they lay together on the couch. From Eli's mom as she kisses Ed on the cheek and hugs him every morning. But mostly I've felt the words just by being surrounded by this loving family.

Eli's eyes shine but he doesn't say anything. I feel like someone just reached inside my chest and squeezed my heart tight enough to leave me bruised. I give him a wobbly smile anyway, biting back my tears.

He might be ready to hear it, but he's not ready to say it back. While I feel like my heart is shattering into a million little pieces, I can't say I blame him.

"Let's go get a drink. Together," I say, pulling my hand back.

TWENTY-TWO

Two Months Ago

ELI

I DON'T KNOW how to deal with Ash telling me he loves me. I don't know how to say it back yet. It's not that I don't feel it, because I do. The problem is that I feel too much and I don't know what to do about it all.

So when he pulls his hand back and says we should get a drink, I blindly follow.

As Ash is grabbing us both drinks, I find Edvin in the crowd of people, throwing the broken glass into the trash can after sweeping it up.

"Hey!" I smile at him in the hopes he doesn't hate me for how I spoke to him earlier and ignored him.

"Eli, you're actually here," he says, startled.

Ouch, okay. I deserve that.

Wincing, I say, "Hey *lapsi*, I'm sorry about earlier.

About everything actually. I should have been trying harder to connect with you over things that are not hockey related."

He looks down at his shoes and at this moment, even though he's the same height as me, he does look like the little kid I remember from four years ago, before I left home and moved to my own apartment, and before I moved to America.

"It's fine, just don't take it out on Ash. He didn't do anything wrong," he says, watching me with his keen blue eyes.

Before I can reply and subtly ask if he suspects something between us, he says, "Ash is your family too. I can tell he's the one you turn to when we can't be there for you. I'm glad you found him. You seem happier around him, so don't let him go."

I take a shaky breath and bring him in for a hug, holding tight. "When did you get so wise, kid?"

"Recently," he jokes.

Ash comes back with a tray of shots and even though I hate crowds and I hate the too loud noises of the party, when I'm with my family, I can tune it all out. They matter to me, so I'm going to try harder to let go of my self-imposed rules and try not to give a shit about what others might think of me, or how they might see me.

We drink and party the whole night and end up coming home wasted. The three of us are clamoring through the kitchen looking for food when my parents emerge from their room, ready for the day.

"Shit, what time is it?" Ed whisper-yells, like we're still sneaking around.

My dad laughs but he moves into the kitchen and starts setting up the dining table. My mom is shaking her head at us, but she's smiling so I know she's not mad about us being drunk and giggling in her kitchen. "It's 6 a.m. Did you boys party all night?"

"Yes," the three of us say in unison.

"Well, how was it?" dad asks.

Ash sighs dreamily, dropping into one of the chairs and says, "Sailboats are fucking cool, Mr. Kalias."

"That they are." My dad gets the orange juice out of the fridge and pours us each a glass as my mom starts on breakfast.

We sit at the table, reliving the night before, and even though we're still kinda drunk, my parents listen with rapt attention, asking us all about it.

"I think I made out with a girl," Ed says, eyes squinting like he's trying to picture her. I can't help but laugh, which then turns into a fit of giggles. I try to smother them with my hand, but that just makes me chuckle more.

"What's so funny?" he says, looking all offended.

"Are you sure it wasn't a mop? You were so drunk you couldn't tell the difference."

Ash laughs along with me and Ed punches me in the shoulder.

"It was a girl, I swear."

"You're right, it was that flirty blond. I saw you two making out," Ash supplies and Edvin beams proudly.

"Yeah, she was hot," he says right as my mom places a big platter of eggs, bacon, and toast in front of us and then smacks Ed across the head for his comment.

"No objectifying women at my table, young man."

"Sounds like you boys had a fun night," my dad says. "Ash, what happened to your hand?"

Ash looks down like he's seeing the bandage for the first time and laughs. "Oh yeah, I almost forgot about it. I broke a glass and—you know—your son makes an excellent caretaker, if I do say so myself." He waves his right arm around before putting it around my shoulder and bringing me close.

I give a short laugh and turn towards him, ready to make a joke, and that's when I panic. Because Ash grabs the side of my face with his free hand, like he's about to—

ASH

I KEEP my bandaged hand around Eli's shoulder and bring the other one to his face. *God, he's so pretty.* I lean in and kiss him, thinking about all the little moments we've shared since he brought me here, to his childhood home. Both Eli and his family have been nothing but kind to me, accepting me from the start and putting up with my personality that my own family deemed to be *too much.*

I don't want to think about leaving this place, but I know that once we head back to Grand Marquee, I'll still have Eli by my side. He is *it* for me. I press my lips harder against his, but I think something might be wrong because Eli is *not* kissing me back. When I pull away, I see the panicked look in his eyes and I hear a fork clatter across the table.

Shit.

Shit. Shit. Shit.

Did I seriously just forget we're having breakfast with his family!? *No, no, no.* This is bad. This is next level *I fucked up* bad. I immediately release him and sit back in my chair, staring at him. Eli closes his eyes and breathes hard through his nose.

He's really pissed.

Edvin has one hand over his mouth but instead of

looking outraged, he's trying to hold in a laugh. I dare to take a look at his parents and they're both looking at us, stunned.

They don't really look mad, but they're also not jumping up and down with joy, and also I'm still drunk, so maybe I'm not the best judge of character right now. Before I can make this worse, I say, "I don't know why I did that, blame it on the alcohol."

No one says anything, and Eli is still stewing in his fury, so I laugh awkwardly and excuse myself, "I should probably sleep it off." I clear my throat, trying to get the lump to go away because Eli still won't say anything or even look at me. "Thanks for the breakfast," I say lamely, grabbing a few slices of bacon off the plate.

In a daze, Mrs. Kalias looks at me and says, "You're welcome, *hani*." I don't say anything else as I bolt up the stairs, shove the bacon in my mouth, grab a pillow, and lock myself in the bathroom.

How could I be so stupid?

Did they believe it was just a drunken kiss on my part, or did I just out him in front of his family?

I feel sick to my stomach and not just from my actions. At least the toilet is right next to me so I can puke my guts out.

Hopefully my humiliation comes out too.

ELI

I COUNT to 100 and I still don't have the courage to open my eyes. I know Ash is somewhere upstairs, probably passing out in our bed.

Fucking hell. Why would he do that?

My hands hurt from fisting them so tight, so I slowly let out a breath and stretch out my fingers, reaching out for a fork and a sip of orange juice. *Stay calm.* Maybe they'll ignore it and think it was a blip.

When I look up, my parents are staring at me, waiting for an explanation, and oh fuck—I think I'm gonna be sick. I rush to the sink and throw up just in time. Ed starts laughing and my mom comes up to soothe me.

Fuck, I can't do this.

"Eli, sweetheart, are you okay?"

"I don't want to talk about it," I mumble and make my way upstairs. When I open the door to the bedroom, I am faced with silence. Ash is not there, and the bed is untouched. The sweatshirt I gave up folding earlier is still there and I crawl over it, clutching it to me before promptly passing out.

ASH

I WAKE up to pounding and a muffled voice at the door. Picking myself off the bathroom floor, I move to it but hesitate with my hand on the handle.

"How mad are you?" I ask through the door.

"Not mad," the muffled voice says. This surprises me and I hurry to get the door open.

"I'm fucking furious, Ash. What were you thinking?" Eli's face stops me dead in my tracks.

He's hurt—really hurt by *me*. My shoulders slump and I reach out to hug him, touch him, something, but he side-steps me.

"I'm sorry," I say, voice cracking. I want to throw myself at his feet and beg him to forgive me, but I know that won't help now. He just needs to process it, that's all.

"You're sorry? What was the one thing I asked of you? The one thing I told you I wasn't ready for?"

I keep my mouth shut and let him yell at me, anything to make him feel better.

"You completely outed me in front of my family, when I told you I wanted to do it on my own terms. When I was ready." He rubs his hands down his face and through his hair, frustrated and angry.

"I really am sorry. I didn't do it on purpose."

He scoffs. "Of course not. You just never think before you do anything."

I look away before he can see the tears in my eyes, because—fuck—Eli being disappointed in me hurts worse than anything else. He's not wrong.

"I just need some space. Maybe you can stay on Mikko's boat for a while. I don't know. I just can't deal with this right now."

I understand the underlying message: I just can't deal with *you* right now.

What a waste of space.

I step away from him. "Okay," I manage to say in a voice that sounds nothing like my own. Eli takes out his phone and steps out to call someone, Mikko probably.

It's like I'm seeing and hearing myself from outside my own body, I'm just moving on autopilot. I grab my suitcase and pack my clothes, most of which are folded at the foot of the bed. Next is my backpack that already has my laptop and chargers in it. I think about grabbing the toiletries but decide I don't need them.

Because I'm not going to stay on a boat when the love of my life is only miles away, wanting nothing to do with me.

I'm not going to show up to practice only to have him ignore me.

I'm not going to stay when I'm clearly not wanted anymore.

Maybe that's the coward way out, but maybe my father was right afterall. I'm just a disappointment, a let down, a fucking idiot. So I'm going home.

TWENTY-THREE

Present Day

ELI

THE BOOK I got at the store is good, but I get way too distracted by Ash's movements outside. Not even the story about a tennis player past her prime looking for glory can take me away from my reality.

I try to keep the memories of this summer at bay, but they rush back to the surface. I can feel them slipping through my carefully built facade. Stolen kisses and illicit touches come to mind when I think back on it. We were spending every waking moment together—being happy. Things were so great until they weren't.

He left. Without a goodbye or explanation, he just left. I drove down to get a hold of Mikko about borrowing the boat for a few nights and when I got back—he was gone.

Ash said goodbye to my family but not to *me*, and that

probably hurt the most. He's not to blame for everything though, I meant what I told him earlier. I let him down too, when he needed me most. He was clearly going through a lot with his dad and it was messing not only with his head, but with his game too.

I should have seen that sooner. I was supposed to be his person, his rock, and yet I didn't see him struggling when he was right in front of me.

I should have tried harder. Ash means so much to me and for the longest time I didn't know how to put into words the feelings I had for him.

I shouldn't have reacted like I did. He was drunk and tired and he messed up, but he deserved more from me.

I take a few deep breaths, coming up with the courage to face him. I'm thinking that it's time to stop running from this conversation. Placing the book on my nightstand, I take a few steps to the door, take another deep breath and open it, only to be met by Ash. His fist is raised, ready to knock, but he slowly lets his hand drop.

We take a second to just look at each other. He looks really good and I'm happy that he's in therapy. That's something I should consider too once the season starts.

"Dinner's ready if you're hungry," Ash says quietly.

"Yeah, I could eat."

He nods and turns around, leading the way back outside. My eyes stray back to his calf and the sailboat tattoo there. I want to ask about it but don't know how.

When did he get it? Was it right when he arrived back home? Or was it more recently?

Does he still love me?

Why is talking about your feelings so damn hard? I look up at the clear sky and try to quiet my wandering thoughts.

We both take a seat at the patio table and reach for the

tongs at the same time. Our hands brush and I let him take them. Ash clears his throat and says, "I can make you a plate, is there anything you don't want?"

Blinking up at him I shake my head. "Everything looks delicious. Thanks."

He nods and loads up both our plates with chicken and veggies. Then, he adds a scoop of strawberry pecan salad on the side. We eat in silence and look out at the lake through the small opening of trees.

This place is beautiful no matter the season. My eyes wander to the fire pit and I smile, thinking about last year and how the four of us were so excited for the new season.

Ash catches my stare and gives me an understanding smile, sad and bittersweet. "I miss them."

"Yeah, me too," I say, taking a big swig of water.

"Robbie says hi."

I pause, fork halfway to my mouth. I need to talk to Robbie, apologize to him for shutting him out, for pushing him away. Realizing I've been a shitty friend, I sigh and finish my bite of chicken.

"I've been avoiding him lately."

"Why?" Ash asks with a mixture of curiousness and weariness.

Well, here it goes, better to get this conversation out of the way before it's too late. "The night you left, I called Robbie. He didn't answer but I left him a voicemail."

Ash straightens up in his chair, lips tight like he wants to ask more, but he holds himself back. I wish he wouldn't. I wish he'd ask me anything that's on his mind.

Does he wonder why I never called him? I picked up my phone so many times, but the thought of him thousands of miles away, angry and hurt because of me made me sick to my stomach.

Does he think that was easy for me? I was a mess after he left, barely even got out of bed most days, except to practice. Keeping my distance was the hardest thing I've ever done.

"I told him everything," I say. "That we were together but that I was mad and hurt by what you did. You not only outed me to my whole family, but you also *left me*. I know it was wrong of me, but I lashed out at Robbie too. I told him he was spending too much time with the non-profit, that he wasn't being a good friend to you, to us."

Ash's face crumples and I want to reach out to him but I need to keep going. "A week later, Robbie called me and yelled at me for my behavior and how I treated you, making you leave. I knew he was right but I wasn't ready to admit it yet, so I shut him out." I take a second to swallow and calm my racing heart.

Ash takes the moment to say, "I didn't leave *you*, Eli. I just left."

"Why?" I ask, voice almost wavering.

He shakes his head and runs a hand over his short beard, scratching at it. "Because I was just a burden to you, and you didn't want me there," he says, sounding exhausted, like this conversation is taking more out of him than he can give.

"That's not true," I frown.

"It is!" he shouts, standing up quickly. "God Eli, you told me you couldn't deal with me anymore and that you wanted me to stay somewhere else for a while." Ash is pacing around, finally placing his hands on the back on the chair, knuckles white. "I had already fucked up enough, I needed to get some help."

"I'm sorry," I say, standing up and crossing over to his side of the table. My fingers itch to reach out and cup his face, pull him to me, hold him. But I don't. That's not what we are anymore.

"I didn't mean it. I was just taking out my anger on you because I didn't know how to deal with my own feelings. I never intended for you to leave for good. Maybe if I had handled things differently we wouldn't have had to go this long without clearing the air."

"It doesn't matter," he says, taking a step back. "You needed to talk to your family and deal with your own stuff, on your own terms, and I needed to figure out my own shit."

"I still regret it. I'm still sorry. *I still miss you*," I say, voice catching on that last part.

"I regret it too, what I did. I'm more sorry than you'll ever know. And I miss you *every damn day*." There's so much earnestness and sorrow in his eyes and I need to fix this thing between us, because I don't know how to be in the same orbit as him but not have him in my life.

"Can we start over? I want my best friend back," I whisper, reaching out a hand.

Ash's fingers are warm when they wrap around mine and I run my finger over the soft flesh between his thumb and pointer finger.

"I'd like that very much," he says and steps closer. I let his hand go and open up my arms. When he falls into my embrace, my only thought is—*I'm finally home*.

ASH

I FEEL like a giant boulder has been lifted off my shoulders, and I guess Robbie was right—I really did just need to talk and be honest with Eli about what happened. I still hate myself for how I behaved, but I plan on making it up to him, especially now that we're getting a fresh start.

Eli helps me wash and put away dishes, and we fall back into this easy routine that we had before. We're both on the cusp of asking for more, figuring out what this new start really means. Are we back to just being friends? Are we going to be more? Is he ready for that?

"Can I ask you something personal?" I say, wiping the butcher block kitchen island with a towel and tossing it in the basket by the laundry door.

Eli looks taken aback by my question. I guess I've always barrelled into his life and taken him by surprise. Almost like going *bar down*. "Sure," he says.

"What happened with your family after I left?" His reaction is immediate and his hunched shoulders relax. What did he think I was going to ask?

Eli moves a couple feet over to one of the couches in the small living area and drops down on it. I follow and take a seat on the opposite side, leaving some space between us.

He clasps his hands together and lets them dangle between his legs as his forearms rest on his knees. "When I came back, my mom asked why I sent you away," he says, frowning. "Honestly, they were all pretty mad at me for doing that. They really like you, Ash."

Eli gives me a small smile over his shoulder but looks away as he continues, "I tried to explain that I didn't mean to, that I just needed some space, but they kept pushing. So I decided to rip off the Band-Aid. My dad was probably the most shocked, Ed seemed unsurprised, and my mom just looked—happy for me."

I nod along even though he's not looking at me. "Has your relationship with them changed at all?" I tentatively ask, my hands itching to touch him at this moment.

"Not really," he says, running his hands up and down his thighs anxiously. "I think they were more hurt that I kept it from them for so long. They're really supportive, even my dad, who is definitely the more conservative one of the bunch."

"I'm happy for you, Eli," I say, meaning it, even though he didn't give me a chance to be there and share that moment with him. But it wasn't about me, and I finally get that now.

My hand reaches out tentatively and I squeeze his shoulder affectionately. Eli grabs my hand with his and rests his cheek on it, looking back at me with misty pale blue eyes.

"Can I give you a hug?" I ask and he nods, letting go of my hand. I slowly trace my fingers from his shoulder to the back of his neck, cupping it gently, then I lean in close. His head falls to the crook of my neck and I bring my other arm around his back, rubbing small circles on his shoulder blades. His hands fist the shirt at the small of my back and I think I might want to stay here, in this cabin, in this moment, forever.

When Eli pulls away, he doesn't go far, just a few inches to look at me. My fingers curl in his hair and I can feel the buzzing tension between us. His eyes linger on my mouth before he leans in and presses his mouth to mine.

He's sweet, and I immediately melt into him, my mouth opening. I let his tongue dance with mine again, and everything is just like it used to be. Me and him, moving round and round in this game of seduction. Our bodies remember each other too well, this invisible force pulling us together again. But for once, I'm selfish. I need more than just his body.

So I pull back gently and say, "Wait..."

PART 2

TWENTY-FOUR

September

ASH

"WAIT, ELI," I say, trying hard not to give in to the taste of him, "we should talk first."

Eli's confused face pulls back. "Haven't we done enough of that already?"

When he starts chasing my lips again, I back away slowly, feeling high on his scent, citrusy with a hint of eucalyptus. *Fuck*, I want him so bad, but I harden my resolve. "I need to tell you something." Eli eyes me warily, his expression filled with concern.

I swallow hard and look down at my lap as I say, "I'm in a really good place right now. Physically, mentally, and"—I glance up, clasping my fingers tightly—"and emotionally. I don't want to jeopardize that."

"Ash, that's amazing. You've come so far and I don't want you to jeopardize it either," Eli says.

I take a deep breath and continue, "The thing is, I don't know if I should be taking this kind of risk right now. Don't get me wrong, I'm not saying you're not worth it, Eli, because you are." My eyes connect with his and hold in place. "I'd give in to every single temptation if it meant I got to have you. But—the past couple of years, I've fallen in and out of love with you more times than I can count."

"*Hani*, I—" he starts, but I shake my head and barrel ahead.

I'm afraid if I don't say this now, I never will. "Every time you pull me in, I'm ecstatic. I feel like I can do anything because I have you by my side. But every time you push me away, you break my heart all over again. Because I could never be enough for you."

Eli's fists clench and it looks like he's trying really hard not to reach out for me. He's giving me the space to get it all out, because that's what I asked of him. But the pure look of devastation on his face gives me pause.

"If you're not going to choose me, Eli, as in really *choose me*, and give us a real chance, then—" My eyes blur and I need to look away from his pale blue eyes. "Then I need to choose myself," I croak.

When I look back at him, his eyes are misty too and I bite the inside of my cheek to keep my emotions in check. I really don't want to fucking cry right now.

Eli scoots closer to me on the couch and gives me another tight hug. My arms instinctively wrap around his torso as his arms cage me in a bear hug.

"I'm really proud of you, *kultsi*," he says softly in my ear. I let out a strangled laugh and squeeze him tighter. Fuck, I needed to hear that. When he pulls back he says, "I do want to give us a real chance. I'm just scared because I still don't feel ready to come out to the team, to the world. But I do want *you*."

I can feel the smile blooming on my face. Leaning in, I kiss him this time and murmur, "That's enough for me."

Eli frowns but I say, "I mean it. I don't need some big announcement to the world that we're together, I just want some stability. Just don't shut me out," I plead and rest my forehead against Eli's. "Don't push me away. I don't think I could handle it. However long it takes for you to come out to the world, I'll be patient with you, *pretty boy,* if you'll be open with me."

Eli drops another kiss on my lips and says, "Deal."

ELI

I'VE FALLEN *in and out of love with you more times than I can count.*

I lie next to Ash on the couch, trying to process everything he told me tonight. He's been having such a hard time finding his footing and I feel like I failed him. Because he's right—I did pull him in only to push him away later. Looking back, I was the one pursuing this friends with benefits arrangement more than he was. Ash would have been content with leaving things as they were and not starting something up at the end of last season.

Hearing him say the word *love* to me—again—must have short circuited something in my brain because now I can't stop thinking about it. *I still love him, I love him, I love—*

"What are you thinking about?" Ash lifts his head off my chest and looks up at me. Even in the cover of darkness, his face is beautiful. I run my hand through his hair, gripping lightly at the base of his head and pulling him in for a kiss. It's shorter than I'd like, and when I pull away, he lets out a content sigh. Like he's right where he needs to be. Like he's home after an exhausting day at work.

"Nothing. Everything," I say, scooting down and shifting so that I'm now slightly on top of him, nuzzling his neck. My arm comes around his torso and I pull him as close to me as I can. Both his hands hold me tight in return, like steel bands around my shoulders. I might not be ready to say it back yet, but I can show him how I feel.

I kiss the soft, warm skin of his neck and move my mouth up to his ear. Taking his earlobe between my lips, I tug at it gently before biting down softly, soothing it with a lick afterwards. Ash's breathing is hard and one of his hands makes its way into my hair, tugging, forcing me to move my head up to meet his. His blue eyes are darker than usual, pupils blown wide with desire, and I can't help myself. I'm helpless and I *need* him.

I press myself harder into him, feeling his hardness next to my own. I brush my lips against his in a tender kiss, then bite and tug at his lower lip. When I pull back, he chases me, moaning against my lips.

With a coy smile, I use my hand to push him back down into the couch cushions. Slowly, I reposition myself to straddle him and bring my hand down to the hem of his shirt, raising it up inch by agonizing inch. When I bunch it up all the way to his chest, he shimmies out of it the rest of the way and my lips immediately land on his blue honeysuckle tattoo. *My favorite one.*

"Will you tell me what this one means?" I whisper against his skin. Ash takes a deep breath, holding it in, but doesn't say anything. "Please."

I feel him exhale and this time both his hands come down to cup my face. I look up at him, reverently, while his thumbs caress over my cheeks.

"It's a birth flower."

"Oh?"

What the hell is a birth flower?

At my confused expression, Ash laughs, but sobers up quickly. "Every month usually has two birth flowers, each with their own meaning. June has two: rose and honeysuckle."

I frown and say, "But your birthday is in December."

Ash gives me a look that says *why the hell would I get my own birth month tattooed on myself?* and my jaw drops open. He got a June flower because that's *my* birth month.

I swallow hard and try to ask the next question but seem to struggle with it. Ash takes pity on me and says, "It means happiness."

There's too much emotion in his eyes and the words are swirling once again in my brain—*love, love, love*. I turn my head and kiss his palm before kissing his naked chest and moving further down. Before I can reach for his shorts, Ash stops me and sits up. He kisses me with a groan. "As much as I want more of this to happen, I really think we should take things slow."

"Are you sure?" I ask, frowning.

"Yeah. I want to take my time with you. I want to date you, even though no one can really know about it yet," he mumbles. "Can we do that?"

"Of course, anything you want, *rakas*."

TWENTY-FIVE

ASH

WE DECIDE to be lazy on the couch and watch a movie, but I can't concentrate the entire time. Being this close to Eli after so much time apart is messing with my brain. I'm aware of every single movement he makes, my eyes drifting to his face more times than I could count, to the point where I feel like I watched him more than I watched the movie.

We end up saying good night and going to our separate rooms and I might be losing my fucking mind for asking to take things slow, but I really don't want to mess this up again.

While Eli forgave me, I still feel like I owe him. I need to make it up to him, and if that means being patient and letting him find his stride until he's ready to make our relationship public, I'm more than happy to wait.

I shoot Robbie and Olivia a text letting them know Eli and I talked last night and that things are going well. Olivia immediately sends back a series of heart emojis in the group chat we have together, but Robbie sends me a private text.

> Are you sure you're fine? Call me if you need to talk.

His message makes me smile. Robbie, always the caretaker of the group. I truly don't know what I would do without him.

> promise I'm good. are you coming up for the red and white game?

I wait for his reply and hope he can make it. The red and white game was always Robbie's favorite. It's this training camp tradition where we get assigned to one of the teams and we get to play against players that are normally our teammates. The game has referees but doesn't follow the normal rules of hockey. There's no checking and no fighting allowed, just a combination of plays that we practice throughout the entirety of the training camp. In all his years with the Manticores, Robbie was always on the red team. And they always won.

> Hoping to, even if it's just for the day.

> cool, can't wait.

THE NEXT MORNING, I can hear Eli moving around the kitchen, so I grab my clothes and a towel and head out into the hallway. I pass the bathroom and poke my head into the kitchen where I find him making coffee. Eli looks over at me and smiles, one dimple popping in his cheek.

"Morning," he says in a low, gravely voice.

I grin back helplessly. "Hey there. Are you hungry? I can make something once I get out of the shower."

Eli shakes his head no and takes a small sip of his black coffee. He grabs the other mug and brings it over to me. I take it with my free hand and sip it and—of course—he made it just right, like always. I sigh contentedly, but my suspicion arises when he says, "I'm actually going out for breakfast."

"Yeah? By yourself? I can join if you give me five minutes to shower." I gulp down more coffee and step around Eli to place it on the counter.

"Oh, um—" He hesitates and I turn back to look at him. Does he not want me to go with him? It's not like I can't keep my hands to myself in public.

"I'm actually meeting Juuse," he says, bringing the mug up to his lips. He seems nervous, his fingers are wrapped around the mug, tapping the side of it repeatedly. His eyes dart around my face looking for a reaction. Is he worried I'm jealous?

Am I jealous?

Of course I fucking am.

Stupid Juuse. Eli basically idolizes him, with his charm and perfect face, and the fact he's also Finnish probably doesn't hurt. I'm sure Eli could use a break from me and spend some time with a fellow goalie.

"Right. Okay," I say, not knowing what else to add. "I'll see you at the arena, I guess." I don't mean to sound as miserable and disappointed as I do, but I can't fucking help it. I want more of his time and attention already.

Chill, Ashton.

I muster a smile and walk by him again towards the hall but Eli stops me with a hand on my bicep. "You seem bothered by it. Why?"

"I'm not, all's good," I say.

"Can we be honest with each other from now on? I don't want you to be upset about something that I don't even know about. I'd like some open communication going forward."

I swallow. *Well, shit.* He's right, communication hasn't been our strong suit up until now so maybe being open is better.

"Okay...well, for the sake of honesty, I guess I'm bothered by the fact that last night you said you'd give *us* a real chance but said you're not ready to be out, and this morning you're going on a date with *Juuse*." His name comes out more like a curse, and I realize I'm being kind of petty, but that's what happens when I'm forced to communicate first thing in the morning. I'm hangry.

Eli's eyes are wide and he lets out a sound that's somewhere between a scoff and a laugh. "It's not a date, *hani*. We're just talking about hockey. He's giving me some pointers and advice, that's it."

"But you realize that he's into you, right?"

He shakes his head and moves his hand from my bicep to my face. Dropping a soft kiss on my lips, he says, "He's definitely not. Do you trust me?"

"Of course I trust you, and I believe you if you say it's not a date. I'm being jealous, I know. But Juuse is definitely into you, did you not notice the way he was checking you out yesterday in the locker room?" I say with a pout.

He chuckles. "I think that's just your jealousy talking. How about I make it up to you for ditching you this morning? After training we can go out to dinner? Just us."

I look away, pretending to think about it. "Hm, I might have to check my calendar." Eli's lips find my jaw and he tilts my head up, kissing me there, teasing me. "I might have some prior engagements, I'll have to get back to you."

I can feel his smile on my lips as he drops another kiss on me. "Okay, *ilo*. I'll make a reservation just in case your schedule opens up."

"Do you need a ride to the breakfast place?"

"No, I ordered a car to get there and I'll get a ride from Juuse to the arena."

I nod and give him room to gather his things. Then Eli finishes his coffee and leaves for his non-date with *Prick*—I mean—Juuse. I take my time in the shower, warm up the rest of my coffee and grab a couple granola bars to eat on the short drive to the arena. The whole time I can't help but let my mind wander to what he's planning for tonight.

Because if I'm not mistaken, Eli and I are going on a date.

ELI

THE COFFEE SHOP is located inside a warehouse market, alongside other local shops. The place is so *blue*, bright, and happy. It instantly makes me think of Ash. I pull my phone out and snap a picture of the mural on one of the walls that has white clouds and constellations painted on a blue sky. Smiling to myself, I text him the picture along with a message.

> This place reminds me of you.

Ash's reply is immediate.

> aww that's so cute. you must like me or something, you think an awful lot about me 😊

You must like me or something. Yeah, or something. I'm about to text him back and tell him how I think about him all the time but a tap on the shoulder stops me.

"Juuse, hey." I pocket my phone and give him one of those awkward half hand shakes and half hugs.

"Hope you weren't waiting for me long," he says, switching the conversation to Finnish.

"Not at all. I didn't even look at the menu yet."

"You need to try one of their bagel sandwiches. Very good."

"Sure, do you want to go first?"

Juuse smiles at me and I notice for the first time how close he's standing to me. Our shoulders are nearly brushing and he's leaning into my personal space. I'm relieved when he steps up to order and I shrug my shoulders, like I can shake off the feeling of anxiety at someone strange being in my personal bubble.

The avocado cucumber bagel sandwich catches my eye and I repeat the order in my head again and again. *Could I get an avocado cucumber bagel sandwich and a chai tea latte? Please.*

So when Juuse asks me something, I miss it. "Sorry," I say, embarrassed.

He smiles again and repeats himself, "I said order what you want. This is on me."

"Oh, well, thanks," I say, a little flustered. "Can I get a cucumber avocado sandwich bagel and a chai? Please." *Damn it*, that was definitely not the right order of words.

Once Juuse pays we head over to one of the open tables

by the mural. I take a seat on the bench that's over-run by frilly pillows and move some around so I can fit. He takes a seat across from me and when he leans both his impressive forearms on the table, I realize just how small this space is.

We're both pretty big guys and when I shift my leg under the table, I accidentally brush his knee with mine. "Sorry," I mumble.

"So, what have you been up to since I last saw you?" he asks, unbothered.

"Since last year? A lot." I laugh.

"Tell me," he says, with an easy smile. I notice he likes to hold eye contact when he talks, so I do my best to do the same. His eyes are a mossy green color and his short hair is blond. It's a darker color than mine but not as dark blond as Robbie's. He's freshly shaved and his smile is blinding. Does he always show all his teeth when he smiles?

And why the hell am I paying this close attention?

Damn Ash, getting into my head and making me question things. Is Juuse into me?

"Well, as you know I've been the primary goalie for the Manticores. Things are going well, I was really happy with my performance in the Calder Cup, even though there's room for improvement."

"Hey, don't beat yourself up, you did an amazing job. Especially that save in the third period and your assist in the final goal."

"You watched that?" I ask, surprised that someone of his caliber would pay attention to the AHL games.

His nose scrunches as he replies, "Well, I watched the highlights. I was back in Finland for the offseason."

"Oh, I didn't realize you went back too. I left after the Calder Cup and spent a few months with my family."

"Right on. Helsinki?"

"Yeah. You too?"

"No, I was in Turku. What else have you been doing?"

"Um, mostly hockey. I usually hang out with my group of friends back in Grand Marquee as well. Not much time for other hobbies during the season, as you know."

"Are you seeing anyone?" His question makes me freeze. Is he asking just because he's curious? Or is he trying to ask me out?

The barista brings over our drinks and sandwiches and I immediately take a big bite just to keep me from answering. Juuse gives me a lopsided smirk and I quickly look away while I chew.

"This sandwich is really good. Thanks, again."

"My pleasure," he says, eyes darting to the corner of my mouth when I lick some cream cheese off. Okay, maybe he *is* into me. Or maybe he's just really observant.

"So, what about you? What have you been up to?"

He takes a bite before telling me more about his trip back home and how he also spent a few weeks in Ibiza with some friends, partying on some boats.

"Sounds like fun," I say, thinking that the only boat I partied on this summer was a sailboat. Bittersweet memories resurface and I think about how Ash told me he loved me that night. Does he still feel as strongly now about me as he did back then?

I must be showing a smile because Juuse smiles back at me and reaches out to grab my hand when I place my chai down. I stare at it, frozen in place. What is happening right now?

"You didn't answer my question earlier," he says, smile still in place. He's so confident and unbothered by the fact that we're in public and he's just casually holding my hand.

"Didn't I?" I think my brain is short circuiting because I

don't know how to react right now. I want to pull my hand away but I don't want to be rude.

"Okay, let me ask you another question. If I asked you to come back to my place tonight, would you say yes?"

My whole body flushes at the question and I swallow a few times before gathering my wits off the floor. I gently pull my hand away, glancing at his face. He doesn't look hurt, but he does look curious, one blond eyebrow raised, waiting for an answer. "Probably not," I say softly, carefully.

Juuse nods and his eyes narrow on me. "Is it because you're not into guys? Or..."

"I'm not," I say quickly and the lie tastes bitter on my tongue. I groan and close my eyes, running a hand over my face. "I am, I don't know why I lied."

"You're not out yet," he guesses and I nod.

"I'm flattered," I say, making sure to maintain eye contact, "but the reason I won't come back to your place is more complicated than just that. I have—"

I pause, thinking of Ash this morning and how jealous he was. I guess he was right about Juuse. "I have feelings for someone else."

Admitting it to someone other than myself feels good. When I had this conversation with my parents, I strictly avoided talking about Ash, because I didn't want them to know the full extent of what he meant to me and how we broke each other's hearts. Normally I would lean on Robbie for this kind of heart to heart, but our relationship is currently strained.

"Well, if that doesn't work out, you have my number," Juuse says with a wink.

I smile and shake my head. Shameless flirt, just like someone else I know.

TWENTY-SIX

ASH

I GET to the arena early and take my time greeting some of the fans that are posted outside. There's a dedicated line near the side of the building where we stop by and chat with people as we come in and out of the arena.

"Meyers, Meyers!"

I turn around and see a kid who looks to be about thirteen, waving a big sign with my name and number on it. I can't help but smile as I make my way over.

"What's up, my man?"

He looks up at me and freezes on the spot. My eyebrows shoot up and he shakes himself out of it. "Woah, you're really tall," he says.

I laugh and point over my shoulder at my teammate who is 6'8" and towers me by about five inches. "No, I'm average for a hockey player, he's the tall one."

The kid's eyes go wide like saucers and just when I

think he's shell shocked, he says, "Could I take a picture with you both?"

"Sure thing. Hey Baz, get over here!" My teammate finishes up signing a jersey and comes over, slapping me on the back.

"What's up?" he asks, looking down at the kid.

"Picture time," I say and motion to the kid to get his phone out. He tries to take a selfie with us but can't point it well enough to have us all fit in the frame. A woman nearby sees this and walks over to help him.

She snaps our picture and we sign his jersey and hat and the kid tells us he's excited to watch the red and white game that's coming up.

Once the kid leaves, Baz moves on to talk to other fans and I'm about to do the same when the woman steps back up to me.

She's wearing a black one piece that kind of looks like a romper, except it has long leg pants that flare wide at the bottom. Her shoulders are exposed, with no straps and there's a lanyard around her neck. Considering that everyone else is wearing a jersey, she looks out of place. My gaze runs down to read what's on her lanyard but she must think I'm checking her out because she crosses her arms and her chest swells with the movement.

She smirks at me but my face goes stone cold when I read one word—media. I don't have anything against reporters and journalists, I just prefer not to talk to them because every time I do, all they ask about is my father.

"I have a question for you Ashton," she says and then pauses, waiting for me to take the bait.

I run my tongue over my teeth and say, "And what's that?"

"Is the rumor true?"

My hands start to sweat and I ball them into fists. She can't possibly know about me and Eli. Not that I would care if word gets out, but I know Eli does, and the last thing he wants is his personal business being scrutinized by strangers on the internet.

"I don't know what you're talking about," I say, forcing my body to stay cool and collected.

"Well you see, there's this rumor that Rhodes Bonavich might be retiring from his position as Detroit's GM." Okay... what the hell does that have to do with me?

"And that your father, Nelson Meyers might have his eye set on us. Any comment on whether he's leaving Boston for Detroit?"

There it is. The mention of my father. I keep my face completely blank but inside I'm panicking. My ears are ringing and I don't even hear the rest of what she's saying. My father *would* be conniving enough to move here just to piss me off, especially after I embarrassed him this summer and cut him out of my life.

Would he actually do it just to mess with my career? Boston is one of the best teams in the NHL and they won the Stanley Cup last year, there's no way he would ever give up on such a great team.

"I don't know anything about this rumor," I say and turn to leave.

"So it wasn't discussed over family dinners this summer?"

"Nope," I say and give her an ironic wave over my shoulder.

JACKSON AVOIDS me in the locker room as I drop my bag and if he's heard the same rumor as that reporter, he probably believed me when I threatened to ruin his career the other day. *Good.*

I mind my own business and hit the upstairs gym, the one that overlooks the ice. I run through a series of squats and Baz comes over to spot me.

"You didn't come out with us last night. Are we too good for you now?" he says with a shit-eating grin, so I know he's just messing with me.

"Damn right, I'm a Calder Cup champion now, don't you forget it!" I let some of my old confidence come up to the surface as we switch spots.

"Ah of course, you forgot about us chumps at the bottom. I see how it is," he teases with a laugh. Baz is on the ECHL team but gets called up to the AHL often. Unfortunately, he wasn't called up while we were playing for the Calder Cup so he didn't get to experience the chaotic playoff games like the rest of us did.

We spend another half hour working out and then we both head out to the locker rooms. The arena has two rinks and the NHL players and part of the AHL players practice on one rink, while the rest of the AHL players and the ECHL players practice on the other.

So far, Eli and I have been paired up on the NHL side, which might be random, or it might show that we have the potential to do more this season.

Baz heads out to the ECHL side and I get my gear ready. Eli walks in with Juuse and his eyes immediately land on me. He smiles and takes a seat across the room, putting on his skates.

"Damn, someone got lucky last night," Mike, one of our defensemen, says to me. I'm confused until he points at my naked chest as I'm getting ready to put on my underlayer. There are at least three visible hickeys on my neck and collarbone. Probably a few lower too. I smirk down at myself and then up at Mike.

"A gentleman never kisses and tells," I say, trying really hard not to look over at Eli and give anything away. I keep my gaze on my gear instead.

"Since when are you a gentleman? Weren't you the one boasting last year about a threesome you once had?"

"It's called growth, Mike. Look it up," I say, giving him a wink.

ELI

JUUSE ASKS ME A QUESTION, but I'm too distracted ogling Ash to reply. I should feel guilty for all the hickeys I left on him, but instead, a weird, primal feeling of pride comes over me. *He is mine.*

I must be smirking because Juuse elbows me and quietly asks, "What's that face for?"

I clear my throat and look away, mumbling something in response. Juuse is too observant for his own good and keeps looking between me and Ash, so I try to keep my eyes trained on something else in the locker room. It fucking sucks, because all I've done since this morning is think about him.

Instead, I put my gear on and head out for practice. I'm dying to tell Ash about the reservation I made at the winery on the peninsula and the tour they'll give us through the vineyard. But that'll have to wait until after.

Today's practice is ruthless as we go through 3v3 overtime plays. This is something both our AHL team and the NHL has struggled with the past season as we kept losing in

OT, so the coaches are coming down on us hard, pointing out all our flaws and coming up with ways to make us better.

Fans come and go on the bleachers and we take the time to read signs and acknowledge them, waving at the little ones. I didn't get a chance to say hi to any of the fans in line when I arrived at the arena with Juuse, and I hope to do that after I get off the ice and take a shower.

The shower bay at this arena doesn't have any dividers, so everything is out in the open. There aren't many guys in here and I walk in, naked. Juuse isn't far behind me, and even though there are plenty of shower heads open, he takes the one right next to me.

What is it about me that says *please, do burst my personal bubble, I'd love nothing more than to chat while naked*? I try to push the irritation down and rush through the shower. By the time Juuse rinses his face, I'm already shutting the water off and wrapping a towel around me.

"I'll see you later," I say, not glancing back.

"Alright man, see ya."

As much as I like Juuse, I need a break from people at the moment. He's an incredibly chatty guy and I can feel my social battery running out after spending the entire morning with him.

THE TEAM PROVIDES us with catered lunches every day and today there is a pasta and salad bar set up in the conference room upstairs. I make my way up there alone, mostly because I need a break, but also because I haven't seen Ash since our drills earlier.

I load up a plate with pasta, breadsticks, and a side salad and take a seat at one of the high top tables that overlooks the ice. I finally see him downstairs by the locker rooms. He looks up and sees me watching him, munching on a breadstick. I should be embarrassed that I got caught staring but instead, I smile.

I haven't been able to stop doing that. Ash smiles back and motions that he'll join me shortly. I leave my food and go load up another plate for him. When he sees me carrying it to the table, he joins me.

"You didn't have to do that, I could have grabbed it."

"Yeah, but what if they ran out of your favorite breadsticks?" I say, waving one around in his face. Ash grins and catches my wrist, stopping my hand. Then he gets closer and takes a big bite of it.

I shake my head at him and say in a quiet voice, "So cute, you're like a little dog."

There's mock offense written all over his face. "Excuse me, if anything, I'm an orange cat. You know, like the ones with only one brain cell."

"You're smarter than you give yourself credit for," I say and catch the end of a shy, appreciative smile on his face.

Ash looks behind me, eyebrows drawn together, then looks back at me. "So," he hesitates, taking another bite of breadstick, "how was your *non-date* this morning?"

I laugh, thinking how right he was and ponder how to tell him. Maybe he deserves to be messed with just a little.

"Oh it was definitely a date," I say and take a big bite of pasta. Ash's eyes go wide and he looks behind me again. I turn to see what or who he's looking at and see Juuse laughing with some other players, grabbing food. He notices us and gives me a wink. *Shit.*

When I turn to Ash, he looks like someone just kicked his puppy. No, he looks like *he's* the kicked puppy. I immediately feel bad for my idiotic comment. *Of course it wasn't a date.*

I don't get to take it back because Juuse comes up and asks, "Mind if I join?"

Ash nods, and turns his focus on the food while Juuse takes a seat to my left. There's an awkward silence but Juuse fills it with questions about Grand Marquee and the Calder Cup. Ash politely nods and smiles along and I hate this subdued version of him. I nudge his leg with mine under the table and watch his profile for a reaction, but he doesn't give me anything. He just ignores it, and that makes me feel even worse.

"Got any plans for tonight?" Juuse asks and it takes me longer than it should to respond so he says, "A few of us were thinking of renting a boat and taking it out into the bay. You're both welcome to join if you want."

He lets the question hang and when Ash doesn't say anything either I make an attempt at a joke. "Nah. Ash doesn't like boats that much."

His head snaps up and he glares at me. At my smile, he bites the inside of his cheek, realizing what I'm doing. *Come on, hani. Play with me.*

"Bullshit. I love boats, I don't know what you're talking about."

"Oh, so you'll come?" Juuse asks. Ash looks at me skeptically to see my response.

"We actually have something else planned," I tell him. "Maybe next time."

"Of course, the offer stands if you change your mind." He gets up, grabs his empty plate and water bottle, then over his shoulder he adds, "On both counts."

"What does that mean?" Ash asks, eying me wearily.

I let out a long sigh. "I'll tell you all about it in the car."

TWENTY-SEVEN

ASH

AFTER SIGNING MORE autographs and taking pictures with the fans, Eli and I finally leave the arena. It's a beautiful day in Traverse City as we drive the M-31 along the bay with the windows down, listening to the local hits radio station. The water is still and a beautiful blue color, and the sun is reflecting off of it. A variety of boats are out, from pontoons, to yachts, to sailboats, and even kayaks and paddleboards. People are riding bicycles in their dedicated lanes and the park along the bay is full of tourists and locals, playing volleyball on the small courts there or lounging in their hammocks or on their picnic blankets.

"It's such a beautiful day," I say, rolling the windows up and turning on the AC.

Eli hums and looks around the bay with as much adoration as I just did. This place is truly incredible and the drive up to the cabin on Lake Leelanau is just as beautiful, with so many trees and greenery the closer we get.

Eli turns the radio volume down and turns in his seat enough to face me. I don't know if I should be concerned or not.

"I'm sorry, about earlier. I—" He takes a deep breath and looks to the side. "Juuse thought our meeting this morning was a date. I made it clear that it wasn't, but I also didn't hide from him. I told him I'm gay."

I nod along, a smile blooming on my face. When I look at Eli, he looks nervous, eyes wearily tracking me for a reaction. "Eli, that's great! I'm so proud of you." His face softens and he smiles.

"I also told him I'm seeing someone," he says, his hand grabbing mine where it dangles from the center console. Eli links our fingers together, squeezing once, before letting go and tracing his fingertips along my palm, my wrist, up my arm and along my vine tattoo. His fingers are warm against my cold skin and his touch leaves a trail of goosebumps in its wake.

"You did?" I manage to get out.

"I did," he says, linking our fingers again and bringing my hand up to his mouth. Good thing there's no one on this road, because I am too distracted by this beautiful man and the way he's touching me. His lips are warm against the back of my hand and I'm left empty and cold when he places it back on the center console. His hand continues to hold mine and that makes me smile.

"You know, if you wanted to go to the boat party, I wouldn't have an issue with that," I hear myself say. I would probably not go since I'm trying to stay sober, but Eli could go enjoy himself. Make some new friends.

"Do you want to go?"

"Not really."

"Good thing we have other plans then," he says smugly.

"So, you weren't lying to him about that just to get out of it?"

"Nope. I made a reservation at Chateau Chantal."

I hope Eli doesn't see the grimace on my face. A winery is probably not that much better than a boat party for me. But I can't say that. He made a reservation. He wants to take me on a date. I smirk and look over at him. "Are you trying to woo me, Eli?"

"Is it working?"

I laugh. "Maybe. But you know you don't have to do anything special or fancy. We can just hang out at the cabin, go kayaking."

"Are you really turning down a six-course meal right now? In favor of kayaking?" he asks, one eyebrow raised.

"I wouldn't say I'm turning it down," I mumble, "just saying I'll do anything with you."

His hand gives mine another squeeze. "I know, *ilo*. I just think this date is long overdue."

My chest swells and I can't help but smile at him. How did I get so lucky to fall in love with the best, most thoughtful person in the world?

ELI

THE SKY IS a beautiful mosaic of orange and blues by the time we park at the winery. The Old Mission peninsula drive is one of my favorites and I'm grateful the weather is nice enough for us to enjoy the outdoor vineyard tour. We get paired up with a few other people for the tour and they all seem to be couples. The two women whispering and stealing kisses from each other in front of us look so happy.

They have matching tattoos on their left ring fingers and I think this might be their honeymoon.

Watching them fills me up with hope. Maybe that can be me one day. Maybe I can be comfortable enough to truly be myself. I look over at Ash who is thoroughly engrossed in what the guide is telling us about the history of the place and the types of grapes they use for their wines. I smile and move closer behind him bringing my mouth to his ear to whisper, "Are you having fun, *söpöliini*?"

When he turns his head just a little to look at me, our eyes hold and I want nothing more than to tell him how much he makes me *feel*. My heart is pounding and he smirks before moving along with the group. I blindly follow him and think, *I'll follow you anywhere*.

I stop behind him again and wait for a response. He turns to give me a glance over his shoulder again and whispers back, "That's a new one. What does that word mean?"

I bite my lip and look around me. There's no one behind us since we're at the back of the group and the rest of the people are too focused on the actual tour, so I take a deep breath and summon some courage.

My hand finds Ash's like it knew exactly how close it was. I let our fingers thread together but don't take my eyes off of him. He looks down, surprise showing on his face but I can't stop smiling. Ash smiles back and pulls me along so we don't fall too far behind. "Are you distracting me with physical touch so you don't have to tell me what that word means?"

I chuckle and decide he's earned this one. "It means *cutie pie*." His smile is wicked as his thumb caresses the back of my hand in acknowledgment. It's a set of different words that won't stop swirling around in my head though.

I love you, I love you, I love you.

But I can't say them yet. I need to show him first that this means more to me now. That I'm not going anywhere.

When the tour is over, we're seated at a small table on the patio. The view of the bay from the top of the hill is breathtaking. Both Ash and I are admiring it when the server shows up to ask us our drink preferences or if we just want to stick with what's paired with each meal on the menu.

"I'm fine with the menu choices."

"I, um, I'd like to hear your non-alcoholic selections, please." Ash takes a sip of water and his eyes dart my way as he listens to the list of options. He lands on ordering some sparkling grape juice and more water.

"Not a fan of wine anymore?" I ask, curiosity getting the better of me.

"It's not that," he says, fidgeting with his hands on the table. The sun is starting to go down and he looks so damn good in his white short sleeve button-up. The contrast between his dark red hair and the green vineyard behind him makes me smile softly. He looks so pretty it's hard not to reach out and kiss him.

"Everything okay?" I ask when he doesn't continue.

"Yeah," he blows out a breath. "I've been sober since I got back from Finland. Since starting to go to therapy."

Oh. Oh, of course.

I'm such an idiot, why the hell did I bring him to a winery?

"I'm sorry. We can go somewhere else if you'd like," I say, getting ready to stand up.

"No, absolutely not. This place is amazing," he rushes in to say.

Fuck, I should have known better, there was no alcohol at the cabin, and he didn't go out partying with anyone the last few nights. Before I can kick myself some more for my stupid decision, Ash reaches out for his glass of water and in doing so brushes his hand against my own in a caress that makes me shiver. "Thank you for planning this amazing date," he says, tongue darting out to lick his lips.

"Anything for you," is all I manage to say.

Ash's eyes drop to my lips and he smirks. "Careful throwing that around, I might actually believe it."

"You should. I mean it."

The intense stare we share is broken by the first course—amuse bouche. When the server goes to set my wine down I say, "Can I actually also switch to the non-alcoholic options?"

She eyes me with a look that says *you came to a winery and you won't drink any wine?* but she gives me a nod regardless and promises to be right back.

"You didn't have to do that. I promise I can handle myself around others drinking," Ash says.

"You already know I don't drink that much to begin with. Besides, I don't need it to have a good time with you."

Ash smiles and we enjoy our six-course dinner, finishing it off by sharing a plate of crème brûlée until the sky gets dark and we're ready to go home.

Under the cover of darkness and other cars around us, I follow Ash to the driver's side of the car and back him into the door. My hand glides to the collar of his button-up and I tug his face closer to me, tasting the dessert we just had on his lips. Ash's hands twist in my hair—which definitely needs a haircut now—and he deepens the kiss.

It doesn't last long, however, and we break apart when we hear someone whoop and cheer from a few cars over. I pull back with more reluctance than I expected and look over my shoulder. The two women from the tour earlier are smiling at us and wiggling their eyebrows. I can't help but laugh and Ash looks at them and gives them an enthusiastic wave.

When we get home, we go straight to Ash's bedroom, but we don't have sex. We spend the night together, cuddling and kissing, and whispering sweet nothings to each other. And I think I want this—*him*—forever.

TWENTY-EIGHT

ASH

I WAKE up in Eli's arms. His whole body is draped over mine and it makes me feel all warm and fuzzy. I'm such a fucking sap. *And I'm so in love with him.*

I want to shout it from the rooftop but I know he wouldn't want that. So instead I keep it to myself, knowing that he feels the same way, but that he's not quite ready to say it.

I can see it in the way he looks at me when he thinks I don't notice. His walls crumple and he looks at me with so much adoration that I don't think I deserve most of the time. But hell if I'm not a selfish asshole for keeping it anyway.

Our training doesn't start until this afternoon, so we sleep in and spend the rest of the morning making pancakes together. "I still can't believe you cook now," Eli says, flipping the pancakes for me as I whisk together a few eggs to make a scramble. The bacon is in the oven and it makes the cabin smell amazing. The small window that faces the back is open and we can hear birds chirping.

I laugh. "Believe it, baby. I've got skills you don't even know about."

Eli smiles as he approaches me and takes the bowl from my hands. He backs me up into the counter and grabs my waist with both his hands. Slowly, he leans in and kisses my jaw, trailing all the way up to my right ear. "I want to, though—I want to know about everything that pops into that beautiful brain of yours, and I want you to show me all your skills. Anything you're excited about, I'm excited about."

My fingers pull at the base of his hair and Eli's scruff scratches along my cheek. He's barely holding on to his control and I miss seeing it crumple at my feet. He pulls away suddenly to take the pancakes off the griddle and when he returns, I'm in the same spot, gripping the counter and breathing hard.

Eli approaches me with a hunger in his eyes and I don't even register what he's doing until his hands grip my thighs and he lifts me up on the counter. Stepping between my legs, he presses into me and I can't help but pull him closer. My hands grip his ass and he grunts as he tips his head up to kiss me.

We repeat that process a few times until the eggs are cooked and the bacon is ready, and then we take our breakfast out on the patio. We eat while overlooking the lake and drink our coffees. For once, the silence is not stifling. There's always so much noise around me with work and I rarely feel like I'm at peace. Except when I'm with Eli. There's this nice quiet calm about him, and I feel more content than I have in months by just being in his presence.

He gives me another one of his adoring looks and I can't help myself from saying, "I love you."

Eli's lips part but I don't wait for his reply. My hands reach out and cup his face and I kiss him sweetly, tenderly. He's the one who deepens the kiss and takes control, and I let him. It's not until I hear a small noise that I pull back a bit. Eli's lips latch on my jaw and my eyes fly open and land behind Eli.

On the people standing there, looking smug as hell.

Fuck.

I spring back, keeping Eli at bay with my arms and yell out the first thing that pops into my head, "I think you got that mosquito, thanks—buddy." I grimace and Eli looks so confused that I want to burst out laughing. Even though our friends more or less know some details of our past, I don't want them to find out about us like this. Not when Eli wants things to be on his terms.

I stand up and the chair scrapes loudly on the patio. *Shit*, this is not good.

"Hey guys, whatcha doing here so early?" I say, keeping my gaze on our friends. At this, Eli whips around in his chair. He does it so fast that I think he might have given himself whiplash, but he stands up too.

No one says anything for a long moment and I want nothing more than to figure out what Eli is thinking and how he's feeling about us basically getting caught necking by our closest friends.

Olivia smiles and runs up to me, giving me a tight hug. "Sorry about the surprise, we tried calling and when we didn't get an answer we figured you two would be at training."

"No, that's not until later this afternoon."

She bites her bottom lip to keep her smile from

spreading as she pulls back from the hug and her hands squeeze my biceps. I widen my eyes and give her a subtle shake of the head. *Please don't say anything.*

She recovers and steps away from me. "Eli, can I give you a hug?" His gaze is fixed on Robbie and the two of them seem to be in some kind of silent brooding stand off for some reason. "Eli?" Olivia asks again, glancing between the two of them.

Finally he breaks the stare and turns to her, a small smile on his face. "Of course, how are you?" She steps in and he wraps his arms around her in one of his signature bear hugs.

"I'm good. We've been really busy with the Blue Line Brigade and I've been skating out more. I found a women's league in Grand Marquee and I've been skating out over the summer."

"That's amazing," he says, letting her go.

I notice that Robbie still hasn't moved from his spot a few feet away. His arms are crossed and he's still glaring at Eli.

What the fuck is his deal? I know they haven't spoken in a bit, but still. This seems extreme. Especially for Robbie, who is the nicest person ever.

"My turn!" Alice yells and runs up to Eli. Her arms go up and she makes grabby hands at him and it's so fucking cute that I can't help but chuckle. The girl is almost a whole foot shorter than us, and Eli indulges her and picks her up. She squeezes him tight and kisses his cheek. "I missed you, you big bear."

"I missed you too, *lapsi*." She scowls at him as he sets her down but she rolls her eyes and tackles me in a hug next.

"Hey," Eli says, taking a step towards Robbie. I know

he's nervous because of the way he fidgets with his fingers, hands clasped in front of him.

"Are we back on speaking terms now?" Robbie says and I can tell he's hurt that Eli iced him out this summer. Olivia gives him a pleading look that probably says *be nice, let bygones be bygones*.

"I'm sorry. I should have reached out sooner."

"Yeah, you should have," Robbie says, but I can see the fight drain out of him. His arms drop to his sides and he takes a step forward. We all watch in anticipation, eyes bouncing from Eli to Robbie.

To my surprise, it's Eli that steps forward and initiates the hug. Robbie gives in immediately and there's some back and forth whispering between them that I can't make out. Then Robbie claps his shoulder, gives him a nod and pulls back.

That's it. No comments are made about the fact that we were making out when they walked in, but I'm sure they're all dying to ask.

"So, if you don't have training until later, what are your plans for the day?" Alice asks, eyes glinting with mischief.

Eli looks at me and smiles and I don't expect it. He knocks the breath out of me with that smile. Walking up next to me, he grabs my hand and links our fingers together. I am too stunned to speak, and I'm sure I just look like a fish out of water.

"We were going to take the kayaks out on the lake," he says, squeezing my fingers.

"Oh yes, let's all do that! You lovely couples can take the tandem kayaks and I'll grab a solo." Alice zips past us to the shed and starts dragging the kayaks out.

Couples. Is that what we are now? A couple? I look at Eli and realize he's still looking and smiling at me. Okay then, he's taking this better than I expected. I thought he might run for the hills and shut me out again.

But no.

He promised me he wouldn't do that again.

We're in this together. And I did want us to be ourselves amongst our friends.

When Alice walks out, handing us all vests, Eli clears his throat. "So, I don't want the team or anyone else to know that we're together yet. Just us."

"But you *are* officially together?" Olivia asks, clicking the vest into place.

Are we?

Eli squeezes my hand and looks at me to say something. Right, I've kind of been left speechless. "We are," I say, pulling his hand up to my lips and pressing a small kiss there.

"Aww, you two are adorable," Alice coos and I roll my eyes but Eli says, "Damn right we are."

ELI

THE WEATHER IS beautiful for kayaking. As soon as we get on the water, it's like things were never strained between us. We go back to bantering and we fill each other in on what's been going on this summer.

Robbie has been living and breathing the non-profit and Olivia has been doing the same during the offseason. Soon she'll go back to reffing and Robbie will have to hire another marketing strategist to replace her. Not only are they a perfect couple but they also work really well together.

As a middle school teacher, Alice has summers off, but

she still works on a few side hustles here and there. She tells us how many books she read (too many) and that she's actually started writing herself but doesn't think it will turn into an actual book. She claims it's a good outlet for her creativity regardless.

I miss Jordan. He should be here too, laughing along and threatening to tip one of us over or trying to race. I wonder how he's doing in Texas and tell myself that I'll reach out to him more from now on.

Truth is, as much as I missed Helsinki and being around my family, I missed this just as much. The family you choose to surround yourself with is just as important as the one that made you into who you are.

I expected Robbie to be more mad than he actually was. When I pulled away after everything that went down this summer, I told myself I didn't need him, but the truth is I've missed his advice. Maybe he could have helped Ash and I to reconnect sooner.

When we hugged earlier he said, "Don't do that ever again. If you need space, that's fine but don't push people away." I agreed and apologized again and then he told me, "Don't hurt Ash, please. I'd hate to kick your ass if you break his heart."

Don't hurt Ash. I'm trying my damned hardest not to, and I hope he can be fine with what I have to offer for now.

We kayak for a couple hours and then head back to the cabin to get ready for training. Olivia, Robbie, and Alice are staying the night, so I move my few belongings to Ash's room so Robbie and Olivia can take mine, while Alice calls dibs on the loft.

Tomorrow is the red and white game which is why the three of them are spending the night. Besides getting tickets to the game, they also want to show Olivia around town since she hasn't been able to experience it yet.

"We're going to go to the beach, drive up the peninsulas, and show her around Main Street," Alice says, following us out the door as we all head to our cars.

"See you guys later. We can meet up for dinner somewhere if you want. Just let us know where you end up," Ash says.

The two of us are taking his car to the ice arena while the three of them jump in Robbie's Jeep. He retracts the top and drives off as we wave at them.

Ash turns to me once they're gone and I hug him, kissing his temple. "How are you feeling about everything?" he asks.

"I'm fine. Why?" I ask, pulling back to look at him.

"I know that's not what you had in mind for how to tell people. And I don't think you were ready to tell them about us either. I'm sorry it was out of your control once again."

"Don't be sorry, it's not your fault and, honestly, I'm kind of glad it happened like that. Now I don't have to stress and overthink every single detail. I think out of everybody, they were the easiest people to come out to."

He nods and kisses me once before dragging me over to the car.

"I do wish we had more time to ourselves though. We go back to Grand Marquee the day after tomorrow and then pre-season starts," he says as we both get into the sedan.

Ash frowns as he turns it on. "I guess I'm just worried that the season is starting soon and we haven't really talked about what that means for us."

I reach out and squeeze his thigh. "Take a breath, *rakas*, we'll have time to talk about it all when we get back to Grand Marquee. Neither of us are going anywhere."

. . .

ASH

THE NEXT MORNING, the day of the red and white game, I wake up being spooned by Eli. He's warm and hard at my back and as much as I love my friends, I kind of wish they weren't in the same cabin right now so I could have my way with my boyfriend.

Boyfriend.

I really, really like the sound of that. I've never really been in a relationship, mostly because I've never had the time for one. Hooking up was way easier than letting someone in only to leave them behind when I would inevitably be on the road or get traded to another team. But with Eli? He just makes it easy to love him, to want to be around him every second of every day.

I turn in his arms and wake him up with kisses, running my hand down his naked chest and the hard planes of his stomach. When I reach further down, I slip my hand inside his boxers and stroke him. His eyelids flutter open and those beautiful pale blue eyes look up at me.

"Good morning, *sunshine*." I lean in and kiss him and he arches up into me, so I reward him with another stroke of my thumb on the head of his cock.

"Morning," he mumbles, one of his hands cupping the back of my head and pulling me in for another kiss.

"Think you can be quiet this morning? We don't want the others to hear."

He nods eagerly and I trail kisses from his mouth to his chest, and all the way down to his prominent V. I pull down his boxers just enough for him to spring free and lick him up, missing the feel of this—of him.

"I won't last long," Eli says, looking down at me, one hand fisting the sheet. "It's been a while." I hum and take him in my mouth, swirling my tongue and hollowing out my cheeks. My hands cup his balls and lightly massage them and Eli all but springs up from the bed. I let him go with a pop and see his chest heaving, hands fisting the sheets so hard he might rip them off the bed.

I smirk at him and it doesn't take long before he does exactly what I expected—Eli takes control and guides my head exactly where he wants me, thrusting up as he starts to get closer and closer. I swallow him down as he comes and, true to his word, he doesn't make a sound, except for his heavy breathing and panting. There's a light sheen of sweat on his chest between his pecs and I lick it off as I make my way back up to him.

I kiss his jaw, his cheek and say, "Good job, pretty boy." I'm rewarded with a bear hug and a squeeze on my ass. When he tries to push me down to reciprocate, I stop him with a hand on his cheek. "Not today. Unlike you, I won't be able to keep quiet."

He groans and burrows his face in my neck. "You're killing me, *kultsi*."

"What does that one mean?"

"Hm, you'll need to work harder for it."

"Harder than a mind-altering blowjob?"

"Yes, much harder," he laughs and I smile as I wrap my hands around his strong back and revel in this moment a little longer.

ELI

. . .

WE LIE IN BED, holding each other. It's on the tip of my tongue again, to say those three little words. After everything, they would hold so much more meaning. Because this time, I don't want to let him go.

Before I can gather the courage to say anything to Ash, we hear commotion in the kitchen and decide it's time to get up. Robbie cooks us all some kind of breakfast pizza with eggs, sausage and cheese. The thing is freaking delicious and we all pull up whatever chairs are available to eat and enjoy our coffee outside.

The air is crisper here in the morning before the humidity takes over, so I take a few deep inhales and close my eyes, listening to the birds and the sounds of my friends' quiet conversations. Ash is asking Alice about her writing, which she's not being very open about, and Robbie excuses himself to take a phone call from Alex.

"Olivia, how do you like Traverse City?" I ask her.

"It's amazing, I wish we'd come here sooner and spent more time exploring, but I'm sure we'll be back at some point."

"You have to come here in the winter, it's gorgeous. Maybe all our schedules will align this year for all-star break and we can finally take you snowboarding," Ash says and Olivia agrees.

I look over at Alice and notice she's unusually quiet. Is she thinking about the last time she was here, just her and Jordan? She never told us what went down that week, only that when the blizzard hit they made it here just in time, only to be stuck inside for a couple days.

"Everything okay?" Olivia asks Robbie when he comes back outside and sits beside her.

"Yeah, Alex was just looking for some feedback on the fundraising gala."

"Gala, you say? That sounds fancy," Alice perks up, popping a raspberry into her mouth.

Robbie rolls his eyes but nods. "It's going to be a pain to organize, but yeah we thought a holiday gala might be a good way to get some people to donate to the non-profit. It's in the early stages, but we're talking about it."

"Count me in, I look dashing in a suit," Ash says and winks at me. I smile. What a shameless flirt.

THE SMALL ARENA is full to the brim with people. Those that couldn't grab a spot on the metal benches are standing in the back along the wall. Everyone is excited for the red and white game. This isn't a usual game, it's more of a combination of plays that we've practiced over the last week that we now get to show off in a game.

There are two 25-minute periods where players from the NHL and AHL level are split into the two teams—red and white. Instead of having backup goalies, four of us are geared up to play, two per each period. Juuse and I are on the red team, while Nadison and Karlsen are on the white team. Juuse and Nadison are in the starting line and they take up their positions.

Ash is on the white team and I look over to his bench and give him a wave. He replies with a grin and a motion that shows I'm going down. I laugh and focus back on the ice. There are referees for this game, but they notoriously take things easy since we're not supposed to get too physical with each other. While checking's allowed, we've never had players fight and drop their gloves during these games.

Most of the first period goes well, with the first twenty

minutes alternating between team red and team white being on a power play, essentially making it a 4v5 game the whole time. In the last five minutes of the period, we switch to 3v3 play.

Juuse lets three goals in, which surprises me, and Nadison currently has a shutout. This changes when one of the guys on my team snatches the puck on a breakaway and takes a shot on him. Nadison is caught off guard and goes into a sudden split that looks bad even from my point of view, all the way across the ice.

The puck goes in but Nadison stays down. He tries to stand up but collapses back on the ice, dropping his stick and shoving it aside in anger. The ref blows the whistle and the team medics go down to check him out. The whole arena is quiet and when I look over at where Robbie is sitting, I see a grimace on his face. I didn't see exactly what Nadison hurt, but from his split, it could be a groin injury. I swallow hard and lift my gaze to the VIP box where our GM, Bonavich is seated. He stands up slowly, gripping the railing, before snapping something at the person behind him.

Shit.

Ash and the two medics help Nadison off the ice and people cheer along as he waves a hand around at them. Karlsen takes up the net for the last minute of the period, and then we all take a ten minute intermission. The locker room is quiet and we wait for someone to give us an update, but they don't.

It must be bad then.

Fuck.

. . .

THE ENTIRE GAME shifts during the second period. I don't let any goals past me, especially fueled by my competitiveness to not let Ash score on me. The second time I glove the puck that he shoots, he fake shoves me and smacks his stick on the ice, all the while smiling. It reminds me of when we were practicing back in Helsinki and how he needed some tough love at the time. Karlsen on the other hand lets in three goals, which ties up the game.

During the last 30 seconds of play, they pull him and they get an extra player on the ice. While they squabble in the face off and wind down the time, the white team gets a hold of the puck and shoots it at me. I stop it with 7 seconds remaining on the clock.

The face-off resumes in front of me and I keep my focus on the puck. The white team gets a hold of it again and shoots it right into my glove. I make a split-second decision and drop the puck right in front of me then wind up and take a shot. With everybody still converging near the face-off, no one sees it coming, and the puck goes right into the net.

Our red team wins 4-3 and my teammates skate out to hug me. We all stay out on the ice longer, waving at fans, and gathering for a group picture with the staff, crew, and volunteers.

As we head off the ice, Ash gives me a hug and shakes his head. "You're fucking amazing, *sunshine*."

"You put up a good fight. Sorry I didn't let you score."

"Are you kidding? I got to show off my cool moves in front of Bonavich, that's all I need. That man's eyes were glued to you the whole time, I swear."

I take a deep breath but can't shake off the anxiety of what that might mean for me or my future.

TWENTY-NINE

ASH

THERE'S no update on Nadison, but the whole team is celebrating the end of training camp. We've all pushed ourselves and worked hard the last few days, and that really showed on the ice. We work well together, no matter what gets thrown at us.

Bonavich joins us for the meal we got catered and he gives us a whole speech about how amazing we're going to do this season and how much faith he has in us. This makes me think that the rumor that my father was vying for his job is bullshit. There's no way Nelson Meyers would give up Boston for Detroit, not when he played there almost his entire career. I breathe a little easier seeing the excitement on Bonavich's face.

Later, I try to find Eli, but he's nowhere in the room. I do see Juuse sitting with a group of NHL players and I make my way to him.

"Hey, have you seen Eli?" I ask.

Juuse smiles at me with his perfect teeth and I still kinda wanna punch him for taking my boyfriend on a date. "Ash, good job out there. I just saw Bonavich pull him aside for a conversation. Guess it's his time."

"Time for what?" I ask, confused.

"Well," he says, standing up and leading me away from the table. "Nadison's injury must be pretty serious," he says in a low voice. "He might be looking at months of recovery. That means I need a backup in Detroit."

I stare at him, understanding dawning on me.

Eli is getting called up to play in the NHL.

I smile, but feel a pang in my chest too. That means he's leaving. I won't get to see him every day like we planned. We won't get to go on dates like we talked about.

My face must show how heartbroken I am, because Juuse of all people gives me a pitying smile and pats my back. "You'll make it work, I'm sure."

As happy as I am for Eli, I can't help but wonder if we will.

ELI

MY ANXIETY DOESN'T LET up as Bonavich takes me aside. I try to focus on what he's saying.

Two months. Groin injury. Secondary goalie.

My heart is beating a mile a minute and I nod along, but my hands are sweating and my breathing is shallow. This is it.

"Are you up for the task?" he asks, and I stare blankly at him. Am I up for the task? It's only everything I've been working towards. Everything I've wanted since I was five years old and my dad was coaching me in little league.

I take a deep breath and run my hands down my face. When I drop them back down, I'm smiling so hard, Bonavich's eyebrows shoot up. He gives me a wry smile back and I don't even get to say anything. He pats my shoulder and says, "You're gonna be great, kid. Keep up the hard work and this won't just be temporary."

Holy shit. Holy shit. This is huge for my career. A chance to actually play in the NHL. Even if it is only temporary, this is a huge opportunity, although I feel bad for Nadison.

I go through a wave of emotions and by the time I go back to the large conference room. I spot Ash at a table and my heart sinks when he looks at me. His eyes are wide and he's smiling hard, but I can tell he knows. I grab a plate of food and sit next to him.

"Well?" he asks, excitement in his voice.

I nod and take a bite of pizza. I keep nodding while Ash just looks at me, waiting for more information.

"I don't know much, just that I'll be the secondary for the next two months."

Ash whoops and tackles me into a side hug. I shush him and look around nervously. "I don't know how much I'm supposed to say right now."

"Sorry, sorry," he says, straightening up. "This is amazing, Eli. *You're* amazing."

"It's not that serious, I only got called up because Nadison is hurt," I say, downplaying it.

"Are you kidding?" Ash says, punching my arm hard enough to lose my balance. "*You* were amazing out there. *You* blocked all the shots that came at you. *You* scored the winning goal. That is not nothing, Eli. Even if this game is all for show and not for points, your performance still matters."

I blow out a shaky breath. When's the last time someone believed in me this much? "When did you get so wise?"

Ash tilts his head and leans in conspiratorially, the corners of his lips twitching. "Someone told me I'm smarter than I give myself credit for."

Then his face gets more serious as he says, "Actually, I think I just have a really great therapist. When in doubt, I ask myself—what would Marge do?"

"I'm proud of you," I say, and he gives me a soft smile and a nod, but a spike of fear still rolls through me. I don't want to lose him, not when I didn't even get to tell him how much I love him.

"We'll be okay, right?" I ask and Ash seems taken aback for a moment.

"Of course, we'll figure it all out when we get home."

"Okay," I say and give him a shaky smile. I really hope we can, but I'm nervous about our future.

THIRTY

ASH

AFTER PACKING up and leaving the cabin up north, we've spent the last week back in Grand Marquee, getting ready for the pre-season. Eli and I have avoided any big conversations about the future, and instead we've spent every waking moment together, torn between staying inside my apartment and going out on a few dates—dinner, movies, bowling.

We spend our days in my apartment, except when he needs to call his family or start packing up his belongings. Since he'll only be gone for a couple of months, he plans to keep the apartment and sublet it to Alice, who recently has had issues with her roommates.

"Ash, can we talk for a moment?" he asks me right as we get back from grocery shopping. I fidget with the last paper bag and fold it down until it's small enough to fit in one of the drawers and I take a steadying breath before giving Eli my full attention.

"Yeah."

"I'm mostly done packing. I'm not taking that much with me since it'll only be a couple months," he says, leaning his arms on the kitchen counter, looking down at my fruit bowl.

"Makes sense," I say quietly. I don't know what to say or what he wants to hear. Should I tell him that everything will be fine? I don't know that.

Eli lifts his head up and looks at me with a sad smile. I blow out a breath and walk around the island to meet him. I wrap him up in a hug and say, "I can't wait to see you kick ass out there."

He laughs, his breath tickling my neck. "I'm going to miss you, *kultsi*."

"I'll miss you too. But you know, phones still exist, and you can text me anytime." I give him a smirk, knowing he usually hates being on his phone. "I know our schedules won't line up, but I'm still here for you."

"I'll be there for you too, always," he says and kisses me. "Any chance you'd want to drive me to Detroit tomorrow?"

I swallow and nod, trying my best to stay excited for him instead of feeling sorry for myself. "Of course, I need to see your apartment."

He scoffs, "It's just a studio downtown. It's not going to be anything fancy."

"I'll be the judge of that."

"Could you do me one more favor?" he asks a little sheepishly.

"Anything, *pretty boy*."

He bites his lip. "Can you give me a haircut?"

"Absolutely NOT!" I rear back like he's burned me or something. Eli just rolls his eyes and runs a hand through his long blond hair.

"Come on, it's killing me. I get too sweaty during games and it looks gross."

I groan, "But you look so hot with it. Like a Nordic viking or something."

"Please," he says, giving me what I can only assume is his version of puppy dog eyes. They're big and wide and damn it, I can't help but give in.

The corners of my lips twitch. "Fine, but I'm not happy about it," I grumble.

I groan and sigh and mumble my complaints the whole time we get set up in my bathroom. Eli takes a seat on one of the counter stools we dragged in here from the kitchen. He takes his T-shirt off in one smooth motion and I can't help but admire his body. He's hard and soft in all the right spots and all I want is to feel the warmth of him on top of me. But I focus on the task he's given me instead.

Eli wraps a towel around his shoulders and I use a spray bottle to get his hair damp. I have no idea what I'm doing when it comes to giving him a haircut, but he trusts me enough to let me do it.

I grab the scissors and thread my fingers through his hair, from his scalp to the ends, repeating the motion. Every time my fingers linger on his scalp, Eli leans into me and melts a little, and I think my heart does too.

"Are you sure about this? What if you end up looking ridiculous?"

He chuckles and places his hand on top of mine where it rests on his shoulder. "It'll be fine. Worst case is you end up giving me a buzz cut."

I choke and sputter as I say, "But you have such nice hair."

Mournfully, I let go of the argument, knowing he won't

back down on this, and I start cutting the longer strands of his hair. I sigh as they fall to the bathroom floor and shake my head.

"RIP sexy viking Eli."

"If it makes you feel better, maybe I'll look more like Charlie Hunnam."

"He is one sexy guy," I say and Eli narrows his eyes at me. "Not sexier than you, of course, my little viking."

"Little?" he asks indignantly.

I don't give him a reply as I grab the clippers and turn them on, carefully readjusting his head so I can better see what I'm doing. When his silky hair falls to the floor, I die a little bit inside.

By the time I'm done, he still has hair left on his head—thankfully. His haircut now resembles mine, with a bit of a fade on the sides and more hair on top. I run both my hands through as much as I can and sigh, catching his eye in the mirror.

"Not much for me to grab, but you're still a sexy motherfucker."

Eli's smile is wide and in one swift movement, he swivels around in the chair to face me and pulls me in close. I step in between his legs and let my hands fall from his hair to his face, tilting his head up. I kiss him tenderly, trying to memorize the taste and feel of his lips on mine. I don't know when we'll get to be this close again.

ELI

THE TWO HOUR drive to Detroit passes by way too quickly, Ash entertaining me with stories of his past, while I do the same. Before we know it, we arrive at my new apartment downtown. The good news is that it's within walking distance to the arena; the bad news is that it's busy as hell. The building has twelve floors and plenty of people are coming and going or hanging out in the common areas.

There's a gym, a lounge area with lots of TVs, an indoor pool, and a coffee bar, all available for tenants to utilize, which is why this place was the most appealing of the bunch. From what I could tell by looking at the pictures, the apartment is small and has minimal utilities but I could see myself here, swimming and sitting at the coffee bar with Ash.

We make our way up to the 8th floor, Ash carrying my suitcase while I carry the other one and my backpack. The place smells like potpourri and I immediately miss home. I want to be back in Ash's apartment cooking something together or watching something stupid on the TV. I'd even play one of the video games he likes so bad right about now. I look over at him and smile, even though it must look more like a grimace. He smiles back, just as awkwardly and as I'm getting ready to tell him what's on my mind, the elevator dings. We shuffle out and make our way to apartment 805.

The place is small, just like I thought, but thankfully it's furnished. There's a queen sized bed near the large window that overlooks the city, a small desk with a chair, and a TV mounted on the wall above it. There's a small kitchenette with no more than two counter cabinets, a fridge, stove and dishwasher, and a closet the size of the bathroom—which is again, small.

"No washer and dryer?" Ash asks and I deflate, dropping my backpack and sitting down at the edge of the bed, hands gripping my hair.

"Hey, no, I didn't mean that as a critique," Ash says,

voice sounding concerned. I feel the mattress dip next to me and right as I let my arms drop between my knees, Ash's hands come around my shoulder, giving me a hug.

"I know, I just feel off about all of this. I didn't expect it and I don't know what to think about it."

"Are you talking about the apartment or the job?" he asks, rubbing circles on my back while his chin rests on my shoulder.

"Both."

"Well, the apartment is temporary."

"So is the job," I say quietly.

"Maybe." I look up and Ash straightens up, one hand holding my shoulder firmly. "Maybe not. You are really good, Eli. And Nadison is fine, but he's also old, in hockey terms at least— he's thirty-five and he just sustained a pretty major injury. Chances are that even if he does come back this season, he might not be around for much longer anyway. So you need to accept that this is happening. You are the future of this team. And when Juuse inevitably retires, you're gonna be the primary."

I close my eyes and take a deep breath. He's right, of course he is. But how can I do this on my own? I know I'll have a team, but I don't know any of these guys like I know Ash and the rest of the AHL players. Like I used to know Jordan and Robbie, how they played and how great we all were as a team. But he's right, I need to accept this.

"I don't want things to change between us," I say. "I—" *I love you*, I want to say. Why does my throat always close up when I want to say it? I've never said it before, not to anyone that wasn't family, and the thought of being so vulnerable when I know he has such a strong hold over my heart is terrifying. Tears well up in my eyes and I blink them away, but a traitorous one escapes anyway.

Ash catches it with his thumb and brings his forehead to mine. "I know, sunshine. *I know*. Nothing will change, I promise."

I look into his deep blue eyes and this time, I believe him.

THIRTY-ONE

November

ASH

PRACTICE STARTS in full swing after I help Eli move to Detroit. He's secondary for a few of the pre-season games and ends up playing a whole game against Boston. I meet up with Robbie and Olivia at their house to watch it, but my excitement sours as soon as I see my father on the TV. Even when I cut out all contact with him and block his number, his disapproving face is still around to haunt me.

A few days later, I get called up to play a game, but Eli is not the secondary, so I don't even get to see him. I'm sure he's in the arena somewhere and I think that maybe I can take him out to dinner afterwards, but we have morning skate the day after and our bus to Grand Marquee leaves promptly after the game.

We get two months of this song and dance. Two months

of missed texts, phone calls, and short video chats at the end of a long day are weighing hard on our relationship. I keep thinking that if I work harder and prove myself, then maybe, just maybe, I'll get called up as well. Maybe one day, I'll be good enough not just for the team, but for him as well. He doesn't need me holding him back.

Selfishly, I am rooting for Nadison's return to the NHL, since that means I get Eli back, but even thinking that makes my stomach turn. He deserves this chance and I would be a shit friend and an even shittier boyfriend if I didn't put his happiness first.

My father's voice comes back stronger than ever, telling me I'm worthless, that I won't amount to anything. Not like Eli will.

I talk this through with my therapist and she tells me it's normal to feel this doubt, especially with the season gearing up, but that I need to think about all the progress that I've made since this summer. It's hard to do that when it feels like all my hard work is not even paying off.

NADISON COMES BACK the day before Thanksgiving and plays a conditioning game at the AHL, but halfway through the third period, as one of the Finchton Foxes gets a breakaway, Nadison goes down at an awkward angle and hurts his groin all over again. He needs to be helped off the ice and I am fucking furious. At him, at myself, at the world.

Why is this my shit luck? I *finally* get Eli and we're happy together, but the universe just wants to pull us apart. I'm at a point in my life where I genuinely feel good about myself—I go to therapy, I don't drink anymore, I'm in love. So why is this happening?

My anger is not rational, it's something that's been

brewing under the surface for a few months now, maybe years. Instead of suppressing it with drinking or hooking up, I let it out on the ice. I've been careful all season, avoiding the penalty box, being the poster child of our team. No one was more surprised than my teammates, and some of them even commented on how tame my game has been. I was just playing it safe, wanting to prove myself, but no one gives a shit anyway. So why hold back?

I play as aggressively as I can for the rest of the game and it pays off. One of the Foxes' players trips me to retaliate for checking him into the boards and that gives us the exact advantage we need to take the lead. As soon as he comes out of the box, he heads straight for me, throwing down his gloves and ripping my helmet off. I should have seen it coming, but the first punch to my face takes me by surprise.

My gloves hit the ice as well and we brawl in the center face off while the crowd is cheering me on. I get a few punches in as well before taking him down on the ice. The linesmen are there to break us up and they have to pull me off of him and keep me away.

Olivia skates up to me, grabbing hold of my jersey and leading me to the tunnel. We're both being thrown out of the game since there are only two minutes left on the clock.

At first, she doesn't say anything, but I know I'm about to get a lecture, if not from her, from Robbie as soon as he finds out. There's nothing worse than having both of them be disappointed in me.

"Ash, what the hell was that all about?"

"Don't worry about it," I say, spitting out blood on the ice and moving my jaw side to side. It fucking hurts and I'm sure I'll have a black eye tomorrow.

"I do worry about it, what happened to staying out of trouble?" she whispers.

I know she's trying to be my friend right now, but I'm too angry as I rip my arm out of her grip and roughly say, "Just drop it, okay? You know nothing about what I'm going through right now, so stop pretending like you give a shit." I expect her to chew me out or tell me I'm being an idiot, but she doesn't say anything.

When I look back at her, I don't miss the hurt look on her face. I want to take it all back, to thank her for always being there for me, but this is not the time or the place. She straightens up and skates away from me without a second glance and I continue walking down the tunnel, feeling shittier than I had at the beginning of the game.

I don't stay to have dinner with the team and instead head across the street to The Arcadian to get some takeout. I put in my order at the bar and take a seat, waiting. My phone buzzes for the third time since I got out of the locker room and I look down at it.

Eli's face lights up my screen and I curl my fingers tighter around the phone. *I miss him.* But I'm in a self-destructive mood right now and the last thing I want is to say something stupid and push him away. So I let his calls go to voicemail instead.

The bartender comes up to me and gives me a wide smile. "Haven't seen you around here in a hot minute. How have you been?"

I scour my brain for their name and land on Gen. I hooked up with them at some point last year after a particularly rough game. "Doing fantastic, Gen, how are you?" I ask, failing to mask my sour mood.

"Oh you know, a little bit of everything. Do you want a

drink? I can make you your favorite cocktail if you want," they say, trailing off and looking behind me.

"No, I don't drink anymore," I say quickly, not allowing myself to think about how good a drink would be right about now.

"Robbie, can I get you anything?" Gen asks, still looking behind me. I groan and drop my forehead on the bar. The last thing I want is a lecture from *grandpa*.

"Two waters, please," he says and takes up the seat next to me.

I don't say anything and neither does he. After Gen drops the waters off, I finally pick my head up and look at him. He's not facing me, but his jaw is tight and he looks me up and down from the corner of his eye. He's disappointed in me. The realization brings a tightness in my chest. Of course he is, I played like shit and was an asshole to his girlfriend.

I don't expect the question he asks me though and I startle. "Why are you avoiding Eli?"

"What? How do you know I'm avoiding him?"

"Because he called me and said you've been avoiding him today."

I grit my teeth and say, "So what, you're here to check up on me? Make sure I don't go on a bender and cheat on him? Fuck you, Robbie." I stand up and consider leaving without my food, anything to get away from this conversation.

Robbie stands too and his arms stop me. I expect him to grab me, shove me, hit me. Something, anything, but instead, he hugs me. Hard.

"I'm not here to babysit you, Ash. You are allowed to make your own choices, even if they're ones I don't agree with. I don't know what happened today, and I don't know why you're so angry at everyone, but I just wanted to tell you that I am here for you. Whether you like it or not." He squeezes me and my arms come up and hug him back. "Your friends are not abandoning you."

"I don't deserve you. Any of you," I say quietly and Robbie pulls back to look at me. He's scowling. It's a ridiculous look on him since he's usually all sunshine and happiness, and I laugh at him.

"Whether you deserve us or not is irrelevant. We're family, and family sticks together, no matter what."

I nod and swallow the lump in my throat. He's right, of course, and I want to tell him everything that's on my mind, but I don't. Not yet. I need to figure out how I'm feeling about it all first. Especially how I feel about Eli not coming back now that Nadison is hurt again.

"Can you at least call your boyfriend? I don't want to be in the middle of everyone's squabbles."

"Yeah, I can do that," I say, laughing. "What about Olivia?"

Robbie's eyebrows go up. "What about her?"

"You're not gonna yell at me for being rude to her?"

He takes a deep breath but says, "I'm trying not to intervene. You'll apologize when you're ready."

I nod. "Of course I will." I just expected him to be more mad at me.

My food comes and I say goodbye to Robbie, walking the five minutes to my apartment building. I watch some comedy special while I eat and before I can pass out for the night, I send Eli a text.

> I'm sorry I've been off the last few days, I just have a lot on my mind. I promise I'm not avoiding you. I miss you.

. . .

ELI

OUR TEAM LOST 5-3 tonight and I can't help but feel responsible for those last two goals. I should have seen them coming, but I didn't. I was being screened too hard for the first one, and the second came out of nowhere on the face-off. It was so quick, I barely had a chance to react.

After the game ended, we got the news that Nadison got injured in his first game back and I was told not to pack up my apartment, since I won't be going back to the AHL for another two months at least. My first reaction was to be excited since I've loved playing in the NHL. I learn every day from both Juuse and the goalie coach and I've improved my game a lot in just a short amount of time. In the last couple of weeks, the starting position between myself and Juuse has been half and half, rather than him starting most of the games like it was intended.

My excitement turned into disappointment pretty quickly as I realized that being in the NHL longer just keeps me further away from Ash.

It feels like he's been avoiding me recently and we haven't had a proper conversation in a while. It's all short texts and rushed phone calls as we move through our hectic days. I miss being in the same room together, I miss holding him, I miss his sense of humor, and his body, and his lips on mine.

Robbie told me about Ash's fight tonight and I tried getting a hold of him, but I know what he's like. Right now, he's probably feeling like the whole world is on his shoulders and he's miserable about Nadison, and he's doing what he does best: pushing me and everyone else away.

If he'd answered any of my calls and texts this week, he would know I'm renting a car and driving down to Grand Marquee in the morning to spend Thanksgiving with him and the Elliots, like we do every year.

I miss Ash more than I imagined I would. It's like there's this hole in my life the exact shape and size of him and I can't fill it no matter what I do. No one compares to him.

His text comes through right as I'm about to go to bed, but I decide not to answer. My backpack is light as I'm only bringing a couple changes of clothes to spend Thursday and Friday night with Ash and drive back Saturday early to make it back for morning skate. I set it by the door and fall asleep as soon as my head hits the pillow.

THIRTY-TWO

ELI

THE ROADS ARE empty so early in the morning and I make it to Grand Marquee in just two hours and park in front of my old building. Since Alice is subletting my apartment, I make my way up to the third floor and instead of going to my door, I go to Ash's, right across the hall. I knock three times and wait. When he doesn't open the door, I pull out my phone and call him. The phone rings and rings until it goes to voicemail. It does that three times.

I knock again, this time a little harder. My heart starts beating faster and I'm starting to worry. Did something happen after he left the bar last night? Did he drink? Did he go home with someone? I feel ashamed for even thinking it, knowing that Ash would never do anything to hurt me like that. But what if he needed a distraction and I wasn't here for him?

The door opens, but it's not the one I'm knocking on. I

turn around and see a rumpled looking Alice. She frowns at me and rubs her eyes, making sure I'm really there.

"Hey, *lapsi*."

"Eli, you're here?"

"Yeah," I say, dropping my backpack and giving her a hug. She looks across the hall at Ash's apartment door and sighs.

"He's fine, don't worry. I saw him briefly when he got home, he had some takeout and looked really tired and you know—beat up. I'm sure he's just resting."

I swallow hard. "Right, of course. I was hoping he'd let me in," I say, chuckling and pointing to my backpack.

Alice smiles at me and pats my chest. "Hold on a second," she says, going back into my—no—her apartment. She comes back and holds up a key, twirling it around her fingers. "I'm only supposed to use this in emergency situations. But I think you being stranded in the hallway is considered quite the emergency." She smirks and with the way her blue eyes twinkle, she looks so much like Robbie.

I smile and pluck the key from her fingers. "Thank you, you're a lifesaver."

She nods and yawns but hovers around the hallway with me until I gain the courage to go into Ash's apartment.

"Hey Eli?"

"Yeah?"

"I didn't say this last time we hung out, but—I think you and Ash are perfect for each other. I don't think I've ever seen you both as happy as you were in Traverse City."

"Hmm," I say, debating how much I should tell her.

"I know your careers are important and that distance might feel like it's a deal-breaker right now, but I don't think it needs to be. If you love each other, I think you can make it work." Alice wrings her hands and gives me a sad look as she says all of this and I get the feeling she's not just talking about Ash.

I ponder what she said for a moment and realize that—she's right, distance shouldn't be a deal-breaker for us.

"Are you okay, *lapsi*?" I ask, picking up on her sadness.

"Yeah, just tired, that's all," she says, managing a small smile. "Someone woke me up with loud banging."

I roll my eyes and gently push her shoulder. She pretends to be mortally wounded as she stumbles and slides herself down against the door. I laugh and she looks up at me, grinning. When I offer her a hand to stand up, she takes it.

"I'm sorry things didn't work out with you and Jordan," I say quietly, patting her arm.

She looks surprised but quickly deflects. "Oh it's—well, it wasn't—"

"You don't have to tell me if you don't want to, but know I'm here if you ever want to talk."

Alice sighs and nods, her eyes moving all over my face. "Maybe one day. Until then, go check on your boyfriend. Make sure he puts some makeup on that black eye, otherwise Mom might freak out and spend all of Thanksgiving fussing over him."

"Would that be such a bad thing?" I ask.

"I guess not. I'm gonna go to sleep for another hour at least before I attempt to get ready for the day."

She slips back into the apartment and I unlock the door to Ash's. The place is quiet and it looks the same as it did the last time I was here, except it's cleaner. There are no dirty dishes around and no clothes thrown all over the living room floor. I make my way to the bedroom and find Ash sprawled out in the middle of the bed, sleeping face down wearing nothing but his boxers. Even though it's not that warm in the room, I know he runs hot at night, which is why the sheets are tangled at his feet. I smile and slowly drop my backpack.

I slip off my jeans and my sweatshirt and kneel tentatively on the mattress next to him. Does he want me here? He said he had a lot on his mind, but did that include me as well? Before I can second guess all my choices, I lie down next to him and wrap an arm around him. He's facing me, eyes closed and his right arm tucked under the pillow, clutching it. My fingers gently trace his shoulders and upper back and I place a kiss on his bicep.

While heat radiates off of Ash, I am cold as hell, so I reach down and untangle the sheets from his feet, pulling them over the both of us. The movement makes Ash turn on his side, facing away from me, which works out great because it gives me the perfect position to spoon him. I bury my face between his neck and the pillow and I press myself tighter against him, relishing the feel of him in my arms again. One of my legs slides between his and my arm holds him close, hand splayed against his heart.

It doesn't take long for sleep to pull me under, and the last thing on my mind is that finally, *I'm home.*

ASH

MY ALARM GOES off and pulls me out of my deep sleep. I was dreaming about Eli being here with me and hugging me, telling me he was home. But that can't be right. He's going to be in Detroit for another two months, at least.

I try to reach for my phone but something around my middle stops me. I blink wearily down at the arm around me and screw my eyes shut tight.

No, no, no.

I didn't bring someone else home, I wouldn't do that. I didn't even drink last night, so why the hell is my memory so foggy? My head is pounding, but that's probably just from the fight.

The arm hugs me tighter and my bleary mind thinks that maybe it is Eli, that he snuck in here in the middle of the night just to spend some time with me. I slide out from under the heavy arm and reach for my phone on the nightstand, silencing the alarm.

Panic takes over when I see a bunch of missed calls and texts from Eli and my stomach drops. Did something happen?

A hand reaches over and flips my phone over and I whip my head around, ready to yell at whoever is in my bed.

"*Kultsi*, come back here," Eli says in a deep, sleepy voice.

I blink down at him a few times, not believing that he's actually here. His pale blue eyes meet mine and for a second I think I stop breathing. My hand reaches out and pinches his cheek and he groans and grabs my wrist.

"Again with the pinching? I told you, you're supposed to pinch yourself, not me."

"Making sure you're really here." I swallow and smile down at him. "I thought—"

"You thought what?"

"Nothing." I shake my head, embarrassed of my own thoughts. "I'm happy you're here," I say, bending down to kiss him. He lets go of my wrist and cups my face, running his hand over my jaw. When his kiss turns pressing, I wince and pull back slightly. My split lip hurts like a motherfucker.

Eli runs his finger over it, then moves over my left eye where I most likely have a massive bruise. He grimaces and pulls me down in a hug. "Are you okay, *kultsi?*"

I sigh and hide my face between his neck and shoulder. "Better now."

"Do you want to talk about the fight last night? Or about Nadison getting hurt and what that means for us?"

"How long are you here for?" I mumble against his skin.

"I have to drive back Saturday morning for an early skate and the home game."

"We can talk about it before you leave. I just want to enjoy our time together for now."

"Okay, *hani.*"

WHEN WE WALK INTO THE ELLIOTS' house, the entire place smells like turkey and herbs. Michael, Robbie's brother, and his wife Tangela are running around after their two daughters and making sure they don't eat too much sugar before dinner. Olivia and Alice are on the couch, reading a romance book together and Robbie and his mom are in the kitchen, putting together some delicious looking appetizers. Robbie's dad is watching the football game and I'm hit by a wave of longing so bad that I stop in my tracks.

This right here is all I've ever wanted from my own family. Casual affection and holiday dinners with close family members has never been a part of my life. Not until now. Holidays were always big, fancy parties with all my dad's business partners and friends. It was always catered meals, suits and ties, and cold shoulders. I didn't realize how much I was missing out on until Robbie brought me into his family and showed me that I could have more. That I deserve more.

Eli notices I stopped in the hallway and comes back to check on me. His eyes roam all over me, concern showing on his face. "What's wrong?"

I shake my head. "I'm just happy to have found this family."

His expression softens and he gives me one of his bear hugs, arms completely enveloping me. His dark green sweater is soft against my cheek when I place my head on his shoulder and he rubs his hands all over my back.

"Hey, you guys made it!" Alice yells out from the couch. She places her book down and runs over to hug us. I expect Eli to pull back since everyone's attention is now focused on us, but instead he grabs my hand and squeezes my fingers. I look up at him and whisper *thank you* before I'm attacked by a tiny blond.

As soon as Robbie's mom sees me, she gasps and fusses all over me, offering an ice pack and having me lie down on the couch like I'm injured. It makes me wish my own mom was more like her, but growing up I never really had this level of care and nurturing. Maybe that's not fair, I'm sure my mom tried, in her own way, to love me, but I was a pretty wild child and eventually I realized that she was always going to pick my dad's side over mine. So maybe I'm also to blame for our falling out.

"I promise I'm okay. Can I help you with the food or anything?" I ask.

"Nonsense," she says, "you and Eli relax and catch up, I'm sure you've missed each other a lot."

I nod appreciatively at her and turn back to my boyfriend who takes a seat next to me on the couch. He hands me a hot cocoa and some appetizers and my heart feels like it might explode at any second.

"Thank you," I manage to say, even though my throat is threatening to close up on me. I still don't think I deserve this amazing man, but I want to keep him anyway. All of them. This family of mine.

THIRTY-THREE

ELI

BETWEEN THANKSGIVING DINNER with the family and Friday brunch with our friends, Ash and I don't get a lot of time to spend alone. The annual holiday game takes place on Friday night and the whole family has seats to watch them play. It's weird being on the other side of the plexiglass.

Olivia is reffing the game, so Robbie and Alice sit on either side of me and pepper me with questions about the NHL while we wait for the game to start.

I've always thought Ash was a great hockey player, but the way he plays now is out of this world. He's faster than ever, easily stealing pucks away from the opposing team and getting breakaways. His shots are better too, so much so that by the end of the first period, he's scored two goals and is on the watch for a hat trick.

"He's been improving a lot," I tell Robbie during intermission.

"I think he's dedicated. He's always been good, but he sometimes lacks motivation. When he encounters a setback, he retreats back into his shell and thinks he doesn't deserve good things. It's bullshit, but I think he's become more self aware recently."

"Do you think he'll stay motivated?"

"I think being with you has opened his eyes more. That there's a future for him alongside you, not just in the NHL, but in life."

I nod, not knowing what to say. As much as I want him by my side, always, this job is so fucking unpredictable. One of us could get hurt, we could be traded to different teams. What then? The last thing I want is for him to resent me, or vice-versa.

Robbie picks up on my quiet brooding and as always, he always knows what to say. "I know long distance is hard. Hell, I miss Olive all the time when she's gone on the road."

I look over at him and expect to see him sad, but he's smiling, lost in thought. "But do you know what the best part is?"

"What?"

"At the end of the day, she calls me, excited about her job and happy to tell me all about it. And not only that, but she's excited to hear about what I'm doing too. The key is to listen to one another. And when we do see each other again, it makes it all that much more special. Because we chose each other and we cherish every moment together, even if those moments are sometimes rare."

"Do you ever worry about Olivia getting transferred to a different region?"

"Sure I do."

"So what's your contingency plan?"

"Well, if she has to move, then we move together. We

spend the season wherever it makes more sense for her career and come back here for the summer. Look, my point is, if you love each other, you'll make it work. There will be compromises and things to worry about, but you need to tackle those together."

I nod and Robbie pats me on the shoulder. I think about asking more but he's right. Ash and I need to communicate and figure things out for ourselves.

Alice comes back with concessions and shares her popcorn with us. The game picks back up and by the end of the period, Ash scores his third goal. The three of us jump out of our chairs, screaming and cheering, tossing our hats on the ice. Ash finds me in the crowd and points at me. I point back at him and turn around, showing him the jersey I'm wearing. The one that says Meyers #1.

The look he gives me is pure joy and during the second intermission I get a text from him.

> when we get home, you're going to wear nothing but that jersey and I'm going to give you the best blow job of your life

> Don't make promises you can't keep.

> oh, I can more than keep it. and when you recover, you're going to fuck me wearing my last name.

"Damn, Ash has a filthy mouth," Alice says, peeking over my phone.

I blush and put it in my pocket. "Don't you know it's not nice to spy on other people's conversations, *lapsi?*"

She rolls her eyes and lightly punches my shoulder. "Whatever, you guys are adorable together. I'm really happy for you."

"Thanks," I say and smile.

THE MANTICORES WIN 4-1 and the whole arena is packed with people. As we head out, we wait for Ash and Olivia before heading out to dinner at The Arcadian. Robbie reserved a table for all of us and we put in our orders, but as soon as Ash puts his hand on my thigh under the table, all I want is to get us both out of here and into our bed.

Halfway through our dinner we see Tangela come in and take a seat at the bar. Robbie looks around, confused. "That's weird, Michael isn't here tonight. He said he was taking the girls to a movie."

"Maybe she's just grabbing some food," Alice says, frowning.

"But would she drive twenty minutes this way just for some food?" Olivia asks.

"No, that's weird," Robbie says. "Maybe I should go talk to her and see—"

He stops, halfway out of his seat and stares over at the bar, mouth open. We all turn to look at the same time and see Tangela hugging a guy. Not just any guy, but one we know too well. One that's been avoiding our calls and texts since he moved away.

Alice gasps out and looks away, busying herself on her phone. Robbie looks disappointed and Ash—well, Ash looks pissed. I'm shocked to see that Jordan is here and that he didn't even tell us, but I can't say I'm surprised. He's been distancing himself from all of us ever since he got traded and moved to Texas.

Robbie sits back down, resting his elbows on the table

and putting his head in his hands. Olivia comforts him and asks, "Do you want to go over and talk to them?"

He shakes his head no, but Ash says, "Fuck that, he owes us at least one fucking conversation." The chair scrapes loudly on the floor, and before I can stop him, Ash is across the room tapping Jordan on the shoulder.

ASH

JORDAN TURNS around and looks at me with wide eyes. I smile at Tangela as she looks between us and then notices the rest of the group behind me, but when my gaze returns to Jordan, it's nothing but angry.

"Ash—"

"No, Jordan. What the actual fuck, man? You don't call or text back for months, and now you're back in town and you don't even tell us? Why weren't you at Thanksgiving?"

My raised voice draws the attention of some of the people nearby and even some servers stop to figure out what the commotion is. I smile apologetically and they move on. I swing back around to face Jordan but he's not looking at me anymore. His eyes are locked on the table behind me, on a particular girl wearing a jersey with #20 on it—Jordan's old number.

His eyes trace the number on her arm and he takes a step forward, almost involuntarily, like he can't help but be away from her for another second. I block his path and cross my hands across my chest. "Don't even think about it," I murmur.

Jordan finally looks at me and he nods, stealing another glance at Alice. "I'm sorry, Ash. You're right, I've been a really shitty friend." He looks down at his feet and the misery on his face makes me pause.

Before I can ask him more questions, he says, "I've been dealing with a lot, honestly, and that shouldn't be an excuse, but I really needed to focus on my mental health."

"Oh, okay," I say, deciding not to push him on the topic since he looks to be on the verge of running. "Look man, I know how that is, and I get it, truly. Just—we're here for you, even though you ditched us for Texas."

He laughs and pushes my shoulder lightly. "Yeah, like that was my choice."

"I know, I'm sorry. That was really shitty. If it's worth anything, our defense kinda sucks without you, man."

Jordan snorts and says, "Yeah that'll make me sleep better at night."

For a moment, we both look over at the table and before I can think better of it, I say, "Do you wanna join us?"

Jordan looks on the verge of running for the hills, but he looks over at Tangela and she nods, grabbing her purse. "I'll see you tomorrow for brunch baby brother." She gives him a hug and heads out, and that leaves Jordan with me.

"Well, come on."

He blows out a breath and follows me along to the table. For a moment, we're all silent, just looking at one another. Eli stands up and offers Jordan a hand, which he takes and turns into a hug. Robbie is next, then Olivia. When he gets to Alice, she gives him a half wave and a meek *hello* and avoids his eyes.

Jordan looks like he wants to say more, but Alice pulls out her phone and ignores him along with everyone else, browsing social media instead.

We pull up an empty chair for Jordan and in a short amount of time, it's like we're the same group of people that we were last year. Like nothing changed. Except in truth, everything has. When Eli puts his arm around my shoulder and I put my hand on his thigh, Jordan stares at us for a beat before piecing it together. When he does, he smiles and says, "You two finally figured it out, huh?"

"What do you mean 'finally'?" I say, indignant.

"Please, you two were always crushing on each other, it was really obvious."

"Says the most oblivious guy ever," Alice mutters, but it's loud enough that the whole table hears. She looks up from her phone and makes eye contact with Jordan. He frowns and she looks away quickly. Olivia gives her a subtle squeeze on her arm and the two of them have a whole conversation with just a look.

"I don't know about you all, but I'm really tired. We're probably gonna head out," Olivia says, giving Robbie a look.

"Right, we should. Jordan, how long are you in town for?"

"I head back on Sunday."

"How about you come over for dinner tomorrow? Ash, you're invited too."

"Gee, thanks for the afterthought, *grandpa*." Robbie rolls his eyes affectionately at me.

Jordan looks between Robbie, Olivia, and Alice and swallows. "Sure, that would be nice."

"Great, we'll see you then," Olivia says with a small smile. "Alice, we'll drive you to your apartment, so you don't have to walk in the dark."

"Okay, thanks. Good night everyone," Alice pipes up and follows them out.

Once the three of them leave, Jordan, Eli, and I stay for another hour, catching up and trying to get Jordan to tell us more about why he's stayed away for so long. He avoids the topic but tells us he missed Grand Marquee and all of his friends.

BY THE TIME Eli and I return to my apartment, we're both beat, but neither of us makes a move to go to bed. Eli comes up behind me and pulls me into his chest. "What's on your mind, *kultsi?*"

I smile and turn in his arms, kissing him and nipping at his jaw. "Tell me what that word means. Please."

Eli watches me as I rake my fingers through his short hair, closing his eyes and melting into me. I press my forehead to his and wait for his answer.

After a long moment of humming content, he says, "It means gold. Or *golden.*"

"Is it because I remind you of a golden retriever?" I joke and he laughs. It's a tired version of his bright laugh, the one I swear he sometimes has reserved just for me.

"No, it's because you're so special to me, Ash. You're incredible," he says and swallows, rubbing his nose against my own. When his lips briefly brush mine he tells me, "You're amazing and I—I love you."

I pull back slightly, making sure I heard him right. I know he's been struggling with those words the past few months, but I also knew deep down that I didn't need to hear them. I can feel how much he loves me through every text, every phone call, every gesture he makes. I've known how he's felt about me this whole time, but hearing him say it after almost a year of this push and pull between us, well —it fills me up with emotion.

My fingers trace all over his face, from his jaw to his cheeks, to his temple, and finding purchase in his hair. I bring him back in for a kiss and pour everything I can into it.

All my love and worry and heartbreak. I want him to stay longer, but I know he can't. That in the morning he'll leave again for another two months, and that I'll have to find a way to be okay with that, because every single little doubt I had about us has been blown to pieces.

Because he loves me.

Eli loves me.

I pull back again and breathlessly say, "I love you too, Eli. More than words can express."

"Show me, then," he says, voice gravelly and deep.

Our hands grip and tug at every bit of fabric as we make our way to the bedroom. In a rare occurrence, Eli lets me take the lead and I back him up until his knees hit the bed. I push him down and crawl on top of him, kissing his swollen lips and straddling him. When his hands slip under my sweatshirt, I pull back so I can take it off. Eli lifts up, leaning up on one hand and caressing my back with the other, his mouth leaving kisses over my tattoos, starting with the honeysuckle one over my heart. His favorite one.

His lips find my neck and he sucks at my skin, lightly biting down before soothing the sting with a lick. I grind on his stiff cock in response and he groans against me. I push him back down and take off the rest of my clothes, moving to remove his jeans next. Once I'm done pulling them off, Eli sits up to take his jersey off.

"What did I tell you earlier?"

"What?"

"You keep that jersey on and I give you the best blow job of your life."

Eli smiles but before I can take him in my mouth, he stops me, a serious look on his face.

"What's wrong?"

"Nothing, I just—I was thinking maybe—"

"Maybe what?" I ask confused.

A beat of silence. Two.

Eli bites his lip.

My eyes widen.

Oh.

"Maybe you can fuck me this time," he says quietly.

I lean down over him and he bends to my will, letting me lead. I press myself flat against him, our cocks aligned and I can't help but grind on him again. He feels so good, so right. We were fucking made for each other.

My arms rest near his head and I bring our foreheads together. "Are you sure, *pretty boy?*"

"Yes," he says, but his shaky voice makes me pause.

"We don't have to do this if you're not ready. If it's some attempt to do it just to make me happy, then you should know I'm happy with anything you give me."

"No, that's not it. I want to. You know I've never done it before though."

"I get that, but just know, if you're not comfortable now or ever, really, then we never have to do it. I mean it."

He nods along, "I know, *kultsi*. I've wanted to for a while now, and I'm ready. Here. Now. I love you, and I trust you."

I stare at him for a moment. "Fuck, I love you so much."

THIRTY-FOUR

ASH

ELI KISSES ME DEEPLY, tongue swirling with mine and I pull him up so we're both on our knees on the mattress. My hand finds his cock and I pump him a few times as he groans into my mouth.

"Turn around," I say, letting go of him and sitting back on my heels. He eyes me intently but eventually does what I say.

As he turns around, I see my last name and number on his back and the feral beast inside me threatens to come out. I've never been possessive of anything or anyone in my life, but one look at Eli in that goddamn jersey makes me want to throw him over my shoulder and take him far away from everything and everyone that could ever harm him.

He looks back at me, confused, and I swiftly move behind him, gripping his hips and grinding into him. Eli's head falls back on my shoulder and one of my hands finds his throat, squeezing lightly.

"Fuck," he breathes.

"Already? No foreplay?" I tease, biting down on his earlobe and feeling him shiver. My other hand trails from his hips down to the coarse hairs on his thigh and cupping his balls. Eli's face turns towards me and I capture his lips in a bruising kiss.

As my hand lets go of his throat, I reach down with both hands and peel the jersey off of him and over his head, tossing it somewhere on the floor.

"Lie down, ass up."

Eli does as he's told and gets rewarded with a swift slap on his right cheek.

"What a good boy you are when you're willing to listen."

All he says in reply is a muffled *fuck* and I smile to myself. He likes this, I think. He likes this a lot.

I move further down the bed and position my face at his entrance, using both my hands to massage his cheeks before spreading him open and licking him in one swipe of my tongue.

Eli groans into the pillow and jerks a little, but my hands keep him in place as I do it again and again. He relaxes more, and I reach around to pump his hard cock. I swipe the precum around and pause, bringing my hand up to his mouth.

"Suck."

Two of my fingers disappear into his mouth and he gets them nice and wet until they come out with a pop. I move back to his entrance and circle both fingers, feeling him tense up.

"Try to relax. If there's anything you don't like, just tell me and we can stop."

"Okay."

I move my fingers around again, spreading the wetness and kissing his back. When I feel him relax more, I dip the tip of my index finger inside of him and hold it in place, letting him readjust.

My free hand reaches around to play with his cock again and the more he relaxes, the further inside my finger slips. When there's no further for me to go, I start curling it, slowly pumping in and out, all the while gripping his cock.

I pull my finger out and reach into my nightstand for lube and condoms and Eli watches me patiently, breathing hard. "Still okay with all of this?"

"Yes. I really want you inside me."

"Fuck, you're driving me crazy here, Eli."

When I return to his ass, I enter him with two fingers this time, slowly working them in until he's relaxed and pliant again. We repeat the process with three, until I'm sure he can take me. I pull back and admire his gorgeous body, slowly rolling on the condom while Eli's eyes are glued to the movement. I pump myself a few more times because fuck if I'm not greedy for the attention. Eli bites his lip as he watches me stroke myself and I can't take the torture anymore.

I tease his entrance with the head of my cock and a groan slips out past my lips. Eli's hands tighten in the sheets as he looks over his shoulder at me.

"Are you ready?" I ask, hoping that he doesn't change his mind because I'm dying to be inside him, but ready to stop if he feels like this is too much.

"Yes," he whispers, relaxing again as I lean in to kiss his cheek, his shoulder, his back.

I slowly push myself inside him and it takes all my

willpower not to drive myself to the hilt. I stop every time he tenses up and coax him with tender kisses and sweet caresses. He feels so fucking good.

When I finally bottom out, I can feel the sweat dripping down my temple. "You're so fucking tight, holy shit."

"Fuck, that—you—feel so good."

"Does it hurt?"

"Yes, but it's a good kind of hurt," he rasps out, and I slowly readjust myself behind him.

"I'm going to start moving now."

I go slow at first, pulling in and out, until he feels ready for more. When he does, Eli starts to push back, asking for faster strokes. I grip his hips as I start fucking him in quick and deep strokes and he grabs the headboard for support.

"Fuck, I think I'm getting close," he says and I pull out completely, flipping him over to face me.

ELI

WHEN ASH KISSES ME, I pull him closer to me, relishing in the feel of his body on top of mine. We're both breathing hard and I'm glad to see that Ash is just as affected as I am by this experience. His face and chest are flushed, freckles stark against his skin. He's *fucking beautiful*.

He kneels before me and wraps my legs around his waist, kissing up a trail from my chest to my lips.

"Why did you stop?" I ask.

"You felt too good, needed to make it last," he chuckles in my ear.

I tighten my legs around his waist and his cock rubs

against me, making me moan. Ash reaches down and lines himself up with me, pushing my legs up so that my knees hit my chest. The new angle is so intense that it makes me grip the sheets, my arms shaking, my breathing hard.

Ash is patient again, taking things slow until I'm ready and asking for more. When I'm certain I can take more, I move my legs back around his waist and pull him against me. I kiss him as he moves deeper inside and I claw at his back, needing him closer.

"Fuck, you feel so good, *pretty boy*," he says against my lips.

"Go harder, I can take it."

"Stop saying things like that or I'm gonna come right now."

I laugh and bite his lip, digging my heels into his ass and guiding him to move faster, harder, deeper. Ash places a hand next to my head and leans up on it, picking up the pace, his other hand reaching down and pumping me. My whole body tenses and I come with Ash's name on my lips and his cock deep inside me.

When I come down from my high, Ash pulls out, takes off the condom, and before he can come all over me, I move further down the bed and take him in my mouth, gripping the rest of him.

I suck the head of his cock, hollowing my cheeks and he shakes and bows over me as he comes. I swallow every drop and then we collapse together in a spent heap.

My hands move all over his body, tracing the freckles on his shoulder. He looks down at me with so much love in his eyes that I can't help but get choked up.

"I love you." My lips find the tattoo over his heart and press there. Ash's fingers rake through my hair and he kisses me. I want nothing more than to stay in this moment forever, to wake up slowly and make love to him in the morning. But I know I can't.

"I love everything about you, Eli," he says, eyes bouncing all over my face, like he's committing me to memory.

THIRTY-FIVE

ASH

ELI LEAVES early in the morning and the whole place feels empty without him. Last night left us both vulnerable and raw. After showering together and packing up Eli's stuff, we had a long conversation about what our relationship is going to look like. We'll text as much as we can and video chat most nights when our schedules align and we're not too tired from playing. We'll try to visit if we end up having a day off at the same time. It'll be messy and hard at times, and we both need to accept that, but it will be worth it. I'm sure of it.

Somehow I manage to pull myself out of bed, tidy up the apartment and hit the gym to clear my head. I take it easy with a set of squats, lifting, and cardio and think about the road ahead. I have no doubts left about our relationship, not after last night. While it's going to drive me crazy being away from Eli for long periods at a time, we're going to make it work.

As I'm on my way to Robbie's house to meet them and Jordan for dinner, I get a call from work. I hit the answer button on my steering wheel.

"Hello?"

"Meyers, you're gearing up for tonight."

"We don't play tonight," I say, confused.

Coach sighs and I can picture him shaking his head at me. "You need to be in Detroit like an hour ago, preferably. Get your ass over there right now and we'll have a crew member bring your gear straight to the arena."

I smile as his words sink in. They're calling me up. "Yes, sir, I'll leave right now."

"Good." He pauses for a beat and says, "Kick some ass, kid. You earned this." Then he hangs up.

My cheeks hurt from smiling like an idiot and I pull into the nearest gas station and call Robbie while I fill up the car.

"Hey, you won't believe what I just found out!" I yell out excitedly.

"Must be good news," he deadpans.

"I just got called up to play in Detroit tonight."

"Wait, really?" Robbie's excitement takes over and he immediately tells Olivia too.

"Yes, I need to head over there. Sorry I can't make it to dinner, tell Jordan I'll have to catch up with him another time."

"Of course, we'll make sure to watch the game tonight, cheer you on."

"You need to relive the glory days somehow, old man."

"Har har, you're hilarious." Robbie pauses for a second and then says, "Are you nervous about playing against Boston?"

Until he says it, I don't even realize that we're gonna be playing against my father's team tonight.

"Honestly, no. I'm done looking for his approval, and even more done reacting to his disappointment. I don't care what he thinks, I'm just gonna play my best and enjoy my time."

"Good. I'm proud of you, Ash."

"That means a lot to me, Robbie. I love you."

"Wow you call me by my actual name and tell me you love me? Your relationship is making you soft." He giggles, knowing very well that he's just as soft as I am right now. "Love you too, man. You got this."

As soon as Robbie hangs up, I call Eli but he doesn't answer. I decide not to text him. If he doesn't know by now that I've been called up, he'll get a nice surprise later today.

ELI

I AM WAY MORE tired than I expected to be. Staying up with my boyfriend until three in the morning probably didn't help when I needed to drive a few hours later. I was slower than usual at morning practice and I got a lot of shit from Juuse about it.

In the last two months, the two of us have become good friends and he's been a good person to confide in about Ash. Once he stopped flirting with me, Juuse showed me that he's actually really attentive and great at giving advice.

I take a seat across from him at our favorite deli near my apartment and he tells me all about how he spent his Thanksgiving with our team captain and his family here in Detroit. When he asks me about how things went with Ash, I hesitate. He knows I've been struggling with the long distance but I haven't talked to Juuse more in depth about my feelings for Ash. He still thinks we're just casual.

"I told him I loved him last night."

Juuse stops with the sandwich midway to his mouth and stares at me. "Are you serious?"

I nod, taking a bite of my own sandwich and chewing slowly. "I think he might be—" I stop, what the hell am I saying? That Ash is the one? Of course he is, but saying this out loud to Juuse feels strange.

"He might be what?" he asks eagerly.

"He might be the one."

"Aw, you're so gay," he says, patting my hand affectionately. "I'm happy for you, but also fuck you. I was still hoping we'd hook up one day and now you just crushed all my dreams."

"No offense, but you're not my type."

He gasps and places a hand over his heart in mock offense. "I'm everyone's type, bitch."

I cover my face laughing and Juuse gives me a wink. A group of people at the table next to us keep looking over and pulling out their phones, whispering to each other.

"I think we might have been recognized," I say under my breath, straightening up in my chair.

Juuse looks over at them and gives them a nod, which brings them over to us, asking for pictures and autographs. We oblige them and leave the deli together, headed to my apartment to hang out before we have to walk over to the arena.

When I get to the apartment and plug my phone in, I see a missed call from Ash and try to call him back, but I end up missing him. I send him a text instead.

> Sorry I missed your call, grabbed some lunch after the morning skate. I'm chilling until the game. Call later tonight?

Juuse sets up the gaming console and we lose track of time playing a racing game until the alarm goes off, letting us know it's time to leave.

THIRTY-SIX

ASH

I ARRIVE at the arena just in time for warm ups, although I am the last to get dressed. Just like coach promised, the equipment is all there. The locker room is completely empty and I take a deep breath when I see my name on the locker plate. While everyone else is in the hallway, getting ready to hit the ice, I quickly put on all my gear and sprint out in my skates, hoping to surprise Eli before he gets in the warm-up zone.

Before I turn the corner to the tunnel, a familiar face stops me in my tracks.

"Dad?" I ask, voice quieter than I intended.

"Ashton," my father says, crossing his arms over his chest. He looks very imposing in his dark charcoal suit and neatly combed brown hair that's now streaked with gray.

Ever since I cut him out of my life and blocked his phone number, I've been wondering what I would say to him if I ever saw him again. I've made plenty of speeches and rehearsed them with Marge in therapy; speeches about how he ruined my life, how he never gave me any of the support I needed growing up, how he always made me feel less than.

Standing here in front of him now is a completely different experience. My mouth feels dry and my tongue heavy. *Be brave, Ash.*

"What are you doing down here? Shouldn't you be up in a private box?" I ask, gripping my stick tightly.

"I came to see my son. Why did you block me?" he asks, moving closer to me. Each step he takes feels like a little crack in my neatly built facade.

"You're kidding, right?" I say, voice tight. Is he serious right now?

His eyebrows climb his forehead and he frowns. "I am not. One moment you were galavanting through Europe, and the next you just disappeared. I was worried."

I laugh and it's loud enough to startle both of us. "Worried? When have you ever been worried?" I want to be angry at him, I really do, but I don't give a shit anymore what he thinks of me.

"I always worry about you, why do you think I'm so hard on you?"

"Maybe because you're a terrible father?" I mean for the words to hurt him but they just slide right off his impassive face. Not a single twitch.

"You know what, Dad? Whatever reason you had for coming down here, doesn't matter. I blocked you because I couldn't deal with your passive aggressiveness anymore. There was a point this summer when I hit rock bottom, and it was mostly because of you and how you've always made me out to be such a disappointment. So much so, that for the longest time I believed it. I didn't think I was worthy of family, of solid friendships, of love," I say, finding that my voice is steadier now as I'm getting things off my chest.

I take a few steps until we're face to face and look him in the eyes as I say, "You always made me feel like I wasn't good enough. It might have started with hockey, but it went way beyond that, and it really messed me up, Dad. So thank you, for coming down here and letting me say this to your face because this is the last time we're ever going to be in the same room together."

There's the barest hint of surprise as his lips part and his blue eyes widen, but I don't stick around for a reply. "If you want updates on my life, maybe tune into the news. I've got my eyes set on the NHL," I say, walking away. Without turning around I add, "It might not be this year, but we're coming for the Cup, old man. We won't let Boston win again."

I finally turn the corner and walk down the tunnel. The crew high fives me as I do and I hit the ice running. I see Eli on the far side of the ice and skate over to him. His mask is on, but I can still see the moment he registers it's me because his eyes widen and he gives me the biggest smile.

"Ash, you're here!"

"I am," I say, hugging him as best I can with all the gear in the way. "I got called up as I was driving to Robbie's house. Sounds like one of the forwards is out for a couple games, and I'll be filling in."

"That's amazing," Eli says. "I'm sorry I missed your call."

"It's fine, I missed yours too. But at least now we'll have a few more days together."

"Kalias, get in the net. We gotta get you warmed up for tonight," Juuse says. Fucking Juuse, always in the way.

"Meyers, good to see you again," he says, smirking at me. I really hate this guy. He's too pretty to be trustworthy.

"Couri, wish I could say the same," I say, calling him by his last name.

He laughs and drops down to stretch as Eli skates over to the net, sparing a backwards glance at us. I don't hear Juuse's reply as I leave him behind and start my own warm up.

As we head back to the locker room, Eli and I keep our distance, remaining professional, as always.

Everyone gives me a warm welcome and the captain gives us all a speech about how important this game is for us, since we have a history of losing to Boston during home games. While I came in thinking I was just going to have fun and not give a shit, I realize that's not a good approach.

The pressure starts to build and I take in deep, even breaths.

Focus.

I'm playing for myself.

I'm playing for Eli.

I'm playing for my team.

No matter the outcome, I'm going to give it my best. For them and for myself.

The buzzer goes off in the arena and we leave the locker room, lining up in the hallway, waiting for the starting players to be announced. I'm on the fourth line, which I expected. I'm ready to bring the energy and help out the team, and maybe even score a goal. I'm still riding high off of my hat trick from the other day and combining that with the fact I'm playing in the NHL makes me excited and greedy to prove myself.

. . .

ELI

THE FIRST PERIOD was the worst I've played this whole season. There are two goals that I'd like to take back, but there's nothing to be done now. Juuse tries to talk to me during intermission but I tell him to leave me alone so I can get out of my own head and focus.

The score is 2-0 for Boston and I can't help but feel like it's all my fault.

"You sure you don't wanna talk about it?" Juuse asks. "It might get you out of your funk."

I give him one of my angriest looks and hope that he'll just leave me alone. He shakes his head but still sits next to me. At least he's quiet.

My phone buzzes next to me on the bench and I pick it up.

> as much as I enjoy seeing you give Juuse the murder glare, is everything okay?

I laugh a little and look across the locker room at him. Ash looks up too and smiles at me.

> I'm trying to get in my zone and he won't shut up.

> sounds like me, lol

> At least I tolerate you.

> WOW, fucking rude

> Kidding, you know I love you.

"Maybe you need to think about something else for a bit, take your mind off the last period," Juuse says. Funny enough, texting Ash was helping, but now that he brought the period back up, my mind is on it again.

I sigh and pinch the bridge of my nose. "Talking about it again doesn't help," I grit out.

"Sorry," Juuse mumbles and rubs my shoulder in what he thinks is comfort. I slowly pull away from him until he gets the hint and lets it drop. My phone buzzes again and I quickly look down at it. I can't stop the burst of laughter that bubbles out of me when I see Ash's text.

> if he touches you again like that I'm going to punch him in the dick

>> You just want an excuse to touch his dick.

> ew, no. I don't get what people see in him, he's not even that good looking

>> He's objectively good looking, but not my type.

> oh, you have a type now?

>> Yeah, chaotic gingers with the attention span of a goldfish.

> you have such a way with words, how did I get so lucky?

>> IDK but you're definitely getting lucky tonight.

THE SECOND PERIOD goes much better, especially as I block two huge shots from breakaways that shouldn't have happened in the first place. The first and second lines are struggling to make any plays and we end up getting two penalties for hooking and high sticking.

When Ash gets on the ice for his next shift, he steals the puck from one of the Boston players and gets his own breakaway. I watch him skating fast but gracefully. When he gets a good opening, he takes the bar down shot, aiming over the goalie's shoulder on the glove side, hitting the bar, which causes the puck to ricochet into the net. The goalie doesn't stand a chance to stop it and the horn goes off, indicating the goal.

The team picks up on the high energy for the rest of the period and our captain scores two back to back goals as well, which puts us in the lead by one.

Everyone is raving about Ash's ability to make plays out of nothing when we get to the second intermission and I can't help but be immensely proud of him.

The third period starts out hot when one of the Boston players boards our captain. It takes him longer than it should to get up, but thankfully he doesn't need a stretcher to get off the ice. This gives us a five-minute power play when the ref calls out a major penalty for boarding.

The team quickly capitalizes on it, Ash scoring another goal almost immediately, followed by another goal by one of our defensemen. In the end, we win by four, which is a huge feat against Boston, and especially with our captain getting injured.

OUR COACHES CONGRATULATE us and the locker room is loud and buzzing with excitement as we begin to undress. Juuse asks me if I want to go out and celebrate, but he doesn't hear my answer. He's looking down at his phone and his face drops.

"Shit," he says, somberly.

"What?"

He looks back at me apologetically and now I'm starting to get nervous. A few other phones ding in the room and everyone seems to be reading the same thing, based on the same surprised faces I see in the room.

I look at Ash and see he's gripping the phone hard, his jaw clenched and eyes furious. He pins his gaze on me and I freeze. I reach for my phone to see what is going on, but Juuse snatches it from my hand.

"What the fuck?"

"Trust me, you don't want to read it."

"What is that supposed to mean?" Is it about me? Is that why Ash is mad? I swing back to look at him and see he's marching over angrily. I think he might get all up in my face, but no—he goes right up to Juuse and shoves him away from me.

"Woah," I say, trying to get between them but Ash gives me a look I haven't seen in a while. He looks angry, protective, and also hurt at the same time.

"What is going on?" I ask, looking between them.

"Are you two gay together?" one of the guys behind me asks and I swear I can feel all the blood drain from my face. I freeze up and look at Ash, then again at Juuse.

Did one of them tell someone? Is that what this is about?

But no.

Ash wouldn't do that to me. Not again. Not from his reaction—Ash is pissed and looks on the verge of punching Juuse. I look at my friend and see a sad expression on his face. Sad, but not guilty.

"Will one of you tell me what's going on?" I manage to say, doing my best to ignore the whispers behind me.

Ash hands me his phone and hits play on a video. It's from earlier today at the deli and it shows Juuse patting my hand and winking, clearly flirting with me. I look happy in the video too, laughing and smiling back. I swipe around, seeing more pictures of us on this stupid blog that focuses on hockey scandals. They've ruined more than one career in the past and I'm starting to panic that this might be it for me.

I can't focus on reading the whole thing, but I pick up on certain words that stick out—*newbie, goalie, couple, spotted together*. From what I gather, the article is speculating whether or not Juuse and I are a couple, and drawing their own conclusion that—yes, we are indeed. I don't make it to the comment section because Ash gently covers the screen with his hand and takes his phone back.

While I'm grateful, I feel like I might either pass out or throw up at any second. I glance behind me and see everyone staring at us.

"Well, is it true?" Mackenzie, one of our defensemen asks me.

"What the fuck does it matter if it's true or not?" Ash asks hotly. I give him a pleading look, silently begging him not to get in a fight with a teammate on his first day up at the NHL. But as always, Ash doesn't take the hint.

Mackenzie looks taken aback but says, "Calm down, newbie. We're just curious. And it's not about you, anyway."

Ash takes a step forward, positioning himself in front of me and says, "No, but indirectly, you're making it about me too. I'm bisexual. I want to know why you're so *curious* to see if it's true or not. Does it bother you to have a gay or bi teammate?"

There's complete silence in the locker room, and Ash

continues. "How exactly does my sexuality affect the way I play on the ice? Do I score fewer goals if I also have sex with other guys? Am I somehow less of a player?" He lets the questions hang in the air for a moment, and when no one answers, he says, "Well, I'm not. So I ask again, why does it matter if the stupid article is true or not? You have two of the most amazing goalies in the whole fucking league right here. You should be supporting them, not questioning what they do with their own personal lives."

Mackenzie looks down at his feet, and if it were any other situation, I would laugh at this 6' 8" man looking chastised. But not everyone in the room has the same reaction to Ash's words. Some of them look angry, but not angry enough to say anything back, and others look at us head on, nodding along.

Our head coach steps in, having listened from the door. He looks around at all of us and points at Ash. "You heard him. We're all a team here and if you want to make it to the fucking playoffs this year, you need to be a cohesive unit. If any of you have any issues, you come to me first and we'll discuss them. Otherwise I expect you all to be courteous and respectful to one another. Understood?"

A chorus of *yes, coach* gets shouted back and everyone resumes undressing. I keep my head down and rush through my shower. I feel bad for avoiding Juuse when he tries to talk to me about it, but right now I just need some space. I need to deal with the fact that, once again, people found out about me being gay when I wasn't ready.

I change into my nice post-game outfit and leave right away, opting to text Ash instead of waiting for him.

> Need to clear my head. Going to walk back to my apartment.

THIRTY-SEVEN

ASH

I LOOK DOWN at my phone and contemplate what to do. I heard Eli telling Juuse earlier that he needed some space. He's clearly got a lot on his mind and the last thing I want to do is crowd him. His apartment is already tiny, he doesn't need me there hovering and worrying about him.

I send a few texts to our friends, giving them a heads up about the situation, in case they see the article too.

A part of me wants to be a little jealous of the fact that Juuse and Eli were so cozy together, but deep down I know there's nothing for me to worry about. As much as I hate to admit it, Juuse and I are alike. We both enjoy physical touch and flirting, and I don't think what he did was anything more than just being friendly to Eli.

My heart breaks for Eli and I want to hug him and tell him it's all going to be okay, but that doesn't seem to be what he needs right now.

I'm searching for a hotel nearby when Juuse walks out of the arena and comes over to me.

"Meyers."

"Couri."

He cracks a smile and pulls me into his chest. I'm so shocked that I just stand there, letting him hug me for a moment. Eventually, he steps back and says, "Thank you, for what you said in there."

I frown at him. "I didn't do it for you."

"I know, you did it for Eli. But—it takes guts to stand up to others like that. I didn't even have the courage to do it, although I'd like to think that I would have said something if you weren't there."

"I'll always stand up for Eli," I say, vehemently.

He nods and tucks his hands in his coat pocket. "Good. It might not seem like it, but he needs you."

I take a breath and look away. He might need me, but not right now. Last time this happened, he sent me away. Eli needs to process things and think them through before he makes any decisions. So I'm giving him the space to do so.

"Where is he?" Juuse asks, looking around. Like a 6'3" hockey player might be hiding somewhere behind me.

"He left early. Went to his apartment," I say, trying to keep the misery out of my voice but failing by the way Juuse looks at me with pity.

"And what? He left you behind?"

"I heard what he said, that he needs space. I'm gonna find a hotel or something nearby."

There's a beat of silence as Juuse considers me. Then he says, "You can stay at my place."

"Why? You don't even like me."

He scoffs. "I like you just fine. Besides, my condo is close by, walking distance to Eli's." Another slight pang of jealousy rolls through me. How often do they hang out together?

"I guess," I relent and type in the address Juuse gives me. I end up following him around in my car and true enough, the condo is only a couple blocks away from Eli's building.

"Make yourself at home," he tells me once we enter his place.

"This is—really nice." I look around, noticing a bunch of abstract art on the walls and a nicely decorated living room and open floor kitchen. The stairs to the right of the entryway lead upstairs to what I assume are the bedrooms. Hopefully more than one.

"Thanks, I paid someone to decorate it."

I laugh and Juuse smiles at me, and for once it's a genuine smile.

"I appreciate you letting me crash here," I say, dropping my backpack on the floor and sinking into the couch, leaning my head back and pressing the heel of my hand into my eyes. What the hell am I going to do? I need to know how badly Eli is freaking out.

I pull out my phone and text him.

> can we talk?

ELI

I STARE AT MY PHONE, not really comprehending what is going on. *Can we talk?* Of course we can fucking talk. Where the hell is he? I figured he would walk over here when he was done in the locker room, especially if he needed to hang back and talk to the coach about the next few days.

I press the call button and wait for him to answer but he doesn't. I will never understand how someone who is on their phone 24/7 doesn't answer a damn call.

Pacing the length of my apartment doesn't seem productive so I end up grabbing a coat and walking around the building a few times, trying to clear my head. An hour later I return to my apartment, feeling lighter and hoping to talk to Ash about everything. But he's not here.

I call him again and this time, he answers. "Hey."

That's it?

Hey?

I can't help but be annoyed when I say, "Hey? Ash, where the hell are you?"

"What?"

I roll my eyes and pace some more. "Where are you?"

He's silent for a moment but then he says, "I'm staying at Juuse's tonight."

Now I'm even more confused than before? Why in the hell would he do that? And why Juuse of all people, when earlier today he was ready to punch him in the dick?

"Ash, what are you talking about? Why didn't you come to my apartment?"

"I—what do you mean? I thought you said you wanted space," he says, quietly.

I close my eyes and sigh. "You're an idiot," I say and hang up on him.

Grabbing my coat off the rack, I put it on for the second time tonight and head out of my apartment. My phone buzzes in my pocket and I ignore it, choosing to stew in my confusion a little longer while I walk over to Juuse's condo.

The light drizzle of rain from earlier is turning into full on rain now and I pick up the pace. By the time I get to the condo, my coat and hair is drenched and I'm fucking cold.

I ring the doorbell and when I don't see any movement, I start pounding my fist on the door. Over and over again.

The door finally opens and Juuse looks at me bewildered.

"Where is he?" My hands tighten into fists at my side and I almost chew him out for even suggesting to Ash that I needed any space tonight.

"He left not long ago, said he'd walk to your place."

"Are you fucking kidding me?" I lean my head back and scream to the sky.

My feet take control and I start running through the rain, leaving Juuse behind.

I slow down when I turn the corner of my building and see Ash standing in the middle of the sidewalk, drenched in the rain and looking down at his phone. Mine buzzes in my pocket again and I pull it out and answer.

"Eli? Jesus, can you let me in the building, it's freezing out here."

I try to catch my breath but I sound ragged anyway. "Why didn't you come home?" I see Ash letting his head drop and shaking his head.

"I—I don't know. I'm sorry, Eli. I thought—" his voice catches and then he anxiously runs a hand through his wet hair. "I thought you wanted me gone. That you needed space, just like last time."

My anger dims when he says it and I feel bad for not making it clearer. "This isn't like last time, Ash. I'm not abandoning you, I'm not pushing you away, we're a fucking team now."

"I'm so sorry. I didn't mean to disappear on you."

"I know, it's okay, *hani*," I say and make my way to him.

"No, it's not. I should have just left early and come with you, I'm such an *idiot*."

I put my phone back in my pocket and reach him in a few strides, cupping his face and pressing my body into his. "No, you're not. I'm sorry I said that earlier."

"Eli," he breathes out in relief. The way he says my name, all breathy and sweet pulls me in and I kiss him. His lips are cold from the rain and I make it my mission to keep him warm and safe.

"You are the best thing in my life, and the only one I want by my side, always," I say, chasing his lips again, tilting his head and kissing him deeper.

After what feels like an eternity kissing in the rain, I grab Ash's hand, scan my building pass and pull him inside the building. We leave a trail of water behind us from the lobby to the elevator and as soon as I press the button for the 8th floor, I turn around and back him into the wall. His gasp is caught by my lips as I devour him, one press of my lips at a time. He tastes minty and fresh as I pull on his bottom lip with my teeth before diving back in with my tongue.

"That article—I'm so mad at them for doing that to you, but I'm also dying to set the record straight. You're *mine*, Eli." Ash's hands grab my ass and squeeze, pulling me flush with his own erection right as the elevator dings.

I don't even try to pull away and we hear the doors open and close. We make out in the elevator until Ash shivers against me. Only then do I take his hand again and we walk over to my apartment. "*Ilo*, I'm so sorry and I need you to know that there's nothing going on between me and Juuse."

"Of course I know that. You wouldn't hurt me like that," he says, squeezing my hand.

I shake my head vehemently and open the door to my apartment. "Never."

As soon as we're inside and the door locks behind us, I peel off Ash's wet coat and his sweater, then do the same to my own. "You were so brave tonight. I don't expect you to fight my battles for me, but it means so much to me that you spoke up when I couldn't," I say.

"I'm not brave. I'm just well-adjusted now, thanks to my good old friend therapy," Ash says, trying to laugh it off, but I won't let him.

"*Kultsi,* you were incredible. And while you've worked a lot on yourself the last few months, this bravery was always there. I'm so proud to call you mine." Ash's eyes shine but I don't give him the chance to ruin this with another joke. Instead, my lips find his in a bruising kiss.

The rest of our clothes come off and I lead him backwards into the bathroom, kissing any part of him I can reach, while maneuvering around to turn the water on. Our passionate kissing and lovemaking turns more tender as the water warms us back up.

ASH FALLS asleep in my arms and we snuggle on the too small bed, but my mind is running through a million scenarios and I stay up thinking all night long. This article can bring me a lot of backlash, but is that really what I care about most? What other people think of me? What strangers think of me?

Ash stirs in my arms and I look down at him. His eyebrows are scrunched up and his nose twitches and all I want is to keep him close. I run my thumb along the bridge of his nose and smooth out the wrinkle in his brows and he lets out a sigh. When I take my hand back I see his lips pulled up in a small smile and my heart is so full. This—*Ash*—he's what I care about most.

When Ash heads out to grab us coffee and bagels, I call the team's PR liaison and ask her to set up a media availability session for me to address the article. She sets it up quicker than I expect and asks me to head out to the arena immediately.

I turn the TV on and pull up our team's channel. Then, I write a note for Ash.

THIRTY-EIGHT

ASH

"ELI?" I ask, looking in the small bathroom and around the room. The apartment is empty and I quickly check my phone in case Eli texted me with an emergency. Nothing.

My first instinct is to give him space, assume that he left or that he didn't want to be around me, but after last night, there's no chance Eli would do that.

I'm not abandoning you.

We're a fucking team now.

I open up his contact and hit call, but the call goes straight to voicemail. After I pace around the apartment, my gaze drifts to the TV that's turned on. The YouTube channel wasn't playing anything earlier, but now a video loads, saying a media availability session is starting soon.

A yellow post-it note is stuck to the bottom of the TV and it catches my attention.

The coffee might go cold, but I'll be back as soon as I can.

Please watch this. I love you,

E

My smile stretches across my face when I read those three little words but it quickly drops as I realize this doesn't explain anything. Where is he?

Before I can call him again, the video on the screen starts and I see him. He's freshly shaved and wearing a red Detroit sweatshirt with our white logo on it. My mind doesn't fully comprehend why he's there until the first question is asked by one of the reporters.

"Eli, are the rumors true?"

I inhale sharply. Why are they asking him this? Why did he agree to it?

It's hard to tell, and anyone that doesn't know Eli wouldn't notice it, but his features let it show that he's a little terrified. His shoulders move slightly, and while his arms are blocked by the table he's sitting at, I can tell he's nervously wiping his palms on his pants.

"They are," he says, looking into the camera.

"No, Eli, what are you doing?" I groan, chewing on my thumbnail. This is torture. Pure torture. The reporters all speak at once and Eli rears back in surprise, not knowing which question to take next.

"Um, you in the jumper, what was your question?" Eli says, pointing off to the side.

"Are you dating your teammate and fellow goalie, Juuse Couri?"

Eli smiles and shakes his head. "No, Juuse is my friend." The room is silent for a beat, and there don't seem to be any more questions. That is until Eli continues talking. "But the article was partly right; I'm gay, and I'm in love with my best friend, Ashton Meyers."

The room explodes into questions once again, but Eli stands up and says, "I've spent a long time hiding who I truly am, but all that's ever done is hurt me and those around me. While I needed to set the record straight, I would appreciate everyone's respect for my privacy. Thank you."

The live video ends and I sit on the edge of the bed. I'm stunned speechless, but I'm so, so proud of him. This amazing man that's come so far not just in his career, but in his personal life too. When he gets back, I don't even let him speak before I jump on him and attack him with my mouth. "I love you, I love you. God, you're amazing, Eli."

He holds me tight and says, "I'm never letting you go, Ash. You're everything to me."

THIRTY-NINE

ASH

ELI and I spend two more weeks together in Detroit and travel around for a few away games. I got to spend two nights filling in for the injured forward I was called up to replace, but with the captain being out after his recent injury, they decided to keep me around longer.

I played six more games and gave it my all and even though we didn't win all of them, getting the experience to play in the NHL was one of the best times of my life.

As I pack up the few belongings I acquired at Eli's apartment, he pulls me into his chest, dropping kisses behind my ear and on the side of my neck.

"I'm going to miss waking up next to you every morning."

My head drops against his shoulder and I sigh. "Me too. But Christmas is coming up soon and we'll have a few days together. Then the all-star break in February. We can go somewhere fun."

"Anaheim?" he asks, bringing up the trip that was the cataclysm of our relationship.

"Fuck no," I say, huffing out a breath, "we can do better."

"We could go to the cabin with our friends."

I hum and turn around, looping my arms around his neck. "Or we could go somewhere tropical. Just the two of us."

"I'll go anywhere with you," he says, pale blue eyes pinning me to the spot.

"Wow, you're so obsessed with me, it's kind of embarrassing."

Eli bends down and grabs the backs of my thighs, lifting me up. My legs wrap around him of their own accord and he tosses me onto the bed, crawling over me.

"Yeah, I really am."

DECEMBER

FOR CHRISTMAS, Eli comes to Grand Marquee, and the two of us go over to Robbie and Olivia's house as they host their first holiday dinner. A week later, I get called back up to Detroit.

My Detroit teammates are a bit wary of me now. They think I'm a little wild, which in truth, I am, but thankfully no one has complained about Eli and I being a couple. Since Eli addressed it head on, the article died down quickly, and with it so did any rumors. While there are still nasty comments out there about us and our relationship, that's not something we want to focus on. Instead, we're focusing on our promising future on and off the ice.

· · ·

JANUARY

AFTER THE NEW Year's game, I'm up for another week where we travel to Canada for a stint of games. The news that Nadison is retiring is not shocking, but it does mean our schedules will continue to be chaotic as Eli signs a three-year contract with the NHL.

He flies his parents and brother to Detroit for the first game after he signs the contract and we all go out to dinner at one of our favorite restaurants, Leila. His family is proud of him and excited for his career to take off and I can finally apologize to them in person for outing their son. They're just as forgiving as Eli and we quickly bond all over again. They seem happy for us both, and I shouldn't have expected anything less.

FEBRUARY

DURING THE ALL-STAR BREAK, we end up going back to Traverse City, sharing a room at the cabin and hanging out with our friends.

In a shocking twist of events, Jordan flies up into town and joins us at the cabin for two days. While his interactions with Alice are awkward as she mostly avoids him, he seems to fit right back in with the rest of us.

We snowboard, we play board games, we drink hot cocoa and we mostly catch up. All of us have such hectic lives that we end up giving each other powerpoint presentations of what the last six months of our lives have looked like.

Robbie has been making a huge difference in the community with the youth foundation. Olivia has been kicking ass as an AHL referee. Alice has been writing a book and blowing up on social media after she shared a snippet of it. And Jordan has mostly been depressed in Texas, even though he does a good job of hiding it. At least he's stayed in contact with us since we reconnected at Thanksgiving.

MARCH

"SIGNED, SEALED AND DELIVERED," I say, closing my laptop and taking a few steps to join Eli on the too small bed in his too small apartment.

His smile is so wide that his dimple is showing and my mouth immediately finds the spot to kiss it. "I hope you're not sick of me yet, I'm about to be in this bed with you for another few weeks at least."

"I could never be sick of you," Eli says and pulls me down to cuddle, one of his hands cradling the back of my neck. I melt into his touch and lean in for a kiss. He tastes like the non-alcoholic sparkling drink we opened to celebrate. "I'm so proud of you, *ilo*. You deserved that contract."

"Even if it's only for two years?" I ask, a bit of anxiety creeping in. *What if they trade me at the end of the two years and Eli and I get separated anyway? What if—*

"Stop," Eli says, pulling me closer into his embrace. "I can basically hear your thoughts, and I can already tell you that no matter what happens, I'm not going anywhere."

I sigh and look around the small apartment. "Think I can move in here for the rest of the season?" I ask, half joking.

"I was thinking..." Eli says, biting his lip. I wait for a response but his confidence starts to waver.

"What were you thinking?"

"Do you know the condo right next to Juuse?"

"The one with the bright blue door? Who paints their door?"

Eli laughs. "Don't get hung up on the color now. Yes, that place. Juuse told me it's available for rent."

"Okay, and?" I ask, not knowing what that has to do with us.

He gives me a deadpan look and waits.

And waits.

Oh. *Oh*.

"You want us to... Together?"

"Yes, *kultsi*. Together. What do you think?"

Instead of answering with words, I tackle him with my body and drop kisses on every inch of exposed skin I can find. *God, I can't wait to live with my boyfriend.*

JUNE

ELI

WE DIDN'T MAKE it to the playoffs. But we put up a great fight, ending the season one point behind the wildcard spot. Ash and I decided to stay in Detroit for the offseason this time, and booked two weeks to visit my family, who were ecstatic to have us.

The sun is up already and shining through the curtains, waking me up from a deep sleep. My hand reaches out towards Ash but all it finds is a cold pillow. I lift up on one elbow and look around my childhood bedroom, the same one Ash and I spent our time in last summer. I expect him to be in the bathroom, but the door is open and there's no light or movement.

I hear shuffling downstairs and I roll over in bed, peeking at the clock. Too early.

Ash opens the door with one hand, balancing something on a plate with the other.

"It's too early, what are you doing?" I whisper.

He softly closes the door and flips the lock and I sit up in bed, letting the sheet fall down to my waist as I lean back against the headboard.

I yawn and rub the sleep away from my eyes, and when I open them again, Ash is in front of me, carrying a tray of breakfast food.

"What is this?" I ask, surprised.

"Happy birthday, *pretty boy*." Ash places the tray in my lap and I look down with a smile on my face. There are heart-shaped pancakes with berries and syrup on top, and bacon on the side.

"You made these?"

"Of course," he says, grinning at me. Ash places one knee on the bed, then turns back to reach some napkins from the nightstand. In doing so, his leg stretches out and hits mine. I cover his calf with my hand, stilling him, and realize this is where his sailboat tattoo is. I rub absently at it, thinking about why he got it in the first place. He said he wanted to immortalize the summer we fell in love, and the first time he told me those words, at the sailboat party. When he twists back around, he fully kneels on the bed and places both his hands above me on the headboard.

"I love you," I say, keeping one hand on the tray and using the other to pull Ash down for a kiss. When I finally pull back, I tell him, "I know I said I didn't want one, but I changed my mind. I want a present for my birthday after all."

"Oh yeah?" he asks, smirking. "Is it my big c—"

"I want a sailboat tattoo."

Ash's smirk turns into a soft smile and he steals another kiss. *"Mina rakastan sinua,"* he says against my lips, and I fall in love with him all over again every time he speaks my language back to me.

EPILOGUE

Five Years Later

ELI

THERE'S nothing better than a home opener. Detroit has some of the most hyped and dedicated fans I've ever seen. Even when we play away games, there's always a sea of red jerseys in the crowd, cheering us on. Tonight is an extra special night for us because Olivia is here officiating her first NHL game.

We're only ten minutes into the game when one of the Toronto players takes control of the puck and moves toward my net. As he gets closer, he passes the puck to his buddy and takes up a position to screen me. He makes it inside the crease and his stick is blocking my glove.

"You better not block me like that, man," I say to him while trying to keep my eyes on the puck. His teammate still has control of it and bypasses one of my defensemen.

He shoots but I can't turn in time to stop it. Dickinson is still screening me, and as I move my blocker arm to stop the puck, he falls back and knocks me into the net.

Olivia blows the whistle and motions that there is no goal. She skates up to the box and calls the penalty. "Toronto, number twenty-two, two minutes for goalie interference. There is no goal."

A chorus of cheers rings out in the large arena, and I pull off my mask and spray water all over my face. Olivia skates up to me and says "Eli, are you okay?"

"All good, Olive." I smile and give her a wink. She turns around and sees Ash skating up, most likely to check on me. "He's fine, get back in the face-off before I give you a penalty," Olivia scolds him and I can't help but laugh.

"Yes, mom," Ash replies but does what he's told.

THE TEAM HAS BEEN incredible tonight and we're all hooting and celebrating in the locker room after a 3-0 shutout. I take my shower quicker than usual since I know Olivia and Robbie are waiting for us so we can go to dinner.

Ash and I walk out hand in hand and see our friends and their daughter talking in the player entrance area.

"How are the wedding preparations?" Olivia asks.

"Jesus, I can't wait for it to be over already. She's such a bridezilla."

I laugh because honestly that's the perfect way to describe Alice right now.

Robbie and Olivia notice us and we all hug as they congratulate us on our win.

"How's my favorite niece?" Ash asks Valerie while grabbing her and flipping her upside down.

She's giggling uncontrollably but manages to say, "Good, Uncle Ash."

Robbie scoffs and says, "I think you mean your only niece?"

"Well, if Alice gets her way, she'll have a whole football team of kids once they get married. Val will definitely have competition then. Won't you, Val?" he asks the toddler and snuggles her.

"Are you excited to be the best man?" Olivia asks Ash.

"Hell yea, I have a speech they will remember for the rest of their lives."

I sigh and shake my head. "*Hani*, you can't embarrass them like that."

"It'll be fine," Ash says.

"Okay, I am starving, what's for dinner?" Olivia asks.

"Soo, about that... Do you two mind if we take a quick detour?" Ash says with his puppy dog eyes.

"Detour from food? Are you insane?" Olivia says as she stops in place and whips around to face him. I laugh and put my hands on her shoulders, making her face me instead. She has to tilt her head back further and her eyes are narrowed on me. This girl loves her food.

"We have an appointment at City Hall and your presence is required," I say calmly, even though I am dying on the inside. I don't think I can wait a moment longer and if she says no, I might actually throw her over my shoulder and kidnap her. That'll get Robbie to follow for sure.

"City Hall? Why? Is someone in trouble?" Robbie asks, worried. Ash grins at me and I can't help but grin back. "We're fine, we just need a couple witnesses, that's all."

"Witnesses for..." he trails off, eyes widening, looking frantically between the two of us. "Wait, are you two getting married??"

"Yes, and we'd like to do it as quickly as possible, please," I mutter.

"But what about Jordan? And Alice? Don't you want them there?" Olivia asks.

"Honestly, we don't want to make a big deal out of this. And besides, we already told them earlier this morning. Alice was a little mad but she'll be over it. She's got her own wedding to worry about," Ash says.

"Holy shit, alright then!" Olivia says with a big smile. "Let's get you two hitched."

"Mommy, language!" Val says and we can't help but burst into laughter.

"Yeah, language, honey," Robbie chastises Olivia with a smile and kiss on her temple as he picks their daughter up and puts her up on his shoulders.

Ash and I fall behind and I steal a kiss from my soon-to-be husband.

"Are you sure you want this?" I ask, joining our hands together and bringing his knuckles to my lips. My sleeve lifts up and the little sailboat I got tattooed on my wrist pokes out.

"You? Forever? I've never wanted anything more in my life," he says with absolute conviction. My heart bursts with pride at his rediscovered sense of confidence and how much he's worked on himself, in and out of therapy.

This absolute goofball of a man has barrelled into my life and made everything better. He's made *me* better. It feels like I'm falling more and more in love with him each day, and there's nowhere in the world I'd rather be than by his side.

THE END.

DICTIONARY

Lapsi = Kid
Helvetti = Hell
Perse = Ass
Vittu = Cunt
Kultsi = Gold
Rakas = Dear (beloved)
Hani = Honey
Ilo = Happiness
Söpöliini = Cutie pie
Mina rakastan sinua = I love you

ACKNOWLEDGEMENTS

Thank you to my family and friends for all your support this past year, especially since you had to constantly listen to me ramble about book ideas. Special thanks to Emma for always being the first one to read my messy drafts and offer me feedback. You're the real MVP!

Maddi! Our friendship this past year has meant so much to me and I'm so happy that I somehow roped you into being my PA and hanging out with me at book events! Here's to many more road trips together!

Thank you to Leanne, Chelsey, and Jen, my alpha readers! I genuinely don't know where this story would have ended up without your feedback. And thank you to my beta readers and street team members for being my biggest hype people!

A round of appreciation for Lorissa is in order—you always know how to capture my characters perfectly and bring them to life on the cover! And thank you to my editor, Ciara, for always keeping me in check!

Last but not least, thank you to everyone that read The

Love Penalty and came back for more Manticores shenanigans! And if you're reading my book for the first time, THANK YOU!

ABOUT THE AUTHOR

Project leader by day, romance author by night, Stef C.R. lives in West Michigan with her husband and not one, not two, but three cats. When she's not working or writing stories, she spends her time reading fantasy and romance, endlessly cheering on the Red Wings, Charles LeClerc, and listening to Noah Kahan.

Are you looking for romances with happily ever afters? Then let's escape into the world of swoony MMCs and unforgettable heroines together. Find more information at stefwritesstories.com!

www.ingramcontent.com/pod-product-compliance
Lightning Source LLC
LaVergne TN
LVHW011944060526
838201LV00061B/4203